The Kansas Connection

This book is dedicated to my friend, Bob Talbot,
who believed in it – and in me – a long time ago.

The Kansas Connection, copyright 2010 by Kathleen Gabriel

All rights reserved under the International and Pan-American Copyright Conventions.
No part of this book may be reproduced or transmitted in any form or by any means,
electronic or mechanical, including photocopying, recording, or by any information
storage and retrieval system, without permission in writing from the publisher.
This is a work of fiction. Names, places, characters and incidents are either the product
of the author's imagination or are used fictitiously, and any resemblance to any actual
persons, living or dead, organizations, events or locales is entirely coincidental.

First published by Aardvaark Creative Publishing
Porthcawl, Wales, UK as Schiller's Road, by Lianne Gabriel
First Imprint Feb 2000

Also published February 2009 by Romance Divas as a Valentine's Day Free Read.

All rights retained by the author.

THE KANSAS CONNECTION

by
Kathleen Gabriel

The Kansas Connection   Kathleen Gabriel

—

CHAPTER ONE

*K*ansas wasn't all that exciting. Sunflowers and the Wizard of Oz were featured in every gas station store as if they were the only things Kansas had going for it. Like most of the country she'd driven through since Oregon, it wasn't at its best in March. Cori found her thoughts drifting as she drove, warm air from the heater splashing in her face, the radio quietly thumping out a country beat, all that came in well on this stretch of road. Soon she would be in Oklahoma City visiting with her mother-in-law, a kind but weary lady who longed for the men she'd outlived. Cori didn't begrudge her the time but could think of cheerier ways to spend spring break.

She'd been studying signs, trying to gauge the size of the towns she passed by and the chance of them having an adequate restaurant and a motel with an indoor pool. She had been driving since six in the morning, a long time ago. She turned the radio up and arched her back. She needed to stop soon.

She checked on the cars around her, very few for this time of day. If this Burney town were any kind of a going concern it would have had some kind of a rush hour. The car behind her in the right lane was a county mounty. Automatically she glanced at her speedometer. Only five miles over. She was okay. She slowed a little anyway and smiled to think what her high school history students might think of her reaction.

The cop signaled to change lanes. So she was going too slow for him, then. Good. Then he wouldn't be behind her. She sang along with the radio, having learned the song from the drive across Wyoming. She was aware of a car on the left, the cop passing, but instead of passing, it stayed beside her. She looked over to see the driver grinning and waving. He was young and handsome, and looked immensely happy.

Good. At least someone was. She waved in return and smiled. He dropped back and she resigned herself to being followed.

Here was the exit for Burney. It didn't have a rush hour, and it didn't have any motels listed on the sign but it did have the wonderful word, "Food" in big letters. She signaled to exit and was startled by flashing blue lights in her mirror. She looked and the cop turned them off and shook his head. She canceled her signal. What the heck?

He pulled up even with her, smiled and pointed up the freeway. Okay, so she was supposed to keep going. Why, she didn't know, but was not inclined to argue with the law. Still, she was tired and hungry and she'd give him no more than two exits to make himself plain.

After just a few miles the cop pulled ahead and motioned her to follow. She followed him off the exit and through a couple of turns into a cafe parking lot. Food. Finally. She was hungry enough to eat whatever slop they came up with. She stretched up and looked at herself in the mirror. She looked pretty rough. Sleepy eyes and wakeful hair.

She grabbed her purse and opened her door, pulled down at the wrinkles in her jeans as she stood. The deputy approached, smiling, hands spread at his sides. "I pray you'll forgive me, ma'am, for my high-handed use of the lights. I just couldn't let anyone from Oregon stop at Burney."

He pronounced it "Orygun," a thing few people east of Idaho knew to do. He stopped four feet from her and seemed to be looking her over, very discreetly, and with sympathy. He didn't look as young close up, slight smile lines on his face, gray at his temples; an adult. "Are you from Oregon? Or is it just your car that is?"

She laughed. "I'm from Oregon. Corinne Schiller, Cori for short." She extended her hand.

He shook it firmly. "Ken McAllister. County sheriff's department."

"No fooling?" She couldn't resist teasing anyone when a clear opportunity presented itself.

He winced comically. "I'm not usually this stupid, ma'am, but I rarely get to see people from Oregon, and I love Oregon. But I bet you're starved. I'll buy you supper if you'll give me the honor of talking about Oregon between bites."

"They have good food here?" She turned toward the café without answering his invitation, just going along with his plan, and they walked together.

"Better than Burney and their alleged restaurant." As soon as they got a booth she went to the restroom, him following behind toward the men's room. It was going to be nice to have company for dinner. This cop was pleasant and she was curious to know why he liked Oregon so well. He wasn't from Oregon, she could tell by his accent, a mix of the Midwest and the South, kind of a cowboy sound. She quickly washed her hands and face and dried them, then put a little hand lotion in her palm and rubbed it around, then touched her hands lightly to the top of her hair, a measure that tamed the monster a bit.

She saw the cop standing at a pay phone by the restroom as she came out. He lifted the mouthpiece slightly and rolled his eyes. "And I said to do your homework first. I can lock you guys out of your computer with a password if you don't..." Cori walked to their table. So, he was somebody's dad. Probably a good, one, too, if he was checking up on them on his dinner break.

She read a little bit of the menu, but there were too many choices. When the cop came to the table a few moments later, he pushed his menu aside. She asked, "How are the kids doing?"

"Oh, they're unhappy I won't be there to make them their dinner and they're fighting over the computer. Their mother works late three nights a week, and this is one of them. I'm supposed to be off now, but somebody else got sick and I'm pulling a double, so they're on their own."

"How old are they?"

"Fourteen and fifteen."

She nodded. "Just my age."

He shook his head, a stern look strangely accompanied by a dimple. "Lady, you're forty-one, and I know it."

"Ran my plates and pulled up my license, huh?"

"Yup. I know it's not fair, so..." He leaned to one side, produced his wallet, dug something out and dropped it in front of her. "Is that fair?"

She picked up his license and looked at it. Not a bad picture. She looked quickly at him to see if his eyes really were blue and couldn't tell for sure in the dim room. Forty-three, licensed in Kansas since he was seventeen. Huh. She handed it back. "First time I ever heard of a cop doing that, Sergeant McAllister."

"They give me a whole hour between shifts, so I'm not a cop at the moment. I'm just Ken."

"It'll be hard to work a double. I feel for you."

"You look kind of worn out yourself. How long have you been driving?"

"Since six."

"That's a long haul. Where are you headed?"

"Oklahoma City to see my mother-in-law. She's lonely and I'm going to visit and take her a bunch of stuff she wanted. Is there a motel in this town?"

"Best Western, next exit." He was gazing at her in a speculative way, she thought.

"Indoor pool?"

"Yup."

"Good."

"What did you decide on?" he asked.

She tipped her head to one side, not realizing what he was asking.

"I mean, to eat?"

She shrugged. "Oh. I'm too tired to figure it out. I'll just get whatever you do."

"That'll work." The waitress was on her way over to them. He ordered grilled chicken sandwiches and salads and coffee, decaf for Cori, since her day was nearly done.

"What do you do, Mrs. Schiller?"

"I'm a high school history teacher, working as a substitute in two different districts, Sergeant McAllister." She sipped her water, keeping an eye on him.

He grinned. "So. Cori. You teach kids the same age as the brats I have at home."

"Yup." There she went, teasing him again. She didn't often say "yup" on her own. "You said you loved Oregon. Have you been there?"

"When I got out of the service I treated myself to a tour of the western states. Oregon was absolutely my favorite place."

"What did you see there?"

"Mt. Hood, Multnomah Falls, Cannon Beach, the Astoria column. Portland has a really nice downtown area. Or it did."

"It's still nice. When were you there?"

"About twenty years ago."

"And you haven't been back?"

The waitress brought their salads and topped off their coffee.

"Never have been back. Always wanted to. What do you like in downtown Portland?"

"Well, I like Pioneer Square. There's always something going on there." Ken ate while she told him about the strolling musicians that were heard on nice days, the speeches and programs, the variety of people that you could see and their interactions. Beggars and business people, mimes and children and strutting teens, people who came to watch people, people who came to sit on the steps while eating lunch or waiting for a bus or train or court date.

"Eat," he said. "I want you to talk, but I'm not going to let you starve."

"That's encouraging," she said and worked on her salad while he told her about the books he'd collected on Oregon, especially hiking books.

"Those get out of date, you know. Mudslides change trails and other things happen."

"Oh, I know. I'll get new books before I start out."

"Coming out, then, huh?" She smiled.

"I think I'll get up the courage pretty soon, but maybe not this year." His smile was gone as the waitress placed their sandwiches on the table and took his salad plate. Once she was gone, he met Cori's eye. "You eat awhile before you tell me about your favorite hikes."

She nodded and said, "Yes, sir."

He talked about things he wanted to see while she ate and listened. "I especially like waterfalls. I want to be sure to spend a couple of days at Silver Creek Falls State Park. I've seen pictures and I think I need to go there."

"Will you stay at the campground? I bet you need reservations way ahead if you're coming out in the summer."

"I don't know. I have camping gear. I'll need to find out about getting reservations. The books tell all that, too. I'll study it out."

"Do you ski?"

He laughed, an honest sound, a happy one, too. "What the heck would I learn to ski on around here? Practice on barn roofs, maybe?"

She laughed and tossed her hair back. It flopped forward immediately afterward. "Well, we have year-round skiing and maybe you can learn a little about it."

"Hm. I might break a leg, but I have sick leave accumulated. What the hey."

"Sheriff's department a pretty good place to work?"

"I like the variety. Not as much shooting as in the cities, and it's not all highway work like the state police. I have a lot of paperwork, but I don't mind it like a lot of people do. You like your work? Is substituting better than working full time in one spot?"

"I did that for a few years, then my husband wanted me to be free to travel with him to conventions and on little vacations." She stopped and shrugged. She was getting close to the big sadness in her life.

"And what does Mr. Schiller do?"

She shook her head. "He was a plumber... I mean a urologist, a doctor. He died two years ago."

"Oh. I'm sorry." She checked his face, and he really did look sorry.

"What does your wife do?"

He smiled. "Well, depends on who you mean. I don't have a wife. My ex-wife..."

She shook her head.

"Okay, the kids' mother?" She nodded. "She's my sister, and she's a pharmacist's assistant. She and the kids moved in with me for a year while her husband's overseas with the Marines. They just moved in last month and we're all still getting used to each other."

She couldn't help laughing at his euphemism. "The kids are trying to see how much they can get away with, you mean?" They would be pushing him, but no one in the world was tested as thoroughly as a substitute teacher was, so she knew what he was going through.

"Exactly. How long do you suppose they'll do that?" He frowned slightly, wet his bottom lip.

"Until the ocean stops making waves."

"Great. Not that this Kansas boy knows a whole lot about the ocean."

"But you say you loved Oregon. Why haven't you ever gone back?"

"The first few years on the force I got lousy vacation times, and I understand November through March is not the time to rely on good weather in Oregon?"

"That's for sure."

"Then I got better times, but I got married and went where my wife wanted to go." Quite a contrast to her own marriage where she gave up her career to go where her husband wanted to go. And usually thought of it as a good bargain.

"And now you refer to her as ex-wife." She thought she saw a jaw muscle twitch, but she wasn't sure. What on earth could this charming gentleman do to drive off a wife? Unless it was working too much, something she was very familiar with, or maybe she had her private reasons. Of course, she didn't know this guy, and he might be on his good behavior.

"That's right."

"So you can vacation where you want."

He took a big bite of sandwich and chewed, so she did, too. He swallowed. "And I want to vacation in Oregon. First summer after she took off

I was too depressed to do anything, then the next summer I needed to rebuild my engine. Then I spent a year with Sandi and the kids while Jerry was overseas, then other stuff came up, then last summer I chickened out but spent the fall planning what I'd do this summer. Then the damned Marine corps has my brother-in-law go back overseas and I have my hands full..."

"Take two or three weeks anyway. Your sister can find a way to manage and the kids will respect their uncle more knowing he puts a priority on his own goals once in awhile."

He looked at her, sandwich suspended. "Do you think so?"

She nodded and wiped her mouth. "Absolutely. It's time to take care of Ken." She was ready to fight for his vacation. She felt strongly about it and she didn't know why.

"I'm not real good at that. Oh, I am as far as the basics go, but there aren't any frills."

"You take care of other people."

He shrugged. "It's what I do."

"Then what...? I'm sorry." She shook her head as she realized how rude her question was, and sipped at her lukewarm coffee.

"About what? What happened to my marriage?"

"It's absolutely none of my business. I almost asked, but changed my mind."

"She ran off with her photographer."

"Photographer?"

"Yeah. She worked part-time as an underwear model and was always trying to get new jobs so she had a lot of portfolio photos taken in different clothes. And lack of clothes. Then one day she was gone." Cori sat still, not knowing what to say, while Ken stared into his coffee. "I wasn't the man I thought I was."

Cori reached across the table and laid her hand on his. "Don't sell yourself short. Some people have a hell of a time being faithful. It's a flaw in them, no one else; certainly not in a loving husband or wife."

Ken covered her hand with his for a moment, then patted it and she drew it back. "Your husband?"

She nodded. "We were okay in spite of it, but there were compromises."

"That's why you gave up your career to substitute?" This man was quick.

"Yes. Now I don't have either - my sweetheart or my career."

"Maybe you could get a permanent job with the school district if you wanted to. And maybe there's another sweetheart for you. You're young..."

"Not really." She tensed up. They had no business talking about such personal things. None.

"...and you have gorgeous hair." She looked up quickly and saw his dimple. Teasing.

"It's scary right now. It usually looks a lot better than this. I leaned against the headrest and I got out in the wind to pump gas and..."

"I can tell what it's supposed to look like and I love it. Are those ringlets natural?" What a flirt he was, and how totally he'd distracted her from his remark about her maybe finding another sweetheart.

"Yup."

"I like the little bits of silver mixed in with the blonde."

"Thank you. You're aging nicely, too." She turned down dessert, and got directions to the Best Western.

Ken paid the bill and walked her to her car. "I'm very glad I got to meet you. Thank you for the encouragement."

"You're most welcome. Thank you for dinner."

"If you'd visit with me some more some time I'd greatly appreciate it." He took out a business card as he spoke, then handed it to her. "E-mail address, cell and home phones. You can even call the home phone collect if you promise to talk about Oregon."

She read the card, his personal card, with no reference to the police department. She said, "E-mail's the way to go. I don't have any cards with me..." Ken hastened to get out another card, along with a pen. She took it and wrote her name and e-mail address for him. Probably they would never get around to talking again, but this was a friendly gesture on both parts.

"Thanks, Cori. Drive safely the rest of your trip." He extended his hand and she shook it.

"Was I driving safely?" she wondered. Surely he would have an opinion.

"Yup. Second thing I liked about you was your good following distance."

"What was first?"

"Your Oregon plates."

CHAPTER TWO

*C*ori stood in the shower with her eyes closed until the water grew cool and turned the faucets off without needing to study to see which way to turn the knobs. Home. Finally.

She dried off, then carefully combed her hair. It was the last chance she'd have until the next shampoo. If she tried to comb it when it was dry, it turned into a huge fluffy mass. It was shoulder length when it was wet, but dry the curls pulled it up so that the longest ends brushed her ear lobes. She liked her hair, but at times it got the better of her. Like on a long car trip. Or camping. Or any time she couldn't wash it in the morning. She had cut it short before, but thought she looked like some old lady. She wasn't ready for that. Also, she needed big hair to balance her broad shoulders.

She put slippers on with her jeans and sweater and padded down the stairs to the kitchen. She started tea, then glanced through the accumulated mail. On the way to the microwave, she stuck her finger in the ivy on the windowsill. Good. Dad had remembered to water it. He deserved a pie. But not today. She made her tea and started a frozen quiche.

She carried the phone to her desk in the corner of the living room and fired up the computer, then dialed her dad while it came up, smiled at his familiar voice. "Hey, how you doing, Dad?"

"Decided to come back?"

"I'm back."

"The charms of Oklahoma failed once more, huh?"

"Boy, did they. Mama Schiller's so lonely. I'm afraid I'm not one of the ones she really wanted to see..."

"She knows what she has to do to see them."

"She'll go soon enough."

"She needs to get out and do something, make some friends."

"She's too tired. She hasn't made any friends in years. Her family was everything. Dave and I should have given her some grandchildren."

"That would have been nice. You couldn't do anything about it, though." That's for sure, since Dave had a vasectomy before they met and didn't bother to mention it until she was already well down the road to loving him.

"That's true. Next time I go see her, though, I'm going to fly. Driving was tedious." She opened her e-mail program. Her medieval history group had been writing a lot since it was spring break. Most of the members were educators or students.

"I bet. Did you get caught in Wyoming this time?" She had gotten a speeding ticket in Wyoming years ago and her dad wouldn't let her forget it.

"I used the cruise control."

"Very good." She could tell he was grinning. She looked over the list on her screen and besides the predictable e-mails, there was one from Ken McAllister.

"Oh, hey, Dad. I did get pulled over in Kansas."

"What for?"

"Dinner."

"It's unethical to pull over a lady for personal purposes."

"This wasn't like that. He didn't really pull me over, just pointed me up the road to a decent place to eat and I went along."

"Honey, you need to quit going along with every hare-brained scheme people come up with."

"I only go along with the ones I like. This was a nice guy who loves Oregon and wanted to hear more about it, is all." She pointed the cursor at Ken's e-mail. She wanted to know what he had to say.

"And if he saw a pretty woman in a car from Montana he'd say he loved Montana."

She frowned. She had thought of that, but Ken was too knowledgeable about Oregon. He couldn't have memorized that much material on every state. Probably not. No.

"You're just a cynic, Dad. And jealous you don't have a nice patrol car to pick up chicks with. Hey, thanks for watching the place for me."

"You're welcome. Talk to you later."

She opened Ken's message. It was conventional, maybe a little longer than the standard thank you note. She'd answer it with a little note after she looked at her other e-mail. There were a lot of messages. Two days down she found another note from Ken, this one just as friendly and funny. She liked one line especially, "...that you and your hair arrived safely home without frightening any little children." He remembered her referring to her hair as scary.

She had to answer this while she had it in mind to do. "My hair and I arrived safely home. I am avoiding scaring the neighbors by staying indoors until I have beaten it back into submission. I fervently hope I'll have enough milk and toilet paper to last the battle. Got your vacation dates yet? Love, Cori."

She pushed "send" and immediately realized that she should have used a standard formal closing as he did - "sincerely" or "yours truly" - instead of writing "love," but it was too late now. Her standard closing would have to do and she hoped he wouldn't notice it.

No such luck. Later that night she went online to answer other messages and found a new one from Ken. "My sweetheart, my darling! I am filled with ecstasy at the thought that you signed your message with 'love.' Uh... do you always do that? Your humble servant, Ken McAllister."

She covered her face with her hands as she laughed. He wasn't this outrageous in person. He was almost reserved. A couple of things he said had been funny, but nothing like this clowning. She had to answer this one right away. "Yup. And if you are *my* humble servant, the good people of Hoskins County are getting gypped. Love, Cori."

The other messages took more thought and she was up late cleaning them all up. She was a participant in a raging debate on the Battle of Agincourt. She didn't feel that she contributed a lot of serious scholarship to it, but she contributed some things and people kept messaging her to contradict her. Most of these were kind enough to do it by e-mail, others posted their messages on the board for all to see. She was tempted to ignore some of them, but she didn't.

She was nearly done when she got an alert from her computer that there was a new message. People kept all hours and lived in every time zone. A message in the middle of the night wasn't unusual. Another one from Ken. She opened it. "Good morning, Cori. I'm going off to gyp the citizens of Hoskins County. Every ticket I write I will think of you. Your sneaky servant, Ken."

She answered, fearing he had taken her joke amiss. "Have fun today, Ken. If you're ever in doubt as to whether or not I'm trying to be funny, be sure that I am. My own darned humble servant, Cori."

He must also have had an alert on his computer that told him when he had new e-mail because his answer appeared within two minutes. "I always choose on the funny side of things unless I'm crying too hard to see it. And what are you doing up? It's two a.m. there. Mine truly, Ken"

She typed and sent, "Haven't gone to bed yet. What are you doing up? It's too early to go to work. Love, Cori."

"Ice on the roads. Sleep well, hairy lady. Love, Ken."

"Be careful out there. Love, Cori." Ice. She had daffodils blooming, and ice was a thing of the past in western Oregon. Kansas was a crappy place. She looked at his message again. Hairy lady, huh?

No more messages came through in the next few minutes so she went to bed. She was surprised to have heard more than once from Ken, but she was glad. She loved corresponding with funny people.

Morning came far too early with a call from Gladhurst school district for her to work that day. Three hours sleep was not enough. She showered and tamed the hair, smiling as she remembered Ken's calling her "hairy lady." Dressing was complicated by her still-packed bags lying on the floor and the awkwardness of stepping over them. She finally hoisted them and dropped them on the bed. She just wouldn't make the bed today.

She felt rushed all day since she had no time to prepare for classes. Fortunately, many of the students remembered her and encouraged the others to behave. All day she only had to take two out in the hall; not bad.

She checked in with the principal as she was leaving for the day.

"You won't be needed tomorrow, Mrs. Schiller. The teacher will be back. Have any problems?"

"No. It went well. Some of them might have actually learned something."

"We can hope."

She drove home and made herself some tea and settled at the computer and looked up her new messages. There were just a few. Two from Ken. "Are you at your computer? Just stopped for lunch and wanted to tell you I survived the ice. Love, Ken." Then another one had come through just a few minutes before. "I guess you must have slept all day. Sounds like a good plan to me. Rest up, and get good ID before you let down your hair, Rapunzel."

She answered, "Slept all day, like fun. I got called in to work. Faced

134 teenagers fortified with caffeine."

She read her other messages, discarded several, answered one. Got a new message. "So what did that do to your hair? Love, Ken."

She sent back, "Bald places where I pulled it out. Do you have yahoo chat? Would love to go one on one with you. Chatting, I mean. Love, Cori."

"I do. What's your nick?"

"I am 'CoriOlisEffect.' Log on and chat?"

No new message came back so she thought he might be offline now. She made more tea and went back to the computer to find a message from Ken. "I am on. Where are you?"

She dribbled tea. How stupid. Of course he would have logged onto the chat program when she said without sending another e-mail. What would she tell him? She logged on as quickly as she could and someone called "SgtHoneyBear" had left a friend request. It had to be Ken. She accepted.

"So there you are. I thought you'd be logged on but it said you were offline."

"Brain was offline. I was in the kitchen making a cup of tea. I sure hope you're Ken."

"I am. And it sounds like you're tired."

"pppppbt."

"That's not nice."

"Sorry."

"Long day?"

"Only because I stayed up too late. I didn't think I'd get called today."

"The kids were all right?"

"Great kids. Only had to flog two. A few examples go a long way."

"Sure do."

"Did you have a good day?"

"After the first half of the morning rush I did."

"Rush hour traffic? Or your coffee rush?"

"Both. The ice melted by eight or so."

"I'm glad."

"Yeah. Got any more of that tea? Pass it over."

She took a big sip. "Here you go, SgtHoneyBear. I'm handing you a big mug of tea with honey in it, just the way you like it. How did you pick that name?"

"I wanted SgtPoohBear but somebody already had it."

"Why a teddy bear?"

"I can't tell you that."

"Why not? The name is in a public place, you know. Surely I'm not the first to ask."

"Yes, but I fear to reveal my weakness to a powerful female person who has met my person in person."

"Oh. And who has your address and your phone number and knows who you work for? I see. Nyah, ha ha. (I'm twirling my moustache.)"

"Yes. And who reveals no weakness to me."

"I would, though. I trust you."

"Why?"

"I just do." She thought about it for a minute. It was true, and she didn't know why she trusted him. "I don't know why."

"That's dumb. I might be some horrible person."

"So might I."

"You don't have a horrible person's record."

"You checked me out."

"Yup. Are you mad at me?"

She sighed. "No. But it's not fair."

"Police departments don't hire criminals. My record is clean as a whistle. Not even a speeding ticket in Wyoming like some people I know."

"Okay. I'm glad."

"I have four sisters. Three are older than me."

"Ummm... is this relevant?"

"Yup."

"Proceed."

"When we were young, a cat had a batch of kittens in Tina's closet. We cuddled those kittens from the day they were born, never let them rest. They grew up to be the most obnoxiously affectionate critters in the world."

"I'd like to have a cat like that."

"I have three older sisters. They cuddled me from the day I was born and..."

She started laughing and typed, "So, you're obnoxiously affectionate?"

"Yup. Been called everything from a teddy bear to a pain in the ass. I like teddy bear better."

"I would, too. But you didn't touch me hardly at all."

"It doesn't go over well with strangers."

"Probably not. I don't have a cute story to tell about a weakness of mine."

"You don't have to tell me anything."

"I want to be fair. Though methinks the thing you told me might be calculated to entice a lady."

"Duh."

"Have you met anybody you met on the Internet?"

"Yes."

"And?"

"Bummer. I am doomed to interact with women on here and if I need to get my cuddlies out I lavish affection on my family."

"That goes over great with your nephew, I guess." Teen boys would rather mow a lawn than hug their parents. Or uncles.

"Takes the form of wrestling with him. And I get a lot out by doing things for people. Cooking is my favorite."

She closed her eyes and imagined good smells coming from the kitchen. Good smells that she didn't work for. "Honey Bear, you tell all these women these things and you're not married?"

"Not married. I am exceedingly fussy in that area. No girlfriend at the moment, no dog, no goldfish."

"A cat?"

"Gotta have a cat."

"Mine split when Dave died. I haven't had the heart to get another."

"Poor Cori."

"Yeah. I'll tell you a weakness of mine now, but it's physical."

"A real one?"

"Your teddy bear problem isn't real?"

"Uhhh..."

"I get migraines. I'm on some stuff that's supposed to help prevent them, but it's not foolproof. And I have stuff to take when I get one that takes them away if I take it as soon as it starts up. So it's not usually too bad, but sometimes it is. And I have to watch out for things in my diet that can trigger them."

"I'm sorry. What triggers them?"

"Red wine, diet pop, chocolate."

"I won't ever send you chocolates, okay?"

"Thank you."

"Unless I'm mad at you."

"I love chocolate. I eat it if it's around."

"You need a servant to go ahead of you scoping out and destroying chocolate."

"Chocolate servants' wages are awful these days."

"It's a pity."

"I like talking to you." She stretched her back.

"But?"

"I am so tired. Going to eat something and hit the sack."

"What will you eat?"

"I don't know."

"I made baked potatoes stuffed with cheese and shrimp. There's one left over. Got a fax machine?"

"You're sweet."

"I'm glad you think so. Sleep well."

"Good night, Ken."

"Good night, Cori."

She logged off and was soon digging through the freezer seeking shrimp.

* * *

At his house in eastern Kansas, Ken leaned back in his chair. She'd seen right through the kitten story. And the cooking remarks. The usual stuff would get him no points with this lady. But she was worth more than the brief flirtation that had become his modus operandi on the Net. She was genuine. Friend material at the very least.

He'd heard things about migraines before, but knew little about them. He sat up and went to a search engine to find information. He was reading his third article when Michael burst in. "Uncle Ken, can you play Master of the Galaxy with me? I want to get better at it before I go online against other people."

He stretched. "I guess I could. Let me bookmark this site first and I'll be on with you." Michael stood and watched for a minute and Ken glared at him. The brat didn't believe he'd get offline right away. He left and Ken dropped the game CD in. His computer and the kids' were networked just for this purpose.

CHAPTER THREE

Cori sat on the couch with a book in her lap, phone pressed to her ear. "Three weeks, beginning tomorrow. That will be fine. May I meet with Mr. Wilson to get some information, and to keep him up to date?"

"I don't think he'll do you much good until at least tomorrow. He's still pretty sedated."

"I understand." Three weeks. It was a longer assignment than she'd had in a long time. She felt sorry for Mr. Wilson and his emergency knee surgery, but his students would have a real history teacher now for three weeks instead of a football coach. She planned to spark their interest in history and do some permanent good.

Ten o'clock. She'd better get to bed so she'd have time to go over lesson plans in the morning at the school. She wrote Ken an e-mail telling him she wouldn't make their morning chat appointment. It was his day off and they were supposed to talk about Silver Creek Falls. She told him about her assignment and what she hoped to do with it. As she wrote, she realized that she was really looking forward to it.

In the morning she sat at Mr. Wilson's desk and read over the lessons for that day. She would be teaching three sections of a freshman history class and two for juniors. The textbook the juniors were using was written in a boring style. She'd come across it before and didn't like it much. She'd have to use it as a starting point, since she couldn't change what the school was using, but she would make the material live for her students.

Things went well. She smiled little and used strategic stares and silences to keep order, the most critical thing for a substitute. Her love of history kept the students interested. If they missed Mr. Wilson's football stories, they didn't say.

She took home copies of the textbooks for both classes and read over the material for the next day's lessons. The more she read that junior text the more upset she became. Some sentences seemed purposely obtuse, others condescending. What were the authors thinking? Or the editors. Authors can write, but editors can make a mockery of what they say. Her father had found this out a few years ago and moaned about it to her when an essay of his came out in a completely different style than he had written it.

She went to her computer, got on the Internet and looked up the publisher's e-mail address. Several were listed. She chose Lauren Tate-Rivera, the managing editor, and told her exactly what she thought. Now she felt better.

On Friday after school, she found an e-mail from Ken. "Will you never talk to me of Silver Creek Falls? I begin to think you've never been there and are stalling. I hope your students were good for you today." He followed that with his schedule for the next few days and a spaghetti sauce recipe he'd been building up. She read it through, smiling. He used a canned sauce with strategic additions. She'd have to think up a similar recipe to send him. She was thinking about what to make for dinner when the phone rang.

"Hi, gorgeous. Have you had dinner yet?"

"Hi, Brian. Dinner with you is just the distraction I need."

"Oh, now I'm a distraction. I like that."

"Better than other things you could be."

"Like history?"

"Yeah, but history is fascinating."

"More than you've ever said about me. I'll be there in about forty-five minutes."

"Drive fast, I'm hungry."

"Will do, beautiful." She hung up and pounded up the stairs to change into a dress. Brian liked her legs and she could give him that much. They had dinner together every couple of weeks and she got all the clinic news from him. She stopped in at the clinic once in a while, and the people who had known Dave were warm toward her, but since his death she felt awkward there. She still cared about what went on, and she had a financial interest in the clinic. Brian formed a bridge for her, along with good conversation and a sense of being cared for.

In a slim purple dress and heels, she decided to answer a couple of e-mails and reread her daily note from Ken. In it, he gave her his schedule. He was online now, she realized, and logged onto yahoo chat, found him online. "Yo. Sgt. H Bear."

He came back with a message. "Hey, Cori. I'm kind of busy right now.

The Kansas Connection   Kathleen Gabriel

Will you be around later?"

"Are you chatting with some woman?"

"Uh..."

"Figures."

"But you're still my favorite."

"Oh, sure. That's obvious."

"I'll get rid of her."

"No, no, no. Go ahead. I'm going out pretty soon."

"Out? With a man?"

"Surely you know I like men."

"Yeah. Hang on a sec." She waited for a few seconds.

"Now. Tell me about this man. If you give me his name and birth date I can check him out for you."

"No need. He's an old friend."

"Aha."

"What does that mean?"

"Nothing. Just 'aha.'"

"Hmmm."

"What does he do?"

"He's a plumber."

"Is he good in bed?" Cori laughed. She doubted Ken would talk this way in person. On the Net he just came right out with it.

"He teaches a class called 'Male Sexuality - How to Please a Woman.'"

"Oh, boy."

"He took over the class from my husband."

"Did he take over anything else from your husband?" Her sex life was none of his business, but he was bold in every area, not just this one. Still. She wasn't sure whether to tease back or tell him to mind his own business. She tapped her fingers on the edge of her desk while she thought.

"Cori? I went too far this time. Forgive me?"

That decided her. Teasing was definitely the thing. "Sure, Honey Bear. Just so you know, I'm only making do with this guy until you can get out here."

"I am throwing clothes in the back of the car as we speak."

"I just know it. How come you're not talking to that other woman?"

"Are you kidding me? When you're online?"

"Aw, gee."

"What's his name?"

"Brian."

"No last name?"

"Not to you."

"Fine. I see how I rate. (Sniff.)"

"Darned snoopy cop."

"Just the facts, ma'am."

"I don't ask you about all the women you go out with."

"Like there're so many."

"Even so. I don't ask."

"Well, I'm just wondering if my presence will upset anyone when I come out this summer."

"Are you going to? Really?"

"Yes. I'm going to do it."

"I'm so glad. You'll get the vacation you've always dreamed of."

"I hope that you'll act as tour guide on a trip or three?"

"I can do that. I need a vacation, too, you know. As long as you aren't too obnoxious."

"Who? Me?"

"Yeah, you."

"You mean my teddy bear problem."

"That's no problem."

"Good."

"But seriously?"

"I can do serious when necessary."

"I think you should know that I am NOT easy. Okay?"

"I never thought you were. Never."

"Good."

"In fact, sometimes you're darned difficult."

"Ken."

"We talk silliness on here, and I hope you don't think I'm really this goofy."

"I'm sure you are."

"I don't think you're as goofy as you are on here."

"Oh, but I am."

"Okay. But I am a perfect gentleman and I'm not easy, either."

"I'm glad. And I'm delighted that you're coming out. When?"

"I'll be there right after Fourth of July weekend. Can I count on seeing you a few times?"

"Sure."

"Will I get to meet Brian?"

"Hahahahahahaha."

"Does that mean yes?"

"He might be in a nursing home by then. I've got him pretty well worn out."

"Wonderful. How old is he?"

"Thirty-three."

"Good grief."

"Yeah. Hey, I think I hear his walker in the driveway now."

"His BMW, more like."

"How did you know?"

"Have fun. Not TOO much fun."

"Like I'd tell you if I did. Good night, Bear."

"Good night, friend."

"Thank you."

"For what?"

"For calling me friend."

She logged off and went to greet Brian. Cori always laughed a lot when she was with him. He loved to tell a story and he didn't care how many people might be around, trying to eat a nice, quiet dinner in a romantic restaurant. He told his stories with broad gestures and sound effects. Cori had long ago stopped trying to reduce his volume. She learned to accept it when Dave was still alive. The two doctors would tell their stories together in a place like this and entertain not just Cori and Brian's girlfriend, but all the people around. Some of their tales weren't suitable for genteel audiences. In fact, most of them weren't, given their line of work. Dave and Brian were best friends for the few months they worked together.

Outside of a little teasing, Brian had been an attentive friend since Dave's death, good for both listening and talking. He had offered more once, but abandoned the subject when she refused. "I think sex is for love, Brian. Not just for comfort or release."

"Well, sure it is. But friends can love, and I'm here if you need me. Savvy?"

"Thank you. A kiss now and then..."

"Consider it done." That's how their good night kisses got started. She felt silly about it for a while but now accepted it as a part of their comfortable friendship. A nice part.

Tonight in her living room, he was taking his leave. "I had a great time, as usual."

"Me, too. Take care, Brian. Maybe I'll stop in and see you at the clinic one of these days."

"Do that. Good night, beautiful."

"Good night." He bent to kiss her and she slipped her arms around his waist. Their kiss was friendly and enthusiastic. She held onto him as she said, "One of these days your girlfriend is going to catch us doing this."

"Nah." He grinned and blew a kiss as he slipped out. She closed the door behind him and couldn't resist the temptation to check her e-mail before bed. There was a message from Ken, as she thought there might be. "A boring evening. I'll probably still be online when you get home. Check and see if you like."

She liked. "Hi, Ken."

"Hi. Did you have a good dinner?"

"Yup. What did you do for dinner?"

"Sandi made stew. Good stuff. How's Brian?"

"Fine. He mentioned Dave and I remembered a story I think you might like."

"Is it clean?"

"Relatively. When we were first married, I once asked if I could visit his Male Sexuality class at the hospital. I wanted to see his teaching style. On the night of the class, I got held up late at the school where I was having a conference with an upset parent. I hurried, but was several minutes late. When I walked into the room, Dave stopped his lecture and said, 'Ma'am, when you're late for this class, you have to kiss the teacher.' He was daring me, something I couldn't resist. I marched up to him and threw one arm around his neck, the arm further from the audience, and while we kissed, I clapped my hand firmly on his butt. The class cracked up.

"The applause was all out of proportion to our little performance and as the class progressed, I saw why. Dave filled his lecture with personal anecdotes. I was the star of these. I was famous in this little circle and I didn't like it much. After class, I led Dave out by the ear, a fitting revenge, I thought."

"It sounds like you two were compatible."

"Yeah. Both nut cases."

"Were you about the same age?"

"No. He was eighteen years older."

"You like older men?"

"Yeah. And younger men. And men my age."

"You said something once about him being unfaithful?"

"I can tell that. If you want to hear it."

"I do. Unless it's too hard."

"No problem. Dave asked me to go to a convention with him, but school was in session and I couldn't get away. So he went alone. A few days afterward I stopped in at the clinic and overheard two of the women talking

The Kansas Connection   Kathleen Gabriel

about another one and what a slut she was and when they saw me they froze. I can make people talk when I want to and I got the story and walked in on Dave during an exam. He pushed me out into the hall and I confronted him there."

"Wow. Did everybody hear?"

"No. I kept it quiet and told him what time I expected him home. He came home at that time and we had what started out as a quiet conversation. He told me how he'd always had to have fun at a convention, have a few drinks and... I told him that he didn't need the few drinks and that his resistance would be stronger if he didn't have them. He went on for a while then I yelled, 'Damn it, you're a thief. What you gave away this weekend was mine. I will not tolerate it. Not one more time, no matter what.'

"'What will you do if I do?' he asked. And I said, 'You will NOT do it again. I have decided.' He looked at me for a long time, and then he nodded. For the next few months, he slept at home when there was a meeting in town, and when there was a meeting out of town, I accidentally lost his plane tickets. That was the last year I taught full-time. After that, I went to every meeting he had with him, and we had a good time at every one of them."

"Was it worth it?"

She sighed. "Yes. But any compromise carries regrets."

"What did Dave give up in this compromise?"

"His taste for strange tail, I guess."

"Ooh, the way you talk."

"Yeah."

"You would never cheat," he typed.

"Never. Would you?"

"Nope. It's a completely foreign idea to me."

"Good," she typed.

"Why do you say good?"

"Oh, I don't know. I guess it just shows we are of the same species."

"We are of the species who sit at home and chat on the Internet on a Friday night."

It was true. Though she had been with someone earlier tonight, he was just a friend. "Maybe we could get a little closer. Send each other pictures or something."

"I have no recent picture. I'll get one of the kids to take one and send it. If you're not joshing me."

"Send it. I'll send one to you tomorrow, attached to an e-mail. It's too big to send on this program and I don't remember how to make the file smaller."

"I still have your phone number..."

"Use it."

"We might feel awkward on the phone. We talk about everything on here, but it's not as close to real as the phone is."

"Call me anyway. Unless you're chicken."

"That's a low blow to a cop. We are big and tough and not afraid of anything." While the words appeared on the screen her phone rang.

She picked it up laughing. "Hello."

"Now that's a greeting I like to hear."

"Hello?"

"No, laughter. I love it."

She cast about for a safe subject. "How's your cat?"

"He's fine. Fat and sassy. He's lying here by me on the bed."

"I thought you were sitting at the computer."

"I am. The bed's right next to me."

"Okay. My computer's in the corner of the living room right by the stairs. I'm sitting here still dressed for dinner."

"What are you wearing?"

"Ken..." Her voice had a definite warning tone.

He started laughing. "Man, that sounded bad. The standard online come-on. I was just curious what you wore tonight. I'm in jeans and a sweatshirt."

"What color sweatshirt?"

"It's a navy blue, I guess."

"I've only seen you once. I don't know if you look good in blue or not."

"Oh, I do. Believe it."

She grinned. "I believe it. I'm wearing a purple dress with silver hoop earrings and black shoes. Heels."

"Purple. A long dress?"

"Knee length. Side slits."

"Hmm."

"What's the cat wearing?"

"A tuxedo. But don't be impressed. It's his only outfit. And he has selective hair releasers."

"What are those for?"

"So he can shed his black hairs on your white clothes and his white hairs on your black ones."

"Most ingenious."

"He thinks he's brilliant. And you ought to see him when it snows. It has to be the wet kind of snow."

"What does he do?"

"He bats at the snow to make snowballs. When one gets too heavy for him, he makes another one. It makes weird tracks."

She laughed. "I don't believe that."

"I've got video I can show you."

"You've been holding out on me. You probably have all kinds of neat stuff to show me and all I get is stories on the Net."

"You don't like them?"

"I like them. Do you see me running away?"

He spoke with a smile in his voice. "No, I don't see you running away and it amazes me."

"How come?"

"Because you're a remarkable person. Someone I'm proud to know."

"Huh. I find that... remarkable."

He said nothing.

"You still there, Ken?"

"Yup. Just sitting here grinning."

"I can't see you."

"I know it. It's no great treat anyway."

"Man, you're fishing."

"Yup."

She chuckled. "You're a fine looking man, Sergeant Honey Bear. As far as I remember, my eyes being clouded with fatigue the one time I was privileged to see you."

"Gee, thanks for that lavish compliment."

"You are lavishly welcome."

"Have you been drinking?"

"No, but it's a good idea."

"Drinking's fun sometimes. I never have gotten into it much."

"Me either. I like to be alert."

"I can see that about you. Your wits are fully present."

"I hope so. I like your wits, too. I mean, your sense of humor but also your smarts."

"Thank you. And I want you to know that I'm no uneducated wit. I went to college and graduated with honors."

"You mentioned college before. So you got your bachelor's degree?"

"Yes, I did. I'm proud of that."

"What major? Law enforcement?"

"Yup. Minor in psychology."

"Did that help you make sergeant so young?"

"It did. They use a point system, not just dazzling personality as a criteria.

"Makes it more fair for the average guys." She was sure he could hear her amusement. She was enjoying hearing his voice, his accent, his laughter. She wished she could see him and touch him. She shook her head. She didn't even know this guy.

"I know you have a bachelor's degree, too, to be a teacher."

"Yeah. History major, education minor, then the teaching certificate. Before I started teaching I went on and got a master's in history."

"I didn't know that. What did you do your thesis on?"

"The link between economic unrest and the persecution of minorities."

"That might be interesting reading."

"It's kind of boring."

"My niece writes stories. Little short ones. Pretty good, what she'll let me read."

"Maybe the ones she won't let you read are even better."

He laughed. "Could be."

"I like talking to you."

"But?"

"No buts." She assured him.

"Good. Tell me a story."

"The last story was mine. You tell me one now."

"Um..." They talked about nothing for just over two hours, then Cori called a halt. "We can't stay up all night talking."

"Why not?"

"Well, it's two hours later over there and you're probably falling asleep."

"I'd be afraid to fall asleep in your presence."

"No."

"Yeah. Dangerous."

"I am not. I'm perfectly safe."

"Oh, sure. I was tired one day and fell asleep on the couch and Jennifer painted my toenails. I bet you're the same way."

"Never. I'd go for fingernails."

"See how you are?"

"Okay. But I'm going to hang up so you can go to bed."

"Are you going to bed, too?"

"Yup."

"I won't tell anyone we went to bed together." It was a joke, but his voice cracked a little as he said it.

"Good. Our secret."

"Well, you handsome rascal, good night. Can we do this again sometime?"

"We can. Good night, sweet lady. Dream well."

The Kansas Connection   Kathleen Gabriel

CHAPTER FOUR

*C*ori's old-fashioned azaleas outdid themselves. She would gladly forgive them for looking like sticks the rest of the year. Their fragrance came in waves as she slogged through her soggy backyard. The rhododendrons were budding out nicely and would put on a good show next month. She wished she had more roses, but hesitated to plant any more permanent plants in this already overgrown yard. She didn't know what she should get rid of, but she knew something had to go. Mowing around all these bushes was a real chore.

She stood still and looked at the sad little tulip patch she made last fall. One hundred and twenty white tulip bulbs she'd planted in an artful crescent in the back here. Fewer than thirty remained. She had pictured what a beautiful display they'd make for her to see from her kitchen and bedroom windows. Now they were gone. Some never even got a chance to bloom.

She squatted next to the remains of a tulip and looked it over. It looked as if it had been cut near the base of the stem. Strange. No one would come into her backyard and cut her flowers. And if they had, surely they wouldn't have done it gradually, a few at a time. They would have gotten them all at once. Maybe. She didn't understand anyone who could steal, so had no idea what they might be thinking when they did it.

She looked around and saw evidence of digging. Not only were her flowers and their foliage gone, but bulbs had been dug up. Whoever did it was sloppy, too.

Cori stood and looked around the yard while she thought. A charming pair of squirrels racing back and forth under the filbert trees distracted her. They stopped and scolded, then ran up a tree. Probably they had nuts from last fall buried nearby and they wanted her to move on so they could retrieve them.

Cori went in the back door and left her garden shoes in the utility room. She washed at the kitchen sink and started water for tea. She went to the refrigerator and got out leftover bean soup and ingredients for a salad. She put a cup of soup in the microwave and took the vegetables to the sink to wash them.

While she washed the vegetables, she looked out the window at her pathetic tulips. A squirrel ran through the patch and stopped by a flower, it looked like he was smelling it. So cute. Now the flower shook. Then it fell. Cori's mouth dropped open as she watched the squirrel dig.

She turned the water off and dashed out to the utility room and through the back door. As soon as she left the walk the shock of cold wetness soaking through her socks reminded her that she should have put her shoes on. She ran through the yard after the squirrel. "Out!" she yelled. "Out of my tulips, you furry jerk!" The squirrel was long gone. He sat high in a walnut tree and chattered at her. Cori stomped her foot, splashing herself with mud droplets.

She whirled and stalked back toward the house. "Hey, neighbor," the man next door called. Figures he'd be out and catch her in her indignity. She grimaced and waved. "Is that a new style you learned from the kids at school?"

"What?"

"Socks in the mud?"

"Yeah, the latest thing."

"Who were you yelling at?"

"Damned squirrels ate my tulips."

"They love tulips."

"Now you tell me." He laughed while she went back inside. She leaned her butt against the washer as she tugged off her soaked and muddy socks. She went upstairs to the bathroom, ran water in the tub, took off her pants and stepped in. She stood there only long enough to warm her feet and to contemplate five or six methods of squirrelicide.

After lunch, she read her e-mail. Ken's told about a fight his niece Jennifer and her best friend got into the night before. He captured the essence of their personalities so that she felt she knew both of them. He often told things about Michael the same way. He loved those kids. It was too bad he wasn't someone's father. She would look over her other mail before answering this one. She'd talk with Ken tonight anyway, as she did every day.

She got several messages from her history discussion group. She wearied of the Battle of Agincourt. It could be time to say goodbye to it. She drummed her fingers on the desk. Surely it was time. She didn't visit the discussions group's site and read everyone's rants, but she did answer the few e-mails she received courteously, one by one.

The Kansas Connection   Kathleen Gabriel

She found an e-mail from someone whose e-mail address was vaguely familiar and supposed it was from another discussion group member. But it was from a Lauren Tate-Rivera. Cori was impatient with hyphenated names. They seemed either pretentious or pitiful. Pitiful that a woman couldn't make up her mind what name to use. What was the big deal? Choose one! It was better than making everyone in the world remember both names.

Cori read Ms. Tate-Rivera's letter with interest. She was that editor with the textbook publisher she had given a piece of her mind. Cori had thought she'd get an answer, but this long message surprised her.

The editor agreed that that text was not their best, and wondered what Ms. Schiller thought of the content, apart from style considerations. She listed several passages and asked her opinion of them. Cori frowned. She had a copy of the textbook here. She got it and read the passages the message referred to.

It took some time, and some study and consulting other books, and a call to her dad, but Cori decided what she thought of those passages. She wrote back to Ms. Tate-Rivera and gave her opinion.

Ken came online sooner than she expected, but when she checked the time it was later than she thought. "Time flies when you're having fun," she wrote.

"Hmm. Dare I ask what you've been having fun doing?"

"Arguing with a textbook editor."

"You're a barrel of monkeys."

"Ha ha. Did you have any fun today?"

"Pulled over a fellow cop, off-duty. He was doing thirty-five in a school zone."

"Uh-oh. That's one of your pet peeves, isn't it?"

"Yeah. He was embarrassed."

"I bet. I didn't have dinner yet. What shall I fix?"

"Snails, watercress salad, frog's legs, turtle soup."

She laughed. He was making fun of her weather again. "It stopped raining for a little while today."

"What did you do with the time? Waded out to look at your flowers, I bet."

"Yup. And caught me a thief." She told the story of the squirrel and Ken was not adequately sympathetic. "You have a walnut tree in the back yard? And you're surprised you have squirrels?"

"A walnut and a bunch of filbert trees."

"What are filberts?"

"Um, you know. Filberts. The nuts they make Nutella out of."

"What's Nutella?"

"I have a lot to teach you, Bear."

"No fooling, what are filberts like? Related to walnuts?"

"No. I'm trying to think." They had another name, but she always called them filberts.

"Take your time. Don't hurt your hair."

"Hush."

"He he he."

"Hazelnuts. That's what the rest of the world calls them."

"Oh, I like those. Do you pick them in the fall and use them in cookies and stuff?"

"No. The damned squirrels got them all."

"Aww. I'm so sorry. Would you rather have squirrels to watch or nuts?"

"Squirrels. But between squirrels and tulips, it's another matter. If you'd been here I would have borrowed your gun."

"I hate to think what a police thirty-eight would do to a poor little squirrel."

"Yuck."

"Succinctly put."

"Thanks."

"But you probably couldn't hit one anyway. You don't know how to shoot, do you?"

"Nope. You'll have to show me how."

"I can do that. We can go to the arcade at an amusement park and I'll show you how to pick off the little duckies one by one."

"Cool! You can win me a teddy bear."

"I'm good at that. That's how I get all my dates. I go to county fairs and win teddy bears for pretty ladies."

"Not really."

"You're right. I win a teddy bear and give it to a pretty lady and it turns out she has a huge boyfriend with a tank top, a skull tattoo and an attitude."

"Poor Honey Bear."

"Yeah. I'll come sit on your lap for a while. Cheer me up, huh?"

"I think you're awful big for a lap pet."

"Maybe that's true. But so is this Sylvester and he gets picked up. Doesn't seem fair."

"I wish I had a cat. I could use some loving tonight."

"Last flight leaves Wichita about eight... if I speed I can just make it. Then right in time for your bedtime... Sylvester will arrive."

She cracked up. "So sweet. You'd even lend me your cat."

"I'd give you just about anything, and that's a fact."

"I'll remember that. Don't be surprised if I come asking for something strange."

"Such as?"

"Hmmm. How about a Holley four-barrel carburetor for my fifty-nine T-Bird?"

"Uh... that might take a day or tow."

"You mean, a day or TWO?"

"No, I meant TOW. You might have to tow it."

"Could be. What if I needed a hundred and twenty little cages the size of soup cans?"

"Um. For what?"

"Planting tulip bulbs in a squirrel-proof way."

"Other flowers are just as pretty and have less tasty bulbs."

"People in Holland ate tulip bulbs during World War II."

"I'm glad there were a lot of tulips there for them."

"Me, too."

"Cori?"

"Yeah?"

"Do you really have a fifty-nine T-Bird?"

He had her laughing again. "I sold it when I was in college to buy textbooks."

"Books are expensive."

"Yeah, they are. But I like them."

"What kind of fiction do you like to read?"

"I like to read cookbooks. I'm hungry."

"Poor Cori. Go eat something and talk to me later. I'll be here and there. If I don't answer online, call me."

"Ladies don't call gentlemen."

"pppppbt."

"Okay. Okay. Later, 'gator." She logged off and scrambled eggs and melted a little grated cheese on them. She ate them with a warm tortilla, salsa and a beer. The beer was in order after battling wild beasts in the backyard.

Back online after supper, Ken wanted to know what she ate and she told him. It seemed silly, but they always exchanged this information. "So what did you have, Ken?"

"Well, Sandi and the kids went out before I got home and the soup they left me looked awful. I felt too lazy to make anything else."

"So?"

"A quart of milk and two Snickers bars. Are you satisfied, now you have learned the depths of my depravity?"

"Ha ha. What kind of milk?"

"Skim."

"That's not as bad as it could have been."

"I lied. It was two per cent."

"Bear, you need someone to take care of you."

"I do not. Um... are you volunteering?"

"I will take care of you when you're here, as far as food goes."

"Oh, no. I want you to have a vacation, too."

"It's a treat for me to cook for someone else."

"I'll let you cook for me, then. But not all the time. Just when we aren't out somewhere on a trail or in a restaurant."

"Restaurant?"

"Yes. I'd like to take you out a few times."

"This is beginning to sound like a very nice vacation."

"I hope you have fun. I'm a little nervous about the whole thing."

"I'm a little nervous, too, but we're just being silly. We really know each other pretty well, don't you think?"

"Not as well as we will. I hope you'll like me."

"I don't think there's much chance that I won't." She picked up the phone and punched in his number.

"I hope you're right. But you never can... hold on. Phone." He said, "Hello?"

She greeted him laughing. "It's Cori. You really need to get caller ID."

"I thought ladies did not call gentlemen?"

"Oh, well."

"Uh, huh. Good to hear your voice."

"Thanks. Is everybody home now?"

"No, just me and this scruffy cat."

"Maybe if he'd been around, those squirrels wouldn't have gotten all my tulips."

"He's an indoor type. And even if he weren't, squirrels are sneaky. They would have found a way."

"Probably." She sighed.

"Hey, lady."

"Yeah?"

"Are you really planning on feeding me when I come visit?"

"Sure, if you'll let me."

"I'm no dope."

"Maybe I'll make us some squirrel stew."

"Yuck."

She giggled. "Hey, mister."

"Yeah?"

"Are you really worried that we might not like each other?"

"No, I'm just worried that you might not like me. You only really met me once."

"I liked you just fine then."

"Yeah?"

"Yeah. I like your smile... and everything."

"Tell me about 'everything.'"

She grinned. "Oh, I don't know. I don't want to be all silly on the phone the way we are on the computer."

He didn't say anything, but she heard him typing and she looked at her monitor. "Maybe we should get back on the computer where we can be mushy."

She typed, "No mush, buddy. Mush makes me nervous."

His voice came through on the phone. "I don't want to make you nervous. I just like to tease."

"I know you do. I do, too."

"No fooling? I never would have guessed."

"So. What do you like to eat?"

"Everything. I always tell you what I eat and I like almost everything. But I went to this Japanese restaurant once..."

Cori sighed happily as he launched into a story.

"And it was kind of dark. I got this seafood stew they recommended. It was good, and there were these little things, about a half a tongue worth in size, that I thought were really good. I wanted to know what they were, so the next time I found one in my mouth I sneaked it back out onto my spoon and held it over near the little candle on the table."

She waited. "And? What was it?"

"It was a little bitty squid."

"Ugh."

"Yeah. Seeing it plum put me out of the mood of eating any more of them."

"I don't remember ever eating any of those before."

"That was the weirdest thing I ever ate, I think."

"I ate snails before."

"Cooked ones?"

"Well, duh. They tasted like garlic rubber bands."

"Must not have been cooked right, then. I've heard they're nice and tender."

"Rubber bands, I'm not kidding you."

"You don't need to cook me any snails."

"All right."

"Or anything fancy. If you want to fry me an egg, I'll be delighted."

"Okay."

"And I'd like to cook for you, too. And do whatever you think is fun. We don't need to look at every square inch of Oregon to make me happy. I don't need to see every one of the Cascades."

"Okay."

"Now the coast is another matter. I do not consider the coast optional."

"I know, I know. Astoria, Cannon Beach, Tillamook, Lincoln City."

"Yes. And any secret beaches you know about."

"I like this one called Hug Point."

"Do I get a hug there?"

"Maybe," she agreed, smiling. "A stage coach route used to go along that part of the coast, and when it got to this place they had to carve the rock for the road, and they still could only use it at low tide. The route hugs the point, so that's where the name came from. There's a waterfall and some caves and rocks you can climb there."

"Sounds good."

"I watched some people making a movie there once. It looked like a pretty stupid movie, but, hey."

"That sounds like a good place. Are there seagulls?"

She scoffed. "Are seagulls an attraction?"

"I like them. I like how they swoop and dive."

"And fight? And steal?"

"All that stuff. Sylvester likes them, too. He woke up when we started talking about birds."

"And we didn't even say the word 'birds.'"

"He's very intelligent, just not so's you'd notice."

"I'd like to meet him."

"I'll send you a picture."

"Okay."

"You can send me a picture of your favorite squirrel."

"Those fluffy-tailed jerks."

"Forget I asked."

"Asked what?"

He laughed, low and lazy. Cori wanted to sit on his lap and mess up his hair. Not practical from a distance of over fourteen hundred miles. She'd have

The Kansas Connection   Kathleen Gabriel

to stifle the urge once more.

CHAPTER FIVE

*K*en sat barefoot at his computer chatting with Cori. He'd left the bedroom window wide open so he could hear the birds and smell the neighbor's roses.

She wrote, "I think we have everything lined out for your two weeks here. Jammed full of trips."

"I think you're an excellent tour guide. I hope you'll come with me on every one of them."

"I might do that. We'll have to see how it goes."

"Did you get me room reservations?"

"No."

"Shoot, Cori. It's getting late. I would have done that from here if I'd known you weren't going to."

"I have another idea. Been thinking about this but I'm afraid you'll think I'm too forward."

"pppppbt." He got that from her, and grinned while he typed it. He suspected what her idea was and it made his grin bigger.

"That's not nice."

"What's your idea?"

"Why don't you stay with me? I have a spare bedroom and I don't mind sharing all the other rooms."

"Really? That would save me a pile of money. I could spend the difference on expensive presents for you."

"Don't think I didn't think of that."

"Ha ha. How do you know we'll get along?"

"If we don't, I'll kick you out."

"That's fair. I like the idea."

"Me, too. Then we can plan stuff better, too. In case some of the trips don't work out."

"I'll do it, if you're sure you don't mind."

"I don't mind."

He had to bring this up, cut down on the awkwardness, maybe, or keep him from fretting. "Wait."

"Wait, what?"

"Will having me in the house hinder your love life?"

"No."

"You're sure?"

"I'm sure. Come on out."

"I'll be there next week." Ken stretched after visiting with Cori. Jennifer and Michael wanted him to take them fishing tomorrow, his day off. He'd do that early, then double check his hiking and camping stuff. He and Cori planned just one overnight trip, a hike to see a secluded lake she said was beautiful. He wanted to use all his own camping gear, stuff he was familiar with, instead of having to coordinate his stuff with her stuff. He was taking two tents for propriety. He'd probably do most of the setting up and breaking down. Cori didn't really seem like a camper.

The offer of her house didn't surprise him. That she waited so long to bring it up did. She was shyer than he thought. He was grateful to stay at her house. Everything would be easier and he'd get to spend more time with her, too, the best part of the whole trip.

About him staying there not hindering her love life, as she assured him it wouldn't, that bothered him. Did it mean she wasn't seeing that damned Brian, her "old friend," as she called him? She never said she was seeing him, but she never said she wasn't, either. Or maybe she was seeing him and wasn't doing anything sexual with him. That didn't seem likely. Such a warm, loving woman would express herself that way with a man she cared about.

Maybe she was seeing that damned Brian and they'd spend the night at his place. Or maybe they'd sleep at her house even though he was there and not care a fig about making noise that would disturb him. And hearing lovemaking in the next room would disturb him, especially when one of the participants was someone he was wishing was his.

And that was dumb in itself, that wish. He didn't know Cori yet. Not really. One dinner together and a few hundred hours on the Net and the phone. He sat back down at the computer. It only took a moment to pull up her picture. There she was. She looked the way he remembered in person, allowing for her fatigue from driving all day. No, he didn't know her face well, or her gestures or physical habits. But he knew her thinking patterns, he knew her sense of humor, her turns of phrase. Now that they had been talking on the phone almost every day he knew her voice, her laugh.

And what he knew, he loved.

* * *

"Why do you want this foolish place so damned clean?" her dad asked as he turned his tea mug around on the table.

Cori straightened up, cleaning rag in hand, feeling a silly grin cover her face. "Are you so amazed that you have to ask again? I do clean once in a while, you know."

"Not like this. If you're doing it to please a man, he's going to be disappointed when he finds out what it usually looks like. If he sticks around to find out."

"Cut it out. I keep it pretty clean. It's just a little cluttered."

"You got that from your mother."

"Ha! I got it from you."

"Your brother's orderly."

"Last time we saw him he was. He could be doing anything now."

"No. Once a neat freak, always a neat freak," he said.

"So do you suppose he's got all his socks in a row in Tokyo?"

"Cheap poetry."

Cori bent to finish wiping the ancient white-painted cupboard door. Maybe she was being silly, but she had no idea how clean Ken kept his house and she didn't want to offend him. Or have him trip over something.

She stood back and looked around the kitchen. She had white cabinets and window trim, and what little wall there was was a soft yellow. One whole wall was windows above the counter with a view of her wild back yard, its overgrown shrubs and flowers tucked in here and there under trees. The kitchen looked good. Not a lot different than before, but she knew it was clean. She had done all the other rooms already, plus her usual cleaning. It was good enough. She poured herself a cup of tea from the pot and stuck her finger in it, then put it in the microwave. "More, Dad?" She paused with her hand on the microwave door.

"As long as you don't stick your dirty finger in it."

"I don't need to, now that I know it's cold. You don't know much for a professor." She refilled his mug and stuck both of them in the microwave. While the tea warmed, she sat at the table beside her father. "I'm glad summer's here."

"Summer's boring without your mother."

"It must be. But Carolyn's free in the evenings."

"Thank goodness. I shouldn't have sold the house. Damned condo has no garden and no character."

"You like your container garden, don't you? And if you want character, just come over here."

"This house has too much character. I never would have sold your old house."

"I couldn't stay there without Dave. Too much history."

He rotated his tea mug on the kitchen table. "I understand. It was the same with me after your mother died."

"I know."

"I would have helped you look for a house, though, Cori. This one's not too practical for someone who doesn't know how to fix things."

"I fell in love with the kitchen, and that's all she wrote."

"It's a great kitchen. This I admit. And the backyard's big. How are your flowers coming along?"

"Good. Let's go have a look."

* * *

Cori had done all she could to get ready. Now all she had to do was wait. Ken would get in some time today. His room was ready, fresh sheets on the bed. She had put some of her flowers in there for him, too, though she felt a little silly. She had stocked up on food, bought some things he'd mentioned he liked. She'd gathered up and washed picnic stuff just in case. She planned to make his visit her vacation, too, and hoped he wanted her around. If he didn't, that would be okay, too. Acceptable, at least.

She wore a red print sundress that was casual and flattering. It was going to be warm again today. She ran downstairs and checked her e-mail. Nothing good since Ken was on the road and not writing anything to her. She went to the bookshelf and dug out a novel she hadn't read in a long time. She carried it to the couch and sunk down, sitting with her legs up on the couch. She opened her book and started reading. She remembered it too well and it was warm. Her eyes closed, and she scooted down. A short nap wouldn't hurt a thing.

* * *

Ken got into Portland a lot earlier than he thought he could, thanks to an early start after waking at four, full of anticipation. He stopped at a gas station despite being very close to his destination. He didn't want to give Cori the impression that he only loved her for her bathroom. He looked himself over

The Kansas Connection   Kathleen Gabriel

in the restroom mirror and combed his short hair. He was wearing his favorite denim shirt with the sleeves rolled up. It was a bit warm for today, but he looked good in it. Though this was not the first time he'd seen Cori, he felt that today he'd be making a first impression.

He filled the tank and it seemed odd to have someone else pump the gas for him. Strange state, Oregon. While he waited, he noticed a car wash. It was free with a fill-up. After he paid for the gas he drove into it and hoped some of the bugs would wash off.

After a quick look at the map he'd printed from the Internet and memorized, he headed for Cori's house. It was on a quiet street, easy to find. He checked the address yet again when he got there. This was a doctor's house?

It was tan with blue trim and it looked like an old farmhouse. It had a couple of huge bushes in front. Impossibly, they looked like rhododendrons. The neighborhood had a mixture of styles from old farmhouses to ranch houses, to the big garage-in-front split-level style of the seventies. There was even a weathered cedar A-frame.

He pulled up in front of Cori's house and parked on the street. It wasn't a doctor's house after all, he remembered. Cori had sold their big house and bought this because she wanted something that was her own, something with personality. He saw it differently now. This was Cori's house. A part of her.

He glanced at his hair one more time, then climbed out of the car and walked up the walk. He got a closer look at the shrub nearest the door and darned if it wasn't a rhododendron. Probably the largest rhododendron in the world, with the possible exception of the one at the end of the house.

He walked up to the entry and stopped. The door was open, a flimsy screen door all there was between the inside of the house and the world. It seemed foolish to be letting the heat in on a warm day like this, but maybe she wanted to be sure to hear him drive up. He peered inside and saw Cori stretched out on her side on the couch, bare feet toward him, the bottom one looped over her calf. He couldn't see her face, that glorious hair covering most of it. Beyond the couch, he saw a painting of a castle with square towers with blooming spring trees in the foreground, and a thunderstorm building behind.

He didn't want to disturb her, but he could hardly stand here staring until she woke up. Slowly he raised a hand and tapped on the screen door.

Cori startled awake. She sat up and he waved to her. She laughed as she jumped up and unhooked the screen. "Hey, here you are."

"I are here." She took his hand and pulled him inside and threw her arms around him. Ken hugged her tight, burying his face in her hair. He had dreamed of such a greeting, but never expected it. Her hair and her neck smelled as good as he'd imagined. She was wonderful.

She slid back from him but let him hold her hand. They stood smiling at each other. She shrugged. "You're better looking than I remember. Not that I thought you weren't..."

Ken shrugged. "It's the uniform. I look like hell in khaki. You look great."

"Thanks. What do you want to do first? Go to the bathroom, I bet."

He grinned. "Got that taken care of. Show me around the house?" He thought that what he really wanted was three or four more hugs, but he couldn't ask for that.

Cori led him through the house. He stopped and stared at the castle painting for a long time, peering at the signature. "This is real, not a print. Who's Amelia Giles?"

"My mother. I have several of her paintings."

"That is so cool." He liked the sunny kitchen, and the older furniture, none of it looking like fussy antiques, just nice old stuff. When she led the way upstairs, he bounced a little on a squeaky step and listened. Oh, well. At least it was her house that was squeaky and creaky and not herself. He stood a long time at her bedroom window, looking out at the backyard. She stood beside him, silent. He turned his head toward her. "Is it all yours?"

"Back to the second fence."

He peered through the overgrown yard and located the fences. The second one was a good hundred feet back. "Wow."

"I've been here for a year now but haven't really had time to do much back there. I planted the flowers but I haven't decided what to do with everything else. Some of it needs to go, but I don't want to start all over, either."

He nodded. "It's a jungle, just like you told me."

"I know it. Maybe next year..."

He chuckled. She sounded like him putting off visiting Oregon. She was his motivator. Maybe he would be hers. "I love your house."

"I have a lot to do on it."

"Well, sure. But it's yours and it has personality. I like your pictures and furniture. Everything feels friendly here." Especially her, but he didn't say that.

"Thank you. I hoped you'd grok it. Want something cold to drink?"

"Thanks, yeah. And I need to get some of my stuff inside." She helped him carry things, with both of them laughing and talking the whole time, and they ended up moving all of his things inside, including the camping gear, which they stashed in the downstairs bedroom.

"Thanks, Cori." He closed the door behind them, wished they hadn't had to leave it open so long, letting in so much heat.

She took him to the kitchen, and they sat at the table and sipped sodas. Pops, according to her. It was getting hot. Odd she didn't turn on the air conditioning. Unless... "Do you have air conditioning?"

"No, not yet. I'll probably have it put in. I think it would be more comfortable on these warmer days. We don't have a lot of them, and usually not 'til August."

"It'll be about ninety today, I think."

"About that. I hate it when it's over a hundred."

"Me, too." He didn't want to offend her, but he was getting downright uncomfortable. "I think I'll change my shirt." She looked a little worried. He stroked the back of her hand with one finger. "You don't have a swimming hole around here, do you?"

She rolled her eyes. "Yeah, but aren't you tired from all that driving?"

"Nah. It was no chore at all."

"Should we take a picnic? I have sandwich makings and fruit..."

"I'll just take you out to dinner afterward."

"This is sounding better all the time. I'll go get my swimsuit on. I hope you won't be disappointed."

He was puzzled. "It's a nice swimming spot, isn't it?"

"No, I mean... It is a nice place. A park with a creek. Bring your water shoes." She got up and ran up the stairs while he watched, following. Water shoes?

Ken changed into swim trunks and an old tee shirt and pulled his jeans back on over the trunks. He found Cori in the kitchen putting a Tupperware pitcher into a canvas bag. "What are water shoes?"

"Shoes you wear in the creek. Fancy people buy special shoes, but old tenny runners work fine."

"Tenny runners?"

"Yeah, you know. Tennis shoes."

"Ha. You talk funny. Let's go." He insisted on taking his car. Cori directed him through the turns while he asked her for the names of plants and trees and birds. She didn't know most of them, but a few she did.

They pulled in and drove up and down looking for a parking spot. They weren't the only people who'd noticed the heat. Cars and vans littered the place. Finally they parked by a huge cedar tree. Ken stood looking up at it while Cori got things out of the back seat. She swung his towel into his stomach. He held it there. "Thanks. This is beautiful."

"Are you sure you've been to Oregon before? You act like everything's new."

"I was here. Twenty years changes memories, I guess. I remember being amazed last time, too, though."

They sat at a picnic table near the creek and Cori changed her shoes while Ken took off his jeans and shirt. "Do I really need to wear shoes in the water?"

"Yup. Trust me."

He sat and slipped on some old shoes he'd brought along, then sat up to watch as Cori pulled off her dress, revealing a blue tank suit, a trim figure and a quantity of smooth, fair skin. He was relieved that her breasts were pressed nearly flat by the snug suit, showing that they were natural, something he was fussy about, considering. Not that he'd ever get a chance to get closer. She raised her eyebrows at him, needing his comment, it seemed. She looked satisfied at his assessing glance and appreciative smile.

The creek was swift, and the bottom was made of rocks of all sizes, not sand or mud like the creeks he was familiar with. It was well populated with people, mostly kids. Ken was fascinated by the fern-covered boulder that protruded into the water and the many tall trees all around. Cori took about five fast steps into the water, then launched herself in, front first. "Aaiee! Mama mia!" she yelled. She stood up and turned around, chest deep in the water, her feet spread wide to keep her balance.

Ken asked from the shore, "Is it cold?"

"No, it's perfect," she squeaked.

He took a deep breath and got in the way she had but got his head under, too, and came up yelling. "Yow! Caramba! Perfect, huh?" He lunged toward her, hands in a strangling position. She laughed and swam away. Several children giggled.

"Hey, mister. My grandpa says 'caramba.' You speak Spanish, huh, mister?" one dark-eyed boy said.

"No. That's about all I know."

"What else can you say?" the kid persisted.

Ken kept moving his arms in the water in hopes of warming up. "Um, taco, enchilada, burrito..."

"No, really."

"I have some stuff memorized." He said something quickly and the kid scowled and waded off.

Cori sounded puzzled. "What did you say?"

"'Step away from the vehicle. Put your hands on your head. You have the right to remain silent.'"

She splashed him. He splashed back, avoiding drenching her hair. They alternated paddling around with standing in the water watching people until the sun hid behind the trees and few people remained. "Thanks for bringing me out here. This is a great place."

"Oh, you're welcome. And it's only the beginning." Ken wanted to take her hand as they walked to the restrooms to change clothes, but she didn't walk close to him and so he didn't. She was, however, checking him out. He tried not to grin, but couldn't help it. She tossed those glorious curls and looked away.

The Kansas Connection   Kathleen Gabriel

CHAPTER SIX

*I*n the changing room, Cori was squeezing the water out of her suit when she realized that she had forgotten a couple of critical items. If she put her suit back on she'd be wet and miserable all evening and the wetness would show. She groaned and pulled her dress on over nothing, hoping she'd look all right. She never went anywhere without a bra, but it might pass. They'd have to go home before they went out if Ken noticed anything.

He was waiting when she came out. She watched him but he was looking at her face, not her chest. Maybe she looked all right.

He pursed his lips as she got close, then said, "This is really dumb, but I forgot my underwear."

She burst out laughing. "I did, too. We sure were in a hurry to get out of the house."

"Man, I guess."

"I wanted to take you to the Ranger on the way home, but maybe we should go change and go somewhere closer, or else eat at home."

"Why? No one can see what we haven't got on."

"They might be able to see what I haven't got on."

His eyes scanned her chest.

Cori felt a sudden heat in her face as she stood still under his scrutiny.

He finished his quick but thorough survey and brought his gaze back to her eyes, smiling. "Nothing out of line at all. Let's go."

She hesitated to take his hand when he extended it to lead her to the car, which added to her embarrassment when he simply waited. On the way to the car, he remarked some more on the height of the trees. She barely listened, but thought that she should show him the redwoods if he liked big trees. That is, if they were getting along all right and could make a long car trip together without her making a fool of herself.

She gave him directions to the Ranger, a place she had stopped often on the way back from trips up the river. Ken's talk about their plans for the two weeks put her at ease on the drive.

The lovely smell of grilled onions greeted them as they walked in the door. The tavern was decorated with all sorts of old forestry and fishing tools, and it was several blessed degrees cooler than the outside air. They looked the menus over in silence, although she nearly had it memorized. After they ordered, Ken stretched a hand across the table to Cori and she took it. He looked as if he were getting ready to say something, so she watched him and waited. A burst of laughter came from another table.

"Can I come sit next to you? I don't want to holler." She slid over and let him into her side of the booth where he leaned close to her ear and spoke softly. "In spite of all our hours on the Net and the phone, I still don't know you well enough to keep from doing stupid things." She shrugged. "You have to remember that I have four sisters..."

What did that have to do with anything? "I know that."

"I'm pretty casual about things pertaining to women, and you're just another woman to me."

"Gee, thanks."

"I'm capable of being polite, but..."

"Oh, quit. I practically asked you to look and you looked and I have no reason to be embarrassed. It's me who's acting stupid."

He let out a long breath. "Okay. But you really do look just fine."

She stared at the table. "Hush."

"Are you going to kick me out?"

"Not yet. You haven't paid for dinner." He whimpered comically and she chuckled. His face was only a few inches from hers and she met his eye for a moment, then looked down only to find his mouth and its dimple close enough to kiss. For just a second she wanted to, but no. She'd only embarrass herself. She met his eye again and saw such suspicion there that she cracked up.

Later that night, Cori met Ken in the hall after brushing her teeth. "It cools down really nicely at night, and I usually sleep with the bedroom door open to get all the breeze I can. It doesn't mean I want company."

He held up his hands. "Oh, shoot. Have I already earned a nasty reputation?"

Sympathy for him washed over her. Surely she had hurt him. She lifted her hand and placed it on his shoulder. "Of course not. I'm just letting you

The Kansas Connection   Kathleen Gabriel

know why I do things so you won't wonder or worry."

"All right. It's cooled off quite a bit. Shouldn't be hard to sleep."

"Shouldn't be hard for you, anyway, after that long drive. I'm surprised you're not dragging butt."

"I am, actually."

"Well, sleep well. I'll see you in the morning."

"Good night, Cori. I'm glad I'm here."

"I'm glad you're here, too." She held out her right hand, laughed as he pulled his head back and frowned. She stepped up to him and held her arms open.

* * *

"If you're sure it's okay," he murmured as he took her up on her offer. She squeezed him hard enough that he noticed a sore muscle in his back. More noticeable than that were her soft breasts tight against his chest. Ken enjoyed holding her but was glad it was a short hug lest he get into more trouble.

While he undressed and got into bed he reflected that women didn't understand that men were not in charge of a certain part of their own bodies. Underdog, his own unruly part, had begun to stir during that hug. What trouble might he cause if they were to snuggle for a good long while, as Ken fully intended to do as soon as he got a chance?

He hoped that Cori understood men well enough to know that he wasn't trying to get anything he shouldn't. Wanting and trying to get were two entirely different activities. He'd been deprived so long that he was surprised he didn't have a misunderstanding with Underdog in the creek, though icy water was one thing that cramped his style.

The creek was so beautiful. The trees, the big ferns and everything. And Cori in her swimsuit, too. She had strong shoulders, graceful proportions. He admired her little belly and how she didn't try to hold it in. The suit hid too much of her. That was his only complaint, and not one he planned on expressing to her.

"Dog, go to sleep, damn it."

* * *

They got up very early in order to get to Crown Point and Vista House before the day's haze impeded the view of the Columbia River gorge. Ken got to the shower first so he went downstairs and made breakfast, French toast and bacon and fresh orange juice. It took some exploring, but he managed since her places to stash implements were fairly logical, even though the old kitchen was big. Spotless, too. He'd have to remember to clean up his act if she ever came to visit him.

Cori made appreciative noises while she ate. He watched her eat and roll her eyes. He liked all of her expressions and gestures.

"You're looking a little stiff this morning. Driving catch up with you?"

"Yeah. I knew it would."

"I can probably help a little." She stood and had him lean forward and explored his back and neck with gentle fingers. Soon the gentleness was turned into focused energy and the sensation in his back was transformed from stiffness to pain, then heat, and then a gradual loosening. She treated each of several spots this way, then had him lean back against her while she massaged his neck and upper chest. Ken found it easy to submit to her ministrations, a bit of a surprise to him.

"There. Did I miss anything?"

"Mmm... nothing, little darling. I feel all new."

"Good." She went back to the table and started gathering up dishes, smiling as she did. He got up and did the same. He moved a lot easier now.

The drive up the highway took a bit over an hour, and when they got there the sun was a few degrees over the horizon. The scale of things was amazing. He couldn't grasp it at all, being able to see so far, and so much. A gigantic river, mountains, forests. As he stood gaping Cori slipped an arm around his waist. He tugged her close. "This is awesome. I mean it in the old sense, not like kids say it for every damned thing."

"I know what you mean.

They hiked several trails that led to waterfalls, then headed back. Ken sang with the radio while driving. Cori was pleased that she'd finally found something he did that wasn't perfect. If he didn't know the words, that didn't stop him. He sang whatever seemed good to him at the time. Some of his invented lyrics made her laugh. She joined in, singing quietly. He leaned over, cupping his ear, and she became bolder. She drummed on her knees, he tapped on the steering wheel.

He turned the volume way down on a commercial. "How about doing a day at the beach tomorrow?"

"We can do that, if you like. I love the beach."

"I've never waded out into the ocean here, just in Southern California and Hawaii."

"You're in for a treat, then."

"How so?"

"Well, did you like the creek we got in last night?"

"Loved it."

"The ocean is even colder. Instant hypothermia."

"Maybe I'll just walk on the beach."

"We'll see."

"Say, Cori. At the risk of getting in trouble..."

"Yes?"

"I'm wondering about the timing for our overnighter to Little Moraine Lake."

"We can go anytime. No rain in the forecast anytime soon."

"Rain wouldn't matter."

"The trails are primitive and steep. Rain would matter unless you have more skiing experience than you say."

"Oh, okay. I was thinking more about bears."

"We have only black bears around here. We'll have to secure all the food in a tree with a rope. Then they won't bother us. They're not very dangerous." She noticed that she was chewing on her thumbnail and forced herself to stop.

"I know. But I was reading about grizzly bear attacks and I got kind of spooked. Do you know what one common denominator is in bear attacks?"

"Someone messing with the baby bears?"

"Nope. And I have read this only about grizzly bears, not any other kind. But still, a bear's a bear."

"What, Ken?"

"Promise not to hit me?"

"Have I hit you yet?"

"It's a woman having her menstrual period. Bears have a keen sense of smell and something about that drives them crazy."

She was appalled. "Gross."

"Yeah. But I want to go on that hike when you're not..."

Now she saw why he was thinking he might get hit. It was kind of a personal question. "Oh. Okay. We have four days or else we have to wait another five."

"You can be that sure?"

"Yup. My inner workings, unlike my mind, are highly organized."

"Okay. I'm sure glad you didn't hit me."

"Why would I hit you? You had a legitimate need to know. I have no problem with that. When I get to know you better I probably won't be embarrassed at anything you say." She looked out the window a moment. "Hey."

"Yeah."

"Do you ever get embarrassed?"

"Only when I do something stupid."

She grinned. "Does that happen often?"

"Well, sometimes. When it does I usually cover for it by getting mad."

"Good plan."

"Not really, but it's the only one I have. So, well, let's go to Little Moraine Lake tomorrow, then."

"Suits me fine."

"You're a dynamite tour guide," he said, "and I have you all to myself."

"Got that right. Remember me next time you want to have a good vacation."

"Oh, I will."

* * *

The next morning, Cori ran down the stairs and found Ken sipping coffee at the kitchen table and staring out at her jungle. "Am I late?"

"Not at all. Coffee?"

"Sure." He poured her a cup while she looked over the stuff on the kitchen table and chairs. She held out her hand for the coffee, still looking. "Is all this stuff going to fit in those two little packs?"

"Yup. Actually, the sleeping bags go on top."

"I knew that." He started putting things in, the heavier things all in his pack.

"What's this?" She lifted a tidy gray package.

"Tent."

"Then what's this?" She hoisted an identical package. "One for the food?"

"Food goes in a tree, as you know. I don't want some bear tearing up my tent."

"Then what?"

"One for me, and one for you."

She tossed the second tent onto a chair. "Like hell, mister. There are bears out there. If one of us goes, we both go."

"So now we're sleeping together, huh?" He fixed a steady gaze on her.

She narrowed her eyes at him. "Maybe you should climb a tree and keep watch while I sleep."

"Oh, sure. If I see a bear I'll point and holler, 'She's in there!'"

Cori started laughing and he joined in. She shook so hard she spilled some coffee on the floor.

Ken cleaned it up.

"I've got you doing all the work around here and I like it," she remarked as he straightened up.

"I know you do. Good thing I'm only staying two weeks or you'd have me putting on a roof for you."

"Actually..."

"Oh, hush." They got on the road only ten minutes after they planned. Cori noticed that they took his car again, no questions asked. She'd have to remember to lead the way to hers soon. It wasn't fair that he should have to do all the driving.

They saw no one else on the trail to the lake. It was rugged and wild, just as Cori remembered it from that other time. There was less chatter on this hike and more enjoying of the scenery. She was watching the trail at her feet and remembering the other trip with Dave and Brian and his incumbent girlfriend when she felt Ken's hand on her arm. She stopped and followed his gaze. A doe stood alert before a thicket, her head raised, big ears poised. Soon she flicked an ear and bent to graze. They stood watching until she got nervous and moved off.

"Beautiful." Ken said. Cori could only nod and squeeze his hand.

They had glimpses of the lake, an incredible turquoise, before they finished the last descent. Then the trees ended and the world opened out onto a perfect lake surrounded by rocks and trees. "Here we are. Do you like it?"

Ken stood staring. "It's wonderful. And no one around for miles. Moraine means glacier, right?"

"Yup. It's right over there." She pointed out the glacier to him, a long narrow strip of dirty bluish white between graveled slopes.

"Looks like plain snow except for there's not other snow around."

"Let's explore after we ditch these packs."

"Is this whole field the campground?"

"Yeah, we just camp wherever we like." Ken tramped around until he found a spot he liked with dry ground and a view of the glacier. Cori went along with it. She helped set up the tent. One tent. She rolled the stones someone else had used for a fire ring back into place while Ken started pumping up an air mattress.

He looked disgusted. "This is pure luxury, you know. We aren't real backpackers with this thing along."

"This backpacker needs the comfort if she's to be able to walk tomorrow. I didn't see you refusing it when I brought it out."

"Well, my body's even older than yours and I like it fine. It's just the principle of the thing."

"Phooey on principles." She walked to where he stood beside the tent, one foot busy with the pump. "I can do this for a while."

"Would you? I'm tired of standing on one foot." He stretched every which way while she pumped and watched him. She chuckled to herself when the thought crossed her mind that he might be hinting for a massage.

They walked around the lake, marveling at the clarity of the water and the boldness of the little animals and birds they saw. They didn't run from them but watched with shining black eyes. Cori wished they could swim but the water was too cold. Ken filled the kettle with some of it for dinner. He said, "When I called, the ranger said it was safe to drink but this needs to boil anyway for our dehydrated dinners."

"Talk about luxury." They ate together, put the food in her pack and tied it to a rope, then tossed it over a high branch. She laughed at how many tries it took Ken to get the rope over, but she knew she wouldn't have done any better. Then they sat by the campfire and talked until the sun had set. They sat in friendly silence as a breeze came up. Cori sighed.

"What is it, lady? Are you wishing for something you left at home?"

"No. I was just wanting to wash my feet but I'm too happy to get up."

"Yeah. It's nice here. How about I make us some herb tea and you go to the lake and wash your feet?"

"Okay. While I still have some light."

* * *

Ken listened to her soft singing, then smiled at the hoots coming from the lake, then the splashing. She came back with her boots untied, socks in hand.

"Success?"

"Yeah. I washed my hands and face, too. Now I'm not sleepy any more."

"The tea has chamomile in it. That'll take care of it."

"Oh, good." She sat near him and accepted a cup from him. It warmed her hands and smelled good. "Are the tea bags food? Do we have to put them in the tree?"

"No. We'll put them in the fire. Everything else is up there. We're safe."

"Good." He lay down in the grass near the fire and she put her tea down and lay down beside him on her side, propping her head on her hand, watching him.

"See any stars yet?" he asked.

"Just you."

He snorted, but was pleased. "When the stars come out there are going to be millions of them, on a clear night this far from city lights," he said.

"It was kind of cloudy when I was here before."

"Who did you come here with?"

"My husband and another couple."

"Was the woman a friend of yours?"

"No. She was Brian's girlfriend."

"Oh." Ken was not reassured in hearing that damned Brian had a girlfriend since Cori used the past tense.

She finished her tea and rolled onto her back. She pointed at the sky. "I see one."

"I see it, too." They lay and watched the stars come out one by one, then by the handfuls, then by the hundreds. When the panoply was complete he took her hand.

"Windows in heaven," he said.

"Big burning balls of gas," she said. She giggled and soon they were both laughing. She rolled toward him and he rolled toward her. Ken laid his fingers on her cheek and she quieted, watching him in the dancing firelight.

He cleared his throat. "How about you get ready for bed in the tent while I change out here. I'll make sure the fire's okay."

The Kansas Connection   Kathleen Gabriel

CHAPTER SEVEN

Cori had never liked changing clothes in a tent, but it was quickly done and she unzipped her sleeping bag and maneuvered into it. "All clear," she called.

Ken crawled in wearing his pajamas and dropped his clothes by the end of his sleeping bag, then zipped up the tent. "I put the fire clear out. Made me nervous to think of it burning unsupervised."

"Hmm. I was thinking about maybe leaving it burning so bears wouldn't think they could join us."

"I don't think there're that many bears around. And we have a good clean camp." He got into his sleeping bag and turned on his side to face her. "This air mattress feels great. Good idea for an overnighter. We wouldn't have room for them on a longer trip, though."

"True." She lay still for a little while.

"Rats."

"What? Forget to use the kybo?" She could hear a note of laughter in his voice, a voice she was beginning to know and enjoy more all the time.

"No. I forgot to get a good night hug."

"I'm right here." He scooted closer and gathered her close. "I'd like to just stay here awhile, if it's all right with you. Think my arm would make a good pillow?"

"Probably not. But I'll try it awhile." She took Ken's arm and let him arrange it under her neck and head. "Feels good to me, but your hand's going to go to sleep."

"I don't care. If I can snuggle with you, I'm happy."

"Tell me a story."

"Hmm." He paused and she waited. "Once upon a time there was a little girl named Goldilocks."

"Ugh. Nothing with bears in it."

He gave her a squeeze. "Go to sleep, then. Aren't you tired?"

"Mmm. Yeah. Night," she murmured. She listened to his breathing slow and deepen. Soon she lost herself to the night.

Cori woke to a snuffling sound outside the tent. For an instant she thought it might be snoring, but it was not like any human sound she'd ever heard. She lay still, her eyes wide in the darkness. Through the tent fabric she saw some large shadow shape moving outside some yards away but couldn't tell what it might be. She heard the sound again. It was something like a pig.

She remembered that bears were related to pigs, and she had heard that they made noises like pigs. She listened and was sure she heard movement on the other side of the tent, too.

She still lay pillowed on Ken's arm, so she knew he was nearby. She reached out and touched his shoulder. "Hey," she whispered.

"I hear it, too. I don't know what it is."

She swallowed. "Bears."

"More than one?"

"I hear something from both sides of the tent." She shivered. He shifted his arm and tightened his grip on her.

"They'll get bored and go away. Probably came to eat some plant or other by the lake."

"It's all gravel by the lake." The snuffling came again, closer than before. Cori wriggled closer to Ken and hugged him around the shoulder. They lay and listened and held on to each other, not speaking or even breathing very loud, for what seemed to Cori a long time.

"This tent has a window. I'm going to look out," he whispered. Cori heard determination in his voice, though he lay still in her arms and made no move toward the window's zipper.

"What if they hear you and come over here?"

"Then I'll go out there and chase them away."

"Oh, sure. Did you bring your gun?"

"No."

She licked her lips. "Then what are you going to scare them away with?"

He didn't say anything. Then he said, "Nothing. I'm going to lie here and wait to see what happens."

"Okay."

"Okay." They lay still, listening to movement and snuffling noises for

The Kansas Connection   Kathleen Gabriel

a while, and then Ken patted her back and reached across her for the zipper on the window. She lay totally still and waited while he unzipped very slowly. He got up on his elbow and peered out. "Wow. Look at this, Cori."

"What is it?"

"Just look."

She raised herself and looked out. Over twenty elk were out there, moving around like the tent was just one more rock. The bulk of the herd was in the lake while a few wandered near the tent nibbling grass. "Not bears. Not bears, thank goodness."

"We still need to be quiet. Don't want to start a stampede and get trampled."

"You're so cheerful. It's what I like about you." Ken unzipped the window further and Cori watched the elk with him until she was too sleepy to watch any more and dropped back down.

* * *

Ken asked Cori to show him her tools. He looked them over, then said he was going out for a little while, but didn't say why. She ran some laundry and cleaned out the refrigerator, doing a little inventory of her own.

A little while later she watched with apprehension as Ken brought stuff in, a big brown bag and a case of some kind. "I thought we were going to rest a bit today. Looks like you have another idea."

"You said I could fix a few things, right? So, I need some stuff to do that. I'm going to put deadbolts on your doors and I'm going to do something kind of noisy." He hefted the case and nodded toward it. Cori didn't know what it was.

"The noisy thing is outside, I hope?"

"It is."

"Better wait 'til after nine to do it, then. Some of the neighbors are retired and might like to sleep in."

Later, Cori had to step over stuff to get out the door to go get her hair cut. Ken seemed happy, and that pleased her more than getting the locks she needed. She stopped and got milk and fresh bread and a little roast. When she got home, she heard a chain saw. She looked out the kitchen window and saw that her dead tree was gone, also a little one she had complained was too close to the fence. Ken was nowhere to be seen.

She put the food away and went into the back yard to see where he was just in time to see the top of her neighbor's tree shake. She went back into the house and walked over to their house to get to their yard.

Ken and the man who lived next to her were proudly watching as his dead tree, a twin to her own, fell to the ground. Ken looked natural holding a chain saw and wearing safety goggles. He grinned at her. Cori didn't want to watch him cut up the tree, so she waved and went back to her house and started the roast in the slow cooker. She had a little bit of a headache, so she took some acetaminophen.

She wanted to see what Ken had done, so she looked at the front and back doors. There was no sawdust to be seen, no trace of the job that had been done. Ken worked neatly in the kitchen and apparently carried the neatness over into other areas. Something on the stairs caught her eye. There were some tools left on a step. Odd.

Ken came in the front door after wiping his feet well. Cori came out from the kitchen and greeted him with a smile. "You sure have been busy. It's great. Even did a good deed, huh?"

"Heck, no. He paid me to drop that little tree. Took me no time at all and I recovered what I spent to rent the saw."

She sighed and smiled. "Good deal. Especially since I'm going to reimburse you for the saw rental and all that other stuff."

"Like fun you are. You're letting me stay here free and tour guiding, too. We will not speak of money."

She nodded. "Okay. Thank you for taking those trees down. They've been bugging me since I moved in. And I like my new locks, too." She stepped toward him but he backed up and held up a hand.

"You're welcome. I'm too grubby to hug, though."

"You aren't going to work all day, are you? Dad wants us to come over early for lunch."

"I'll quit pretty soon. I need to know if you use that squeaky step as a warning device? Or if you like it for some other reason?"

"I don't like it particularly."

"Good." He walked off and she watched him sit on a step, pick up a hammer and give the step a solid whack. She winced and retreated to the kitchen.

She cut up the vegetables she'd cook later to go with the roast and put them in the refrigerator. Then she mixed a little spice cake and put it in the oven.

Ken came around and leaned in the kitchen entry. "Something smells good in here."

"Dinner. I have a roast started."

His face fell. "Darn. I wanted to take you out. Get dressed up and call it a date."

Her breath caught. She nodded. "Sounds good. We can dress up to eat

The Kansas Connection   Kathleen Gabriel

here, maybe. And afterward we could go out dancing in the living room."

He raised his eyebrows and his dimple showed. "Dancing, huh?"

"We don't have to always be on some trail, do we?"

"I guess we don't. Let's do it. Oh. Come and step on your formerly squeaky step."

Before they left for her dad's about an hour before lunchtime, Cori took some ibuprofen, since the acetaminophen alone wasn't working. She didn't know what kind of a headache this was, but it wasn't typical of any of the types she was familiar with. It had been building since she woke up.

"We always take your car. Let's take mine this time."

* * *

"Okay." Ken readily agreed. He would agree with anything that she came up with since she'd be dancing in his arms that evening. They got to her car and he expected her to give him the keys. But she didn't. She crossed to the driver's side and got in.

Ken wondered if their friendship could survive this trauma. He was never comfortable in any vehicle he did not control. He got into the passenger side.

"How far is it to your dad's place?"

"About three miles. Cozy, huh?"

"It is." She started the car. He put on his seat belt. Was she going to put hers on? He kept silent, watched her belt herself in. He tried to relax.

Cori pulled out. He had seen her drive before, and she did a good job. He would be just fine. What could happen in three miles?

Cori made a few turns and they were suddenly in traffic. She followed a gray Honda. She followed it rather closely. Ken kept quiet. The Honda was braking.

"That's a Honda in front of you."

"Yes, it is," she agreed.

"It's slowing down."

"Uh huh."

Ken's hands doubled into fists. He knew he should shut up. He knew it. "You're going to hit it."

"No, I'm not." The car in front of them stopped at a stop sign and she stopped neatly behind it, about three feet from its bumper.

"Oh, I see. You were just going to drive up its tailpipe."

The other car pulled away and Cori moved to the stop sign and checked her rearview mirror before turning to him. "What's wrong?"

"You were too damned close."

"I thought you liked my following distance."

"I do, on the freeway. You need to allow more room in town, too, and when you stop."

She was looking into the mirror. "We've got to get going. How about I pull over and let you drive?"

"Yes. Please." She got off to the side and they traded places. "Thank you, Cori. You're babying me and I appreciate it."

They pulled neatly into traffic and Ken got directions for the next few turns.

She sounded strained when she asked, "How come not stop so close?"

He glanced over at her, saw her tense face. Damn. "Because of the person who might come up behind you and hit you and send your car into the car in front of you. And because the person in front of you might have a clutch they're not used to or a sudden need to back up."

"Oh." She rubbed her forehead. Darned headache.

"Are you hurting?"

"Headache, since I woke up."

"Migraine?"

"No. They start with blurred vision, then a pain in my right temple. This is more on the left side."

"You wouldn't notice blurred vision if you were asleep."

"That's true. But the pain would have wakened me, if this really was a migraine. They start off pretty emphatically in me."

"I hope it goes away. Did you take something?"

"Yeah."

Cori's father lived in a condo, a nice second story unit with a balcony filled with flowers that she pointed out as they walked up to the building. Henry, who had Cori's rascally eyes with bushy white eyebrows, opened the door and admitted them, then Cori made the introductions.

"I've heard a lot about you, Ken. I'm glad you came here to create a diversion for my girl."

Ken smiled at this assessment of his current function. Cori was looking around the living room, then she called, in an affectionate tone used for a favorite child, "Hey, Sweetheart."

Ken turned to see who got treated to that affection. A little Siamese cat came bounding into the room. Cori laughed and squatted and the cat rubbed her face on her and meowed and batted at her hair.

"Cori loves cats, and they all seem to like her, too."

"I wonder why she doesn't get another cat?"

"I think she's still heartbroken over the last one. It left when Dave died, you know."

"That's what she said. It's too bad."

"The whole thing was. How do you like Oregon so far?" Ken told him some of the things he had seen and marveled at. All the time he watched Cori on the floor with the cat. Sometimes she would sit still for a little bit and stare at the floor. He wondered if it was memories or the headache that bothered her.

Henry put sandwiches out for lunch and Cori took only a half and nibbled at it and drank nothing but a little water. "Headache?" Henry asked when she turned down cheesecake.

"Yes."

"Migraine?"

"It's starting to feel more like one. Wrong side, though."

Henry brought her a cup of coffee. "Caffeine helps," he said to Ken. "Drink this, take your pill and Ken'll take you home to bed."

"I wish," she murmured.

Ken raised his eyebrows, looked quickly at Henry and caught a knowing smile.

They stayed another half-hour but Cori's headache now prevented her from focusing on anything but the pain. Ken saw her take another pill in the car. Most of the ride she sat with her eyes closed. He got her to lie down in the downstairs bedroom and unbuckled her sandals and took them off. He sat beside her and rubbed her arm. "Cori. What can I do to help?"

"It'll be better in a half hour."

"That's what you said at your dad's house."

"Do you like him?"

"I love him. He's great. Hon, I saw you take another pill in the car. Aren't you supposed to have water with them?"

"I don't feel good."

"I know. I'll get you some water." He went to the kitchen and when he came back with the water, she wasn't there. He listened for her and heard her throwing up in the downstairs bathroom. He went there and she was washing her face. "Are you all right?"

"Yeah."

"The first pill should have worked by now, and you probably just lost the second one."

"They only work when you take them as soon as it comes on. I was several hours late because it sneaked up on me. I'll have to ride it out."

He put his arm around her waist and gently caught her head to his shoulder. "How long do these last?"

"Last time one started this way it was four days."

"Oh, God. There has to be something we can do. I'll call your doctor. What's his name?" She handed him the prescription bottle from the shelf.

David Schiller, M.D., it read. "Oh, no. Who's your doctor now?"

"Haven't got around to getting a new doctor."

"Then I'll take you to the emergency room."

She closed her eyes. "No."

"Why not?"

Tears flowed out from under her closed lids. She whispered, "I can't go there. I just can't."

Ken kissed the top of her head and inventoried his brain for any medical information about her that he could think of. "Brian. Are you still friends with him?"

"Yes. But he won't help me. I'll go back to bed now." He supported her as she walked back to the bedroom.

She lay down and he said, "I'm going to call Brian."

"Whatever." Her eyes were closed and she lay stiff on her back.

Ken went to the bathroom and retrieved the prescription bottle. The phone number was probably the same. Only after the receptionist answered did he realize that he didn't know that damned Brian's last name. "I'd like to speak to Brian, please." The receptionist said nothing. "This is Ken McAllister and I'm calling regarding Cori Schiller. It's urgent."

"Dr. Wright is in surgery now. May I have him call you in a few minutes?"

"Thank you, yes." He gave Cori's number and went to check on her, then came back and waited by the phone. He was in surgery. Was he at the hospital, then? Would he get the message?

He snatched up the phone when it rang. "This is Brian Wright. Who are you and what's going on with Cori?"

"I'm a houseguest..."

"Ah. Her Kansas cowboy."

Kansas cowboy? "She has a migraine and it didn't start out as typical and she didn't take her medicine in time..."

"Ken, I'm not her doctor and migraines aren't my area of expertise. She needs to call her doctor."

"She doesn't have a doctor, she says."

"Aw, damn it, Cori," he murmured and sighed. "Take her to the emergency room, then."

"She won't go. Wouldn't say why, but she was insistent." And she'd cried, too, which he didn't mention.

"There's little I can do, even if I wanted to. I'm in surgery all day.

The Kansas Connection   Kathleen Gabriel

You'll just have to take her to the emergency room. Don't let her tell you no."

Ken sighed into the silence. "You're a doctor. And she said you were her friend. I kind of thought those two together..."

"Oh, son of a bitch. Bring her in. And if she doesn't get herself a doctor after this, I'm going to kick her pretty little butt."

"Thank you. We'll be right there." He went to Cori and spoke softly while he put her sandals on her. "I'm taking you to the clinic. You'll have to give me directions."

"Brian? You're kidding."

"I'm not kidding. But he's ticked at you." Light made the pain worse so Cori wore sunglasses in the car, where she sat impassive the whole ride, not saying a word other than telling him where to turn.

Once at the clinic, a medical assistant took them directly to an exam room. After a few minutes, a tall young man in green scrubs burst into the room. He nodded to Ken, tossed a file onto the counter, then turned his attention to Cori. He took off her glasses and looked at her face, the dark circles under her eyes. "Aw, Cori, you look like hell. You need to find yourself a doctor. You're overdue for a pap smear. Surely you don't want me doing that for you, too?"

She groaned.

"All right, then. I'm sorry about the light, but I need to do an exam."

Ken watched as he shined a penlight into Cori's eyes and had her touch her nose and do other things that resembled the sobriety test he was so familiar with. Brian looked satisfied with the results. "Okay. I asked the neurologist down the hall and he says this is what you need, provided everything checks out, which it does." He took a little bottle and drew most of the contents up into a syringe. "I need a bare hip."

"Put it in my arm, Brian." It was the first time she'd spoken to him.

"That's not the way it's done. Hop down and drop 'em." Ken wasn't sure whether to leave the room, but Cori simply unzipped her jeans and pulled them down a little ways. It was enough for the injection.

"It feels hot."

"You might get sleepy. Go with it, okay? I'll check on you tonight."

"Thanks, Brian."

"Thank Ken. He shamed me into it. Nice meeting you, by the way." He nodded to Ken and glanced at the clock. "Got a guy scrubbed and waiting for his vasectomy. See you."

He had been there less than five minutes.

The Kansas Connection

Kathleen Gabriel

CHAPTER EIGHT

*C*ori woke and stretched, worn out and feeling thick, but free of pain. She hung onto the handrail as she went downstairs. She saw Ken at the computer writing his daily e-mail to the kids. Cori knew they wrote back, even shared their fights with him, proof that he had made the grade with them. She came up beside him and laid her hand on his shoulder. "Hi."

He looked hopeful and then happy as he looked up and wrapped his arm around her waist. "Hi yourself. Are you better now?"

"A lot better. Still sleepy, but I had to say thank you."

"I didn't do much."

"Made me get help. I'd still be lying in bed in pain if you hadn't. I was actually asleep in there just now."

"Good." He squeezed her.

"Scoot back?" He looked puzzled but scooted his chair back. She watched the amazement on his face as she sat on his lap.

He recovered and wrapped his arms around her. "Thank you for this great honor. But..."

"Yes?"

"Are you still doped up or something?"

She laughed. "Probably." She leaned against him and enjoyed his closeness while they talked about their plans. Ken seemed amazed that she still wanted to go to Silver Creek Falls in the morning. She grew sleepier and yawned.

"You should go back to bed, my friend."

"I love it when you call me that. I don't take friendship lightly." She

The Kansas Connection   Kathleen Gabriel

hugged him around the shoulders. "I'll take another nap. Don't let me sleep past our date, okay?" She got up and looked back at his goofy smile.

Cori slept in a warm cocoon, safe and happy, nothing to disturb her until she smelled beef and onions. A good smell, now that her stomach was at peace. The change in light showed her that it was evening. Better get dinner finished up. She got up slowly. No pain, no dizziness. She stretched and walked out to the kitchen barefoot.

Ken was there, frosting the cake. "I made cream cheese frosting. Is that okay?"

"Good. What can I do?"

"Tell me what to do with those potatoes and stuff you cut up?"

"Boil them for ten minutes, then I'll make pot roast gravy to go over them."

"Give me a break. I know how to make gravy."

She stood still, at a loss at what to do with a competent man in her kitchen. "Well, I guess I'll go get dressed."

She chose a dress she thought he'd like, a light blue one that brought out her eye color. She put on some heels, but it was too warm to mess with pantyhose. Her hair took some work to repair to non-fuzziness. She tried out a new lipstick she thought would be good with the dress.

Ken tapped on the door. She opened it and found him in a dress shirt and slacks, a thing she hadn't seen before. "You're looking good," she told him.

"And you're... wow."

"Do you like this lipstick?"

He came in to see better, then nodded. "Nice color."

"It's new. It's not supposed to rub off on stuff. I don't see how that can be." She considered her chances of getting away with it, decided the odds were good. She stepped close and kissed his cheek. His dimple appeared and she inspected his cheek. "Huh. It works."

"Speaking of experiments, dinner's ready. That's what I came here to tell you. I think." She peered out after him as he ran downstairs, lightly stroking his cheek with his fingers.

After dinner they put on some music and took their shoes off and danced in the living room. Their first slow dance, Ken's embrace gently possessive, verified what Cori had been hoping. There was romance in the air. It was wonderful to have a friend, but Ken was becoming something more. There might be a real possibility here, if he didn't live halfway across the country. She wouldn't think about that tonight.

Later in the evening, Cori was snuggled into Ken's arms as they danced, her temple resting on his jaw. She wanted to kiss him but was afraid he wouldn't accept it. She still didn't know how he felt about her. Not for certain. She heard a knock at the door. Ken stirred. "Expecting someone?"

"No." She shook her head, then nestled again.

The front door opened and Brian walked in. Ken and Cori stopped dancing and stepped apart. "I thought maybe you couldn't hear the door. I guess you're feeling better?"

"I really am, thanks."

"You still look like someone punched you."

Ken gripped her hand. "She says the bruised look fades in a day or so."

"Yeah, it does," he agreed.

"Lemonade, Brian?"

"Sure, thanks." He sat on the couch, and Ken dropped into the armchair nearby. When she got back with the lemonade, he and Ken were talking about the trips they'd been taking.

"So Cori's going along with you on everything instead of just sending you off."

"Yup. And I like it real well."

"She's a lot of fun. I went with her and Dave and my ex up to a place called Little Moraine Lake once. It's beautiful."

Cori said, "Ken and I just went up there. No one else around. No one else human, anyway." She told about the scare that the elk had given them.

Brian laughed and stood. They both got up, too. Ken shook his hand, then Cori gave him a hug. Brian lifted her chin with one finger. Cori shook her head, but Brian chose not to get the message, and bent and kissed her anyway, full on the lips. A three second kiss, at least, then another little one right after it. He looked into her eyes. "Take care. And get yourself a doctor."

"I will. I promise." She looked at the carpet.

"And what do you have against the emergency room?"

She closed her eyes. "That's where they took Dave when he died and I wanted to be alone and there were all these strangers and I never want to go there again."

"Oh, that's right. That was awful. I'm sorry." He squeezed her shoulder. "Good night, you two. Nice meeting you, Ken."

* * *

Ken's thoughts ran fast in several directions at once and to no conclusion. Cori lured him to the couch and sat down beside him. He wanted to know, but he was afraid to know. If she had a boyfriend, why was she so friendly toward him, letting him stay at her house and being so cuddly? And if that damned Brian was her boyfriend, as he obviously was, why was he so casual about him staying there? And why wasn't he more attentive? He even had to be talked into a five minute office visit, for crying out loud.

Cori deserved better. She deserved a good man, a loving one who would always be there. Someone like himself. But in his own way, he was worse than that damned Brian. Most of the time he was nowhere near. He was in Kansas. No, Brian was better for her than he was. He would have to forget his dreams. Cori had someone, and he was her choice, no matter how poor a choice Ken might deem him.

"What are you thinking about, Ken?"

He told himself to focus. "I was wondering about how Dave died. You said a heart attack."

"Yes. He never would go to a doctor himself, wouldn't get a checkup, ignored symptoms. I guess that's where I got it. One day he was feeling sick at work and told them he was going home. Brian feels guilty still that he didn't try to find out more about how Dave was feeling. He could have saved him. I was working that day and came home and found Dave lying dead on our bed."

Ken put his arm around her shoulders and tugged her close. "I called 9-1-1 because I didn't know what else to do. I knew he was dead, but I called them. I guess that's what most people do in a situation like that. An ambulance came and took us to the emergency room. People were staring at me and I was so upset with all the questions. Brian came and kept them away from me after a while."

"So he's been your friend for quite a while."

"Yes. He and Dave were close for the short time they knew each other."

"It's a good thing to have a friend."

"Yes, it is." She snuggled up to him and laid her hand on his chest. Ken didn't know what to make of her. She and Brian kissed as if they did it all the time, yet here she was with him. She didn't talk about Brian much, and they never talked on the phone as far as he knew. Maybe he should just enjoy her company while he had it, take her affection for what it seemed to be and not try to define things.

Like hell. He asked, "I'm your friend?"

"Yes, you are. My teddy bear, too."

"I like that," he growled. "Cori, am I the same kind of friend Brian is?" He could feel his heart beat seven times, eight, nine, ten, while he waited for her answer.

"Basically the same kind," she said at last.

He wanted to urge her along into telling him more about her and Brian, but at the same time he didn't want to hear. Provoking her was the only way to get at the truth. "Then I suppose I should be getting kisses, too."

"Absolutely. I've been wanting to kiss you for years."

That wasn't what he expected to hear. "You've only known me four months."

"Feels like years."

"I feel the same way about you. Seeing you kiss Brian has thrown me a curve, though. Do you kiss everybody like that?"

"Only him. And you."

He shook his head. "I'm not comfortable with this at all."

She sighed. "I thought you might not be."

* * *

Cori rested against Ken. She wished she could give him some assurance, but she knew it looked bad, and there was nothing she could do about it. She had kissed Brian, solid evidence for whatever Ken was thinking. That dumb Brian had no sense at all to do that in front of him. She tried to stop him, but that probably looked bad, too. She sighed again.

"Hey, are you getting sleepy?"

"No."

"You're sighing there."

"I'm feeling bad that you're feeling bad and I'm doing wishing sighs."

"What are you wishing?"

"Really want to know?"

"I think so."

"I'm wishing Brian hadn't come over tonight. We'd still be dancing."

Ken tightened his arm around her. "Let's go dance some more, then."

They got up and danced and although he held her the same way, Cori felt it wasn't the same. Conversation might fill the gap. "I want to take you to see the redwoods. And Crater Lake. I've never been to Crater Lake myself."

"Let's go, then. Our itinerary isn't written in stone. But the falls tomorrow?"

"Of course." They talked about where to go and where to stay until they were both getting tired. Cori wouldn't be able to sleep for hours since she slept all afternoon, but she didn't mention that since Ken was obviously tired.

They walked up the stairs together, holding hands. "Step doesn't squeak."

"I can put the squeak back if you miss it."

"Don't do that."

They took turns with the bathroom and she saw him in nothing but pajama bottoms in the hall. She liked the way he looked but didn't tell him so lest he think she was some kind of loose woman. Surely, that's what he was thinking after she said she wanted to kiss him right after he'd seen her kiss Brian. Though they had cuddled most of the evening she still looked forward to their good night hug.

Cori walked up to Ken and into his arms. He held her tight for some time, his breath warm against her head, his skin intimate beneath her hands. He released her far enough to look into her eyes. His gaze went to her lips and her heart picked up speed. He met her eyes again and smiled. He patted her back, backed up and turned away.

Now she would never have his kiss. Her stupid game with Brian had taken her chance with a man she thought the world of, a man worthy of anything she could give. She hadn't cried herself to sleep in over two years, but this night, behind a closed door, she did.

* * *

The redwoods were majestic. Ken gazed up for a long time, until Cori had the idea to put an open sleeping bag down and lie down to look up. They stayed out in the forest until they were hungry, then began looking for a camping space. In the middle of the week it should have been easy to find one spot for one night. But no camping places were to be found in the redwood parks they went to. Every one was full.

"A motel, I guess. Same as last night." Last night had been cozy, except for the sleeping, which they did in separate beds.

"Fine with me," she said. "Running water and all."

"You're a very civilized person, Cori."

"Oh, I know it." They stopped at several motels and found the situation much the same as at the campgrounds. Ken went in and checked at places and came back shaking his head. Finally he came and got into the car and said nothing for a bit. "What is it?"

"This place has a room."

"Good. Since we know where we'll sleep, we can get something to eat."

"Not that simple. It only has one bed."

"So? We slept together camping."

"Yes, with separate sleeping bags and without all the connotations of sleeping in a bed and in a motel, no less."

"It'll be all right. I won't jump your bones. Go get the room before someone else does. I hate sleeping in cars."

Ken nodded and left. Cori felt wicked at looking forward to sleeping with Ken. She would enjoy the snuggling, but he, being a man, would probably be uncomfortable in a certain very physical way if he felt about her as she thought he did. If they were more intimate, she could ease him, but he would never allow her to help, and his pride would prevent him from doing anything about it himself.

After lunch, they went for a swim in the Smith River. They played and splashed and swam back and forth across the river in the perfectly clear water. Cori liked standing still and watching little fishes swim around her feet.

Ken lingered over dinner until she thought he was avoiding going to the motel. On the way there he said, "I'll bring in the sleeping bags and we can use them."

"That's dumb."

"I can wrap up in the bedspread on top of the bed."

"Oh, brother. We won't have any problem as long as we don't kiss while we're in bed." And there was little chance of that since they hadn't kissed anywhere. "Am I so repulsive that you don't want to sleep with me?"

"Exactly the opposite. Maybe you don't know a lot about men..."

She interrupted with her laughter. "Oh, please."

"All right. But this is no picnic for me." They got to the room and got ready for bed, both in sedate pajamas. Ken got in bed first and lay on the edge.

"I want to cuddle, Ken. Be my teddy bear."

He scooted closer to the middle and she got next to him and wrapped her arm around him and draped her leg over his.

Ken hugged her, then groaned. "I'm already in trouble."

"How so?"

"You know how so, but I am not going to discuss it."

"Okay. You know where the bathroom is. Why not be comfortable?"

"That's tacky."

"Do you prefer pain over tackiness? Of course, I could help you out."

"No chance." He lay still for a few minutes, then patted the leg she still had over him. She withdrew it and he got up and went into the bathroom.

When he got back, she didn't say anything but got close to him again as they arranged arms and legs. "Cori. What you said about helping me out."

"Yeah?"

"Would you have?"

"No. Not at this stage of our relationship. I just wanted to get you to take action."

"Would you help Brian that way?"

"No. I wouldn't even get in a situation where the subject would come up."

He was quiet and she began to wonder if he'd fallen asleep. "I thought maybe you were lovers."

"No, just friends."

"But you kissed him."

"That bothers you a lot, huh? It's just for fun, those good night kisses. We've been doing it for ages. I never meant for you to see, because it doesn't mean anything."

He was quiet for a moment, then said, "Does making love mean anything?"

"It's everything, it's getting closer and loving and... it's only for people who belong together. For them to be more together. When I was younger I didn't know that, but now I do."

"Me, too. I'm glad I asked you about it. Assumptions can be so ridiculous. I was afraid that you might be more casual about... things than I am."

"I told you once before that I wasn't easy."

"Oh, I never thought you were. But more casual, maybe. I feel better now."

"I'm glad. I think you know I'll ask you anything I want to know."

"That's good. I sure want to kiss you."

"Not in bed. Leads to trouble." She rejoiced. They were all right again.

"I'll kiss you tomorrow, then."

"Okay."

"Roll over." She rolled over and Ken fit himself to her. He started to slip his hand under her pajama top.

"Uh-uh, buddy."

"Just your tummy, no further."

"No. Unless you give me something in return."

"Such as?"

"His name."

"Whose name?"

"The friend you took with you into the bathroom tonight." Ken was silent. "I know you guys name them."

He chuckled. "Underdog."

She cracked up. "Underdog! Why Underdog?"

"He was my favorite cartoon character. Say. Who was your favorite?"

She pretended to think, then said, "Underdog."

"Horse hockey." He tickled her. "Tell the truth."

She laughed and swatted at his hand. "Okay! Okay! It was the Roadrunner!"

He held still for a minute, then chuckled. "Figures."

"Why?"

"Your favorite cartoon character shows what your personality is like. I am a dashing hero, like Underdog. And, yeah, I can see you as the Roadrunner. He's such a smartass."

"Ha! Then your favorite ought to be..." She cast around for the perfect insult. "Foghorn Leghorn!" She cleared her throat and lowered her voice to do a Southern imitation of the yacky rooster, "I say, I say, I say, Son!"

He laughed. "I do not have an accent!"

She snorted.

He tugged on one of her curls. "Let's go to sleep so we can get up early and see some more stuff."

"Okay." She kissed him before he could object, just a quick kiss. Then rolled back onto her side and settled against him. She felt him slip his hand under her pajama top, and was pleased that he didn't rub the bottom of a breast with his thumb in the classic sneak approach. "Good night, Ken. Good night, Underdog."

"Hush."

She was quiet for a little while, then couldn't resist. "I always thought teddy bears were nice and soft all over."

"You hush, woman."

The Kansas Connection   Kathleen Gabriel

CHAPTER NINE

*I*t seemed far too soon, and far too sudden, but Ken's car was packed and he was standing before her in front of the door, looking at her face as if he were memorizing it. He stood in this same spot less than two weeks before, the spot she had hugged him and laughed, so happy to see him. She had begun to get used to having him here, to feel he belonged here. Now it was over.

Her eyes stung and she hugged Ken and hung on to him so he wouldn't see her tears. Foolishness. They were only friends, after all, and they would go right back to spending a lot of time visiting on the Net. Ken slowly rocked her from side to side while he nuzzled her hair. She never had gotten the kiss he promised, the kiss that might have changed everything. But what was the use, since they lived in two different states?

He whispered, "Thank you, Cori, for everything. This has been the best vacation of my life."

She nodded against him, not trusting her voice.

"Getting to know you was the best part of it. If you'll let me, I want to come back."

She nodded again. Of course he could come back. Of course they would have fun together and of course her heart would break every time he left.

He pulled back to look at her and she was surprised to see tears in his eyes as well. She laughed and hiccupped. "We're both stupid."

"Damn straight." She kept looking into his eyes until there was nothing to do but kiss. She let her eyes close as his face drew closer, then he kissed her, warm and smooth, all tenderness and devotion. She responded in kind and, tightening her arms around his neck, held him near when he would have withdrawn. She felt the beginning of his smile against her lips as she kissed him in return, an emphatic kiss that cut his smile short and occupied his lips thoroughly. He caught her to his chest and hugged her hard. She could feel his heart beating as if he'd been running. He held her there until it settled.

As his hold relaxed, Cori let go, too. Ken lifted a hand to her face. "If I don't get time off soon enough to suit you, let me know and I'll send you a plane ticket."

"Okay."

"You don't think I'm being too forward, do you?"

She laughed and the tears threatened again. She looked down. "Be sure to let me know when you get home. I'll miss you between now and then, when we can get back on the Net."

"I'll call when I stop for the night. Oh, and I got you a present. Left it by the computer. It's a game I play with the kids over a connection between our computers. Maybe we could play it together over the Net sometime."

"I've never done anything like that."

"It won't be the same as being with you in person. But all the building and shooting should cheer us up."

She watched him drive away, then walked to the computer to take her first look at Master of the Galaxy.

* * *

Sandi and Michael and Jennifer were glad to see him, but they hadn't missed him all that much, he could tell. They had a new routine that worked well and didn't include him. He tried to stay busy but kept finding himself at the computer, chatting with Cori or writing to her if she wasn't there.

One night he was writing her an e-mail when Jennifer came in and laid her hand on his shoulder. He gave her his attention, the thing fourteen year old girls need the most. "Writing to Cori again?"

"Yeah."

"What are you telling her?"

"I'm telling her how snoopy my niece is."

"Huh-uh."

"I'm commiserating with her about some blackberry vines in her back yard."

"What's commiserating mean? I've heard it but I don't really know."

"Figure it out. What's 'com' mean?"

"With."

"Right. And the rest?"

"'Miserating' sounds like miserable."

"Right again."

"And you're miserable without her."

He sat back and studied her young face, so much like her mother's at that age. "Does it show real bad?"

"Oh, please."

He scratched his head. "I guess it does. We had a lot of fun together."

"Did you kiss her?"

He narrowed his eyes, but answered. "Yeah."

She patted his shoulder. "You probably shouldn't have done that. Mom says kissing's when the trouble starts."

"I know it. Don't tell her, huh?"

"Course not. We never nark on each other."

He laughed and hugged her.

* * *

Cori worked on figuring out Master of the Galaxy. When Ken asked her to play with him and the kids, she said she needed more practice. The game was full of detail, and she didn't know which details would be significant under what circumstances. She wanted to know why it was easier to win some times than other times so she could develop some strategy. One day she sat looking at another scenario where her ships were all dust and decided she needed expert help.

She got on the Internet and cruised her favorite online bookstore. There it was, the Master of the Galaxy Strategy Guide, for ages twelve and up. Just what she needed. She ordered it and got it the next day. Now she'd get this thing whipped.

* * *

Cori had hoped to get a call to teach this day so there would be less time to remember, but neither district called. She knew the evening and night would be hard enough without having time to think in the daytime as well. She planted crocuses in the backyard to supplement last year's, purple and cream. If they all survived it would be beautiful. Before she was done she took off her sweatshirt, she felt so warm.

Today was not as bad as last year had been, and that had been easier than the year before. Dave had died three years ago today. Parts of the nightmare she remembered plainly, others had faded. She wished she could talk to her mother, but she was gone before Dave. He had helped her through that.

She went in and washed and made pea soup and a sandwich for lunch.

Her dad called but he was between classes and couldn't talk long. "Just wanted to let you know I was thinking of you."

"Thanks, Daddy." She wanted to talk to Ken, but he didn't know what day it was today and she didn't want to cry to him. She looked at his schedule to see when he would be home. It was two hours later there, but still not time for him to get home.

Getting out among people would be good. She changed out of her garden clothes and into good jeans and a sweater. She drove to Fred Meyer and bought fruit and some flowers. Happy flowers. She walked to the garden center and bought yet more bulbs. Can't have too much color, and the front yard deserved some, too.

On the way back home she passed the road that would take her to the clinic. It was the last place she should want to visit. She drove around the block and headed there anyway. She sat in the parking lot for a few minutes, then started the car and drove home.

She put her garden clothes back on and planted crocuses in the front yard out by the road where not much grass grew.

She got online as soon as she knew Ken would be getting home and chatted with other people until he came on. "There you are, buddy. Been waiting for you."

They talked about this and that and she felt like it was their usual banter, but Ken asked, "What's wrong?" and she started to cry.

She typed some reply, but it must have seemed off to him because he called her on the phone. He got her to talk, and she felt better. Much better.

* * *

Ken got a formal request for a game from Cori one day. He and the kids were all excited. Finally someone outside of the three of them to play with. Ken set up a time with her and he and the kids plotted who to be. Ken and Jennifer would be one alien race, Michael, the best player, on the other computer, would be another and Cori would be whoever she wanted.

When the time came, Michael was appalled at Cori's apparent choice of races. "She's a darned rock eater! I always kill those off first," he hollered from the next room.

Ken typed, "Use 'private message.' Your mom'll have our heads if we yell. And be good to Cori. She's a beginner."

Early in the game, when the diplomatic visits began, they were surprised that Cori, as a rock-eater, was able to communicate with them. "I thought they were always repulsive, that they couldn't communicate except to declare war and the most basic stuff like that." Jennifer was puzzled. So was

Ken.

A private message came from Michael in the next room. "She's playing a custom race. Look at her racial characteristics."

They played awhile and noticed that Cori had more technology than they did. Then they noticed that she was colonizing other systems like crazy. She shouldn't have been able to move so far so fast. Then, while they were trading technology among themselves, she wiped out one of the other competitors, a computer player.

Ken typed a private message to Michael. "I think we're in trouble."

"No shit, Sherlock? Your rock-eating girlfriend is using cheat codes."

"We'd better, too, then."

"Do you know any?"

"No. And Michael? Don't say 'shit.'"

After a couple of hours, in spite of a non-aggression pact, Cori placed war ships in each of Michael's star systems. Not really an aggressive act. Not officially. Then she demanded ten per cent tribute. Michael refused. Ken and Jennifer moved their ships into Michael's systems, too, to back him up. Cori sent ships to one of Ken and Jennifer's systems and nabbed it. All of those colonists were now captive, working and making money for her.

Ken and Michael each got the same message from Cori. "Hey! This is a really fun game! I think I'm getting the hang of it."

Michael typed back, "Die, rock-eating scum." He took out one of her outlying colonies.

"Ha ha! You violated the non-aggression pact. Now you're fair game, jellyfish eater." Michael was an aquatic race, so he was subject to this kind of abuse.

"You violated it first."

"Against Jennifer and Ken, not against you." She declared war. Michael requested an alliance with Ken and Jennifer. After a hurried conference, they refused. Ken sat back, only shoring up colonies that needed a boost, while he watched his nephew's demise. As the last colony bit the dust Jennifer said, "I always wanted to do that to him."

Michael typed, "I can't believe you kissed that monster." He forgot to make it a private message, so Cori could read it, too.

"Ken, you have a big mouth. For that your colonies shall die."

"They were dead as soon as you came on the scene."

"Michael, thanks for the fun," her message read.

"Oh, sure, rock-eater. Any time."

Ken chuckled at the sarcasm.

"Kiss your uncle and sister good bye. They're next."

Ken let her get him down to just four ships and led her on a merry chase around the galaxy. Jennifer and Michael both watched until the bitter end when Cori built a stealth ship and he ran right into it.

"Wow. She is an awesome player," Jennifer said.

"Yeah. She is."

"It won't be any fun if we aren't on even footing, though," Michael said.

Since the game was over, the game server's chat function wouldn't work any more; Ken got on yahoo chat.

"What's new, Ken?"

"I just got slaughtered and you want to know what's new."

"That's a fun game."

"Probably your last chance to play it with any of us."

"How come?"

"Because you cheated."

"Cheating is fun."

"I know. But we don't know how to cheat and you were just shooting ducks in a barrel."

"(Happy sigh.) Wasn't it great?"

"It was novel."

"Wouldn't it be fun if we could all cheat together? One big happy family. Or, galaxy. My little demonstration convinced you, I hope?"

"Yes! Teach us to cheat, oh ravenous rock eater."

"I am hungry, actually. Maybe I'll give you the codes after I make myself a granite sandwich."

Michael shook his head in disgust. "She's awful. I can't believe you'd hang around with a teacher, but a cheating teacher? And a tease?"

"Yeah, she's horrible," Ken agreed, grinning in admiration.

Cori typed, "Got a pencil and paper? I'm going to give you the codes and what they're for."

Ken pushed back from the desk to get a pen while Jennifer ripped paper out of the printer.

"The first one is for accelerating your research."

* * *

Cori was about to begin a day of substituting, and she had visitors in the classroom for the third time in a month, three of them this time. One was a repeater. They were called "community observers," but they dressed and looked like academics - tweedy and hawk-eyed.

At one minute before the second bell, she heard a young male voice in the hallway. "Old Greenwood's sick. I wonder who we got as sub?"

She couldn't hear the murmured replies, but did hear the first boy speak again. "Oh, shit! Not Mrs. Schiller!"

Most gratifying.

* * *

It was Ken's task to take the kids to the mall this Saturday. He didn't mind, since Sandi was working and he liked watching people. The mall was a great place to see all kinds. The hairdos alone would be worth the trip. He remembered the one mall he visited with Cori in Portland. It was much like this one, but the outfits and hairdos were more varied.

Michael was in a shop that sold software and Jennifer was looking at jeans. Ken looked toward both stores before he went to a jewelry display. One ring stood out above all the others. The sales woman was kind. Ken did some quick figuring, decided he could do it.

"Do you know her size?"

He took out his wallet and pulled out a little slip of paper with a circle on it. "I traced this from the inside of a ring that fits her."

Later he met Jennifer at the jeans store, carrying a receipt in his pocket that proved that he believed in dreams.

* * *

Cori played the game with just Michael one evening while Ken was working and Jennifer was at a girlfriend's. They swapped tips on how to build the best colonies for various purposes. Michael maintained that he saw the advantages of being a rock-eater, but still liked all of the other races better.

"Don't you feel funny about killing off people?" he asked.

"It bothered me at first. But it's just pretend."

"It bothered Uncle Ken a lot at first. I think it's because of his job."

"He's never had to shoot anyone."

"He's fired warning shots before, so he was ready to shoot if he had to."

"Part of being a cop."

"Yeah. I guess. I'm going to work with computers."

"Good. Not much shooting there. Hey. Humans sneaking up on your Proxima system, I think."

"Oh, shit!"

* * *

Time went by slowly for Cori once the fall and winter rains got started.

No more walks in the woods or puttering in the garden. It got dark early, long before Ken was off work and available to chat. She spent more time with her father and his cat. He told her that she came to see the cat, not him. She denied nothing.

Christmas was a few days away and she hadn't yet mailed Ken's box to him. She kept meaning to, but didn't get around to it. Now she'd have to overnight it. Decorating the tree and mantel took up some time. Too many decorations were from her years with Dave. The more sentimental ones she wrapped up and hid from herself.

One night she was online while eating dinner at the computer, waiting for Ken to come on. She chatted with a few other buddies. One was a lady in Tasmania, a place she had never thought of anyone actually living until she met her. They traded recipes every once in a while and had to explain the ingredients to each other. She remembered telling her once, "No! I don't have any kangaroo meat," only to find she had been teasing.

Cori cleaned up the kitchen and checked on the computer occasionally to see if Ken was around. It was odd that he wasn't, but maybe he had to work over. He had a lot of paperwork to do every day after turning in his patrol car for the next shift's use. Christmas season with increased traffic and shoplifting made it busier than usual. He had to work over before, though, and he called to tell her so. She sat and wrote him an e-mail, hoping he was well and letting him know how her day went.

At eight o'clock, she felt sure something was wrong. It was ten o'clock there. At eight-forty she called him. Sandi answered, her voice strained. "This is Cori. I haven't heard from Ken tonight and wonder if everything's okay?"

"Oh, Cori. Ken's all over the news." She started to cry.

Cori felt she'd been slugged in the stomach. "What is it?"

"They keep showing him talking to the newsman and he's crying and..."

Thank God. If he was crying, then he wasn't... "Sandi? What happened?"

"A kid robbed a convenience store and Ken was there and he shot at him and Ken shot him. He was only fifteen."

"Oh, no." That would almost kill Ken. "Will the kid be okay?"

"I don't know. He's in critical condition. But he's a robber and he shot two people in the store and if a robber shoots at you, you have to shoot back but they're making a big deal about him being only fifteen."

She trembled and dragged a hand through her hair. "Was Ken supposed to get his ID before he defended himself?"

"I guess so."

"Where's Ken now?"

"At the sheriff's office, talking to Internal Affairs. They have to get all the information from him while it's fresh."

"Okay. I hope he's okay. When he gets home, tell him I called and to call me. It doesn't matter what time it is."

"Wait." Cori could hear the TV news in the background, but couldn't distinguish the words. "Oh, God. The boy's dead."

Cori held her breath. "The robber? Or one of the people he shot in the store?"

"The robber. And his best friend came on earlier and said the kid had told him that he knew an easy way to get Christmas money. This is terrible."

"It really is." They talked awhile, Cori trying to calm Sandi while her own heart was racing, her tears choking her. Poor Ken. That poor family.

Cori went to bed and tried to sleep but the pictures of what happened kept flooding in. She didn't need the news coverage, and she felt sorry for Sandi who had seen too much. The phone rang and woke her and she struggled to orient herself before picking it up. "Hello?"

"Cori. It's Ken." He sounded more weary than she had ever heard him. "How are you, sweetheart?"

He sighed. "You can call a baby killer sweetheart?"

Her throat seized up. "You're no baby killer. A good man doing your job, a necessary job."

He started to weep and it triggered her tears. After some time he said, "I don't know what I'm going to do."

"Tell me what you mean."

"I don't know if I can face Christmas. I'll ruin it for the kids."

"I see what you mean. It would be unnatural for the kids to miss it, though."

"I know."

She waited a minute. "Are they done with you, the questioning?"

"Is it ever done?"

"I don't know how it works. Can you, do you want to, come to me?" She hurt for him, wanted to hold him and care for him. "I'm here. I'm here for you. If you want to."

Ken was quiet. "I'm on administrative leave until I feel I can come back. I'm supposed to see a psychiatrist."

"We have those out here."

"Yeah. Of course."

She waited but he didn't say anything else. "Ken?"

"Yes?"

"I'll be here for you, whatever you need."

"It's good to know that. I'm going to bed now. I'll think about your offer. I'd feel guilty being with you when that boy's family doesn't have him."

"I understand, I think. But he chose to do what he did. You had to act, and you know it." She hoped he did know it, then he could deal with it better.

"You're right. But it's still going to be hard."

"I'm sure. I'll be thinking of you."

"I'll be thinking... well. Good night, Cori."

"Good night, Ken."

CHAPTER TEN

Christmas Eve at the airport was a wild mixture of impatience and goodwill with a huge number of rushing people, the volume thrice what it usually was. The crowd at the security checkpoint was so huge that she fretted that she wouldn't be able to see Ken coming up. How lonely he would feel if she wasn't there. She called, "Merry Christmas" back to strangers who said it to her, and tried to smile.

She waved when she spotted Ken and he wove his way toward her while she dashed toward him. She hugged him around the neck while he wrapped his arms around her and nuzzled into her hair, just as she remembered. It wasn't a satisfactory hug with their big coats on, but the connection was real.

"Aw, sweetheart. I'm sorry I couldn't get here until today."

"It's okay. No problem at all. Got baggage?" She sincerely hoped that his carry on was all he had because the baggage claim area would be shoulder to shoulder, wall to wall, with people in back hopping to see over others in hopes of spotting their baggage.

He lifted his bag. "This is it."

"Good. Let's begin our sojourn." She gripped his hand as they started out and didn't let go.

"Are you afraid I'll get lost?"

"Yes. This place is so crowded. Was it like this on your end?"

"Not as crowded, but it was worse."

She spared him a glance. Wichita had a much smaller airport, with no international traffic. "Worse?"

"A couple of people recognized me from the news and said some shit."

"You're kidding."

"No. Sandi laced into them."

"Good. I like her."

"She likes you, too." They got out to the front of the terminal just after sunset and boarded a shuttle bound for the parking lot and squashed in, shoulder to shoulder with a bunch of other people in big coats. The windows were steamed up. Someone had drawn a smiley face. Cori watched a young guy draw a Santa hat on it. She held her purse close to her on her lap, gathered the strap in so it wouldn't be in anyone's way. She exchanged smiles with the Asian lady across from her.

"This place is too big," Ken said.

"Yeah. Always under construction, too."

"Reminds me of me." She examined his face, his tired face, for a moment, then raised herself and kissed his cheek. He turned and kissed her mouth. The bus lurched over a speed bump.

When they got to the car Cori opened the trunk for Ken's bag. He dropped it in and she handed him the keys. His smile was sheepish. "You remembered."

"I remember everything about you."

"Oh, man, I hope not."

As he buckled in and started up the car, she asked, "How was the flight?"

He shook his head. "Well, actually, the pilot did a perfect job, but you know me and my stupid driving thing."

She rubbed his thigh. "Aw, poor Bear. They wouldn't let you fly the plane, huh?"

He rolled his eyes. "At least the parking shuttle was a short ride."

She directed him through traffic that was heavy at the airport, lighter later. He was quiet and she respected that while talking to him about what was going on, her dad coming over for Christmas dinner, the things she still had to do to get ready. "I got the pies made already, though."

"Rats. I like helping with pies. What kind?"

"Pumpkin and apple."

"Yum. No mincemeat?"

"Nope. You sure you don't mind doing Christmas?"

"It'll be fine. A small group, no kids."

She nodded. Once home, Ken helped prepare food, as she knew he would. She had taken the tree down, left only the mantel decorated and some mistletoe hanging in the kitchen entry in a strategic spot. She caught him under it several times and he always cooperated.

The Kansas Connection   Kathleen Gabriel

When all the food was ready, they faced each other in the kitchen. "What now? Do you want to talk?"

He shook his head. "I don't want to talk about what happened."

"Dance?"

"It's kind of late."

"I think you need a long hug." He stood looking sad. "Like an all night hug." He grinned and she felt relief flow in like rain from a downspout after a cloudburst. He could still smile. He'd be all right.

"Do we dare?"

"I don't see why not. I've missed you so much and it's not dangerous as long as we don't kiss."

He was nodding. "We'd have to be sure to be up before your father gets here."

"No problem. Although, I am of age."

"Okay."

Cori dressed in her most proper pajamas as she always did when there was a chance Ken would see her. He did the same. "Candy cane stripes, it looks like."

"From Michael and Jennifer. I never wear pajamas except when they're staying with me or I'm with you."

"I like nighties and pajamas about the same. You usually sleep in your shorts?"

"Yeah. Enough of this talk. Get to bed." They snuggled together, moved around until they both were comfortable. "Happy Christmas, Cori. I'm sorry I'm not more fun."

"It's all right. I'm so glad to have my friend back."

He hugged her tight, only relaxing his grip as he fell asleep.

* * *

Ken slept late, and she dressed in the room while he was there, since he was sleeping so heavily. She dressed in slacks, a deep red sweater and an apron with a Santa face on the bib. She waited as long as she could, then woke him by shaking his foot. "Hey. Dad'll be here soon. Shake a leg."

He groaned, then stretched and smiled. "Merry Christmas to you, too, pretty one."

"Merry Christmas. Now get up."

"I slept like a baby."

She smirked. "No you didn't. Babies wake up in the night to breastfeed."

"Cori" he warned.

She laughed and ran downstairs and started singing along with the Christmas music and setting the table. She was bent over the oven checking the meats and stuffing when Ken came in.

"Did you get your package from me?" he asked.

"Yes, about the tenth. Been trying to figure out what everything is."

"Today you shall know. Um, I never got a package from you."

"I never got around to sending it. I have it here."

"Then you did get me a present." He sounded smug.

"I did. Just some little stuff. One is something I think you need badly."

"Christmas is not for stuff you need."

"I know it."

"Cori, love, can we open the gifts to each other before your dad gets here? To spare him all the sentimentality?"

"Ooh. Sentimentality. I like the sound of this." She also liked the way he sounded this morning. He was close to normal, close to the Ken she knew. She glanced at the clock. There was time. "Maybe save one apiece to open when he's here?"

"We can do that." She got her cocoa and poured him some and gave him a candy cane to stir it with. "This is a good idea."

"I've always done this on Christmas."

"Doesn't cocoa give you a headache?"

"Mine's white chocolate. It's not nearly as bad, and I only have one cup. I'll be fine."

They sat on the couch with a plate full of sliced apples and oranges, and opened presents. Cori laughed at the truly ugly pajamas he gave her, tan with crooked black and olive stripes.

"I thought of you when I saw them."

"Wonderful."

"Nothing can make you unattractive, but these might make a fair disguise."

She loved her mug with his photo on it. The other side had the words, "Good morning, Sunshine." "This will be my morning mug now. Thank you."

"I knew you wanted it, you hinted broadly enough, though why you want to look at a thing like that first thing in the morning is beyond me."

Ken's favorite present was the Master of the Galaxy Strategy Guide. He laughed and patted the cover. "This is the secret to your success, isn't it? Even with us using the cheat codes you're hard to beat."

"That's the present I said you needed so badly. You know, if you really want to drive Michael crazy, don't tell him you have this."

"That's an idea. He gets frustrated with you, though, you know."

"I know it. He's so sarcastic when he's losing."

"And you get exuberant when you're winning. It's funny to watch."

"I like those kids."

"They're all right, for sure." He went quiet, staring at the fireplace. He sighed and said, "I have a present for you in my pocket. Do you want it to be the thing your dad watches you open? Or this bigger box here?"

Cori looked at each. The bigger one was maybe some clothes. The one in his pocket had to be something small. Maybe it was a last minute purchase, or maybe it was something he didn't want to trust to the mail. "What do you think?"

"Doesn't matter to me. How about you save them both?"

"Okay. Now let's get this paper picked up." Ken picked it all up while she went back to the kitchen with the cocoa cups. While she washed them, Ken came up behind her and put his hands on her shoulders. "Coffee. Do you want some? Will your dad?"

"Make a full pot. Somebody'll drink it."

She peered into the refrigerator but found nothing to do there. It was all ready to eat or ready to cook at the right moment. She took Christmas cookies out of the cupboard. Ken paused, coffee carafe full of water in hand, to nab a coconut one. Cori was carrying them out to put on the coffee table when Henry came to the door. She greeted him with the platter in hand.

"Let me put this stuff down first. Good grief, girl." He put his packages down by the fireplace and turned to get a hug.

"Merry Christmas, Daddy."

"Merry Christmas to you, too. Ken around?"

"Right here, Henry. Merry Christmas."

They shook hands, and Henry gripped his shoulder. "I'm sorry about what happened."

He nodded. "I feel a lot better now that I'm here. Cori's a big help."

"It's her mission in life."

"Cocoa, Dad?"

"Only if you have candy canes."

"Well, duh." He followed her to the kitchen entry. She turned around and kissed his cheek.

He looked up. "Mistletoe."

Ken feigned disgust. "Is that all it is? She's been kissing me all morning and I thought I'd suddenly grown attractive. Darn."

"Be quiet, Ken."

Henry grinned as he stirred his cocoa. Ken got more cocoa for himself, mixed it half-and-half with coffee. Cori got coffee and led the way out to the living room.

"Presents," Henry said. "Let's get to them. Enough lollygagging."

They settled close together, Cori on the floor at her father's feet, an elbow resting on his knee. Ken was close enough to touch. He dragged the presents close. "I see one here for Cori."

"No surprise," Henry said. "She always gets the most presents." She got several items of clothing from her father and a book on the duchy period of Bavarian history. "Ooh, Daddy, thank you. My German's pretty rough, though. I would have preferred it in English..."

"No one's translated it. Sorry, toots. Ken, have you noticed that I'm Daddy whenever I've been especially good?"

"I see how it is."

Henry laughed at the frog wind chimes, and tried on his new jacket immediately. While he did, Cori got up and stretched and moved to a spot on the couch. Ken smiled at the wool socks Cori gave him. "Just what I need, and I mean it. My feet get so cold when my two pair are in the wash. I never remember to buy more."

Cori opened another gift. "Ken, I already have some jeans exactly like these."

"I know. You look good in them, except for the paint stains."

"The right size. How did you know that?"

"I do laundry with my eyes open."

Henry said, "A good policy, I'd say."

Ken got a good shirt from Henry. Henry got a good shirt from Ken.

"Thanks, Ken. I think it's a little too big, though."

Ken nodded and looked at his new shirt. "Mine's going to be a little tight." He looked up and their eyes met. Ken slowly handed him the shirt he just got while Henry handed him his. "Merry Christmas," they both said while Cori laughed.

"Time to get dinner on?" Henry asked.

"One more present." Ken got a velvet jewelry box out of his pocket. Cori's heart lurched. He handed it to her. "I didn't wrap it. Sorry."

"That's okay." She took a deep breath. There was no way it could be any kind of a ring. Not presented this way, and in front of her dad. She opened it while both men watched closely. Earrings, beautiful, blue earrings. She was relieved and disappointed at the same time. "Ooh, pretty. Thank you."

"You wear a lot of blue, but I never saw you in blue earrings, so..."

"Let me see," Henry said. He took the box from her and looked at them. "Sapphires. They sparkle nicely. Put them on, honey. Ken and I'll get dinner going."

She patted Ken's knee and kissed him again before getting up and running upstairs. She took off the earrings she was wearing and put the new ones on. They did sparkle nicely, as her dad said, and she would always remember Ken when she wore them. She sighed. She didn't want to remember him; she wanted to have him around.

Henry said the blessing at dinner, and while they ate, they talked about things that happened at other Christmases. Ken seemed to enjoy hearing the family stories and told a few of his own. Cori thought how her brother would like Ken, wondered if they would ever meet. But he had lived in Tokyo for years and while he traveled a lot in Asia, he never came home. Sadder was the thought of how her mother would have liked Ken. Ken looked over at her while she thought of these things and tipped his head. She smiled and shrugged.

Henry led the way in clearing the table, the others joining in. "We have pie, too," Cori said. "For later, I guess."

"Yes, for later. If I ate any more now I'd be comatose for a week," Henry said.

"Ken, didn't you want to call your sister and your folks?" Cori asked.

"Yeah, I need to do that."

"Tell them hi from me."

"From me, too, though they don't know me from Adam," Henry said.

"Sandi and the kids have heard of you."

"I shudder to think what you must have told them." Ken left to make his calls. Cori put food away while Henry loaded the dishwasher. "I like him, Cori."

"I like him, too."

"I can tell. He'll recover from this latest thing."

"I hope so. He seems kind of deflated."

"What are you going to do about him?"

"What do you mean?" She turned and peered at him.

"You know what I mean. Am I about to lose you to Kansas?"

"He hasn't asked me to make that choice."

"If he did, what would you do?"

She had spent a lot of time thinking about that. "I don't know."

"Good. Then it's not time yet for me to be polishing my good-bye song."

"Oh, Daddy."

* * *

Ken came back and put some music on, dancing music, and joined

Cori and Henry in the kitchen. He watched Cori working in rhythm to the music, swish swish with the dishrag, plunk plunk, forks in the dishwasher. Henry finished his job first and watched her until she let the water go, then took her hands and danced in the kitchen. Ken stood by until they worked their way out of the kitchen, then he wiped the counters and range.

On the next song he stepped in and danced with Cori. While they danced there was a knock at the door. Henry answered it and Brian shook hands with him and walked into the room. He stood grinning. "You guys dance all the time."

Ken shook his hand, Cori gave him a quick hug and they exchanged Christmas greetings.

Brian said, "I didn't know you were in town, Ken."

"Got in last night."

"Another vacation?"

"Not exactly," Cori said. "You guys want some pie?"

"That's what I came for," Brian said. "Oh, and to give you this thing." He handed her a wrapped box.

Henry got the pie plates and forks and Ken got out the pies and whipped cream while she opened the package. "All right. I love this stuff. Thanks, Brian. Hey, guys, smoked salmon and several kinds of cheese, some other good stuff."

Brian backed up a little and when Cori turned to find him, he pointed up at the mistletoe. She laughed and stretched up to kiss his cheek. Ken turned away, but was sure she'd caught him smiling.

Later, Brian took Ken aside. "So, what brings you here? I got the impression there was a story to be told."

"Well, there is, but it's not something I'm proud of." He told him about what happened, and the treatment the news stations gave it.

Brian listened quietly, giving him his full attention. "Death comes in my business, too. I see some that could have been prevented, but you just do what you can. I know it's little comfort, but you might have saved a lot of lives. If he shot two people before he went after you, he might well have killed a lot of innocent people in his career."

"I've thought of that. But I can also see his face, the look of bewilderment he had before he lost consciousness, lying on the sidewalk." He stopped, then shook his head and went on. "He was somebody's little boy."

"I'm really sorry. You did well to come to Cori. She has more compassion in her little finger..."

"She's a treasure."

"She is. Dave was a lucky man."

Ken silently agreed with that.

"Your turn, Brian," Henry called.

Brian got up to dance with Cori. Her cheeks were pink, her smile wide. Ken watched her with a longing he couldn't define.

* * *

When everyone had gone, Cori took Ken by the hand and drew him to the couch. She sat close to him and held his hand until he withdrew it and put his arm around her and tugged her close to lean on him.

"How was Christmas?"

"Good. Your dad's a great guy. And I think I could be friends with Brian."

"Did he get you to talk about what happened?"

"Yeah, he did."

"I thought he might." She sat, comfortable with him, comfortable with the silence.

"How come you didn't kiss him?"

"Brian?"

"Yes. Even mistletoe only got him a peck on the cheek."

"I haven't kissed him since July."

"July?" He frowned. "July?"

"Yup. Since the first time I kissed you."

"How come?"

She drew circles on his leg with her fingertip. "A game can't compare with something real."

"Oh." He rubbed his chin, and said again, "Oh." She couldn't help smiling, but tried to hold it back. He tightened his arm around her. She shifted toward him and laid her hand on his chest. She didn't know she'd fallen asleep until he nudged her.

"We're getting all too comfortable here. You need to get to bed, and so do I."

"With me?" She raised her eyebrows.

"No way. I'd love to, but we'd better not."

"How come? It worked great last night."

"That was then, this is now. You know we can't be making love, and that's what we'd want to do."

She felt the truth of his words. "We would want to, no doubt. What would be so bad about that?"

"It would make us even closer and, I don't know about you, but I'm already over half in love with you. That would push me over the edge and then when it was time to go home my heart would break into ten thousand little pieces. Now you don't want that."

"No, of course not. I'm in the same boat and don't want to see either of us hurting. One day we'll figure things out."

"That's right. And we will, I promise. Meantime, please try not to tease me."

"It's not teasing if I intend to deliver."

Ken blew air out of pursed lips. "Now what did we just talk about?"

"I mean someday. I think we're headed in that direction."

"It would take some time for me to wind up my obligations in Kansas, but... Cori, if I have any chance with you, I'll be moving out here."

She hugged him, her eyes closed. It was the closest he'd come to saying anything like this when he wasn't teasing. "I'd say your chances were very good."

He squeezed her tight. "I'm so glad."

"But Ken? I wonder about the timing, here. Should you be making any major decisions when you've been through something so hard?"

He shook his head and smiled. "There's no decision being made here. I've known since this summer how I felt about you. I just wanted to tell you in person. Some things are too important to tell on the phone, you know."

She nodded and kissed him. "I had a hard time letting you go home in July, you know that?"

"Thought so. I know I didn't want to go. The day we met, I felt we'd be friends. I was drawn to your caring, your concern for me even though I was a stranger."

"And I was puzzled about why I cared so much about your vacation. I wanted you to have your dream."

"And now you are my dream. Did you know that?"

She raised her head and looked into his eyes. "I don't think I've ever been anyone's dream before."

He skimmed the hair back from her face. "That's impossible."

CHAPTER ELEVEN

Cori called the leader of the grief-counseling group she attended after Dave's death for a recommendation of a psychiatrist to see Ken, someone who regularly worked with police officers. Ken said, "I appreciate it, Cori. Now how about you do something else for me?"

"Sure."

"Call and get yourself a doctor. You have that list from Brian."

"Okay. I'll do that." She got up from her desk and started toward the kitchen. He caught her arm. She stopped and stared at him.

"Sweetie, I want you to do it now. You've put it off for three years, and that's long enough."

She frowned at his hand on her arm and he let go. She placed her hands on her hips and scowled. "Are you planning on bossing me around?"

"When you had that migraine it scared the hell out of me. And..."

"And what?"

He shrugged and looked ashamed. "And on Christmas Brian told me to use muscle if necessary."

She turned back to the kitchen. "Men." She got a cup of coffee, found Ken right behind her. She handed it to him and poured herself another one. "You going to get out of my way, or what?"

He held up his hands and stepped aside. She went to her desk, pulled out the long-avoided list and started calling. Ken bent and kissed her cheek while she was on hold. She leaned into it a little and apparently he was encouraged because he kept giving her little kisses. While she talked with a receptionist, he kissed her just below her ear and she almost lost her place in the conversation. He kissed her neck again and she pushed at him with her elbow. Ken chuckled and kissed her temple.

This doctor was not taking new patients, but might make an exception for her since she was Dave Schiller's widow. The receptionist would check and call her back. She hung up and turned to Ken. "I like being rewarded, but you cannot kiss my neck."

"Why?"

"Because, you just can't."

"I'd like to know why. I like your neck."

"Because it drives me wild, that's why."

"Oh. Have I found one of your weak spots?"

"You can call it that, if you like. Now, behave or I'll make you stand in the hall."

"Okay. Just a couple more, though, huh?"

"No way. I like it too much." She turned back to her list and her phone. That one receptionist might not turn up anything and she had to keep going or it might become another excuse to put it off.

* * *

Ken got his first appointment a couple of days after New Year's. "I have an appointment with the shrink tomorrow. Suppose I could have the car for the morning?"

"Sure. If I'm working you can drop me off at the school and pick me up."

"Do you think maybe we could do a trip, between my psychiatrist visits? If you can take some time off the sub list."

"Where do you want to go?"

"I hear storms at the coast are awesome. So if one's brewing, maybe there?"

"I'd like that. Get reservations, though, to avoid problems. Any other ideas?" He shrugged, got a silly grin on his face.

"I've never been to Disneyland."

"You're kidding."

"Nope." She laughed. At the psychiatrist's office after his appointment, Ken borrowed the phone book and looked up an address. He drove there and walked into the office. The small waiting area was strictly separated from the front office, with a window the only communication between them. There was a door with a card lock. Good. Efficient. Secure.

A woman in a tan uniform rose from her desk when he came in and walked to the window. "How may I help you?"

"Hello. I wonder if you might be taking applications for employment."

She looked him over quickly, what she could see from the window. She spoke cautiously. "We occasionally have openings for deputies, but aren't actively seeking applicants now. If you have some police experience..."

While she spoke Ken had been getting his badge out of his pocket. He opened it before her now on the counter between him and the window. She raised startled eyes to his face. "Please wait right here, Sergeant. Don't move." She rushed out of the room. Ken felt his dimple form but held it in check.

* * *

Cori was getting used to seeing Ken sitting across from her at the table. She watched him whenever he wasn't watching her and they talked and laughed in between.

Ken seemed to be doing well. He was sometimes quiet, and often looked as if he hadn't slept, but he always said he was fine and had a huge hug for her in the morning. He rarely talked about the reason he was here, but mentioned it in a natural way when it was called for.

One morning he picked at his food, and stared out the window until she had to ask, "What?"

He measured words out slowly. "Can I go to work with you today? I want to see you in action."

"You're kidding. It would be completely boring. I teach the same class five times at this school. A junior history class, required. You'd hear about the holocaust five times the same way each time."

"I want to come anyway." She knew there was more, and waited to hear it. When he went on, he shrugged one shoulder in an attempt to look casual. "Besides, the shrink told me I need to try being around teenagers. Can't think of a place where there would be more of them."

Her heart caught. She couldn't think of a place where there'd be more, either. It didn't seem like a good idea to her, but it was his business. "Do you think you're ready?"

"Yeah, I do. Are you allowed to have an observer in class?"

"Yes. I get them fairly often, weirdly enough. I have to call in, though, and let the principal know."

"Please do. Unless you don't want me." He stuck out his lip.

She rolled her eyes and went for the phone.

* * *

Ken's stomach clenched at the sight and din of all the kids walking through the parking lot and on the sidewalk. There were boys with pants too big, and girls with pants too small. They had big backpacks and small electronic things. Some gabbed, some giggled, some walked alone with their heads down, some horsed around. Their hair was blond and brown and black and purple and green and absent. They were regular kids. He took a deep breath and went inside.

He took a seat at the rear of the classroom and nodded to any students who noticed him. Cori introduced him by name and instructed the class to ignore him, then went about her business. In the first period class, a paper airplane appeared at her feet. She picked it up and dropped it in the trash, made no mention of it.

Ken loved watching Cori. She took charge of her class. She allowed brief sidetracks, but always brought the discussion back to the subject. She looked cute, too, the way she walked and talked, the way she leaned forward to listen to students. She wore a navy turtleneck with tan slacks. She looked conservative, respectable; altogether teacher-like. She sometimes perched on a stool, then got down from it and paced. He couldn't help watching, and neither could most of the students. She held their attention, and he was sure some of them were learning, not just enduring a required course.

In the second period class there was one boy who made little jokes, plays on words, and he imitated people as well. Cori kept smiling at him and Ken wasn't sure that was the right approach. She frowned at one interruption and motioned to him to follow her. They went out into the hall for a minute. A girl near the front gestured for everyone to be quiet. She appeared to be listening, but shrugged when others asked her what was said.

Cori came back into the room, followed by the boy. He walked just like she did, a swing to his shoulders and precise carriage, a jaw first toss to his head to flip his hair back. The class was gasping and laughing. Cori turned around and he imitated the way she stopped, one foot up, the heel touching the floor, one eyebrow raised. They stood and looked at each other while the class quieted. Cori shook his hand. "Thank you for breaking up a sad subject with your humor."

"You're welcome, teacher. May I stop now?"

"Yes. Please."

He returned to his seat and Cori went back to work. Ken had never seen anything like it. After class, he came up to her. "It was great, what you did with that boy. What did you say to him out in the hall?"

"A kid like that wants attention. I gave him attention and he ate it up. Out in the hall I asked him to help me, and he did. Helped himself, too, by getting attention from the whole class. If I'm here tomorrow I'll have to think of something else for him to do."

"I enjoy watching you work, Cori. You're a real pro."

She swallowed and shrugged. "Thank you, Mr. Community Observer. Now go sit down before more come in."

"Yes, teacher." The third period class went well, too. Ken was getting tired of hearing about the holocaust. He wasn't tired of watching Cori handle the students and keep them alert. It was right before lunchtime, and he knew many of the students had skipped breakfast and were hungry and distracted. Cori kept it all together.

He waited for all of them to leave. Cori stretched.

"Where is there to eat?"

"Cafeteria, faculty lounge, outside. That's about it."

"I don't want to meet all the faculty."

"Me either. I'll stop in to say hello when I get our sandwiches out of the fridge and we can eat by the flagpole."

"It's not raining, last I looked."

"That's good."

They ate side by side on a bench, huddled against the cold, and talked about the students and the class material. "They have to know, every generation has to know, the mistakes that were made before so that we can maybe avoid similar disaster. We need to be careful to look into the backgrounds and beliefs of people we elect to office. Hitler was elected to the first government position he held. He didn't just appear out of nowhere."

"I know. It's scary. Is that why you teach history? Because you believe people should know?"

"Yes, and because I like to know. It fascinates me. Sometimes people made what seemed to them intensely personal decisions and it affected lives for years."

"Like the choice of a mate?"

"Exactly. Or, say, it's snowing in St. Petersburg, so you attack Moscow instead."

"Snow's the pits without snowplows. I'd go after some warm city."

She smiled. "And some of those decisions we never will hear of, like a wife decides to stop fighting with her husband one night..."

"And, voila, Napoleon is conceived." They laughed.

In her fourth class of the day, a girl voiced an opinion. "I think that maybe the Germans were so hard on people because their language is so hard. It always sounds like you're cussing or something." A few people giggled. Others nodded and turned to the teacher.

Cori nodded. "Language affects all of life. I wonder." She paced a few moments before saying anything else. "English is actually very closely related to German."

"But it sounds nicer," another girl said.

Cori nodded. "And one of the loveliest languages is Spanish. Do Spanish-speaking nations treat people better?"

"Yes, they do," one said. There was dissension and loud discussion on this. One boy said, "They're good to people, but they're hell on bulls." That brought laughter.

"In the Second World War, which we are discussing, the Russians committed atrocities, too. Does anyone here speak any Russian?"

All of the students turned to one boy. He sat up straight in his seat and raised his hand.

"Please give us an example of the language. Just recite a nursery rhyme or some such."

He did so, and the girl who brought up the question of language said, "See? It sounds rough, too."

Cori nodded to her and continued. "And the Italians, too. Who speaks Italian?" A girl raised her hand. She was tall and blonde and Ken doubted her Italian ancestry. "I only know musical terms."

"Say some for us, if you will." She recited musical terms for tempo and expression. Several people said, "Ooh."

"I'm sure you know that Italian is a Romance language, as are French, Spanish and Portuguese. Can anyone to give us an example of French? Spanish?"

A boy gave the words of a song in French. The consensus was that it sounded good, sexy, even. "And Spanish?" No one volunteered. She knew many of them had taken Spanish in school.

Eyes darted toward one girl. "Osiris speaks Spanish better than she does English," another girl sitting near her volunteered.

Cori raised her eyebrows toward her. "Osiris?"

She shook her head and ducked behind her open textbook.

Cori turned to Ken at the back of the classroom, a challenge in her eyes. "Mr. McAllister? Do you know how to say anything in Spanish?"

Everyone turned to look at him. This was beyond embarrassing. He went ahead and gave the Miranda warning, fast. The Mexican girl laughed with her hand covering her mouth, but the others shook their heads, not quite getting it.

A boy raised his hand and said, "The Japanese did some awful things, too. Their language sounds like chopping."

Cori spoke some Japanese for them. "But every language is used for every purpose where it is used. In movies, we're used to hearing German used for giving orders. But German is also used for everyday conversation, for joking, for singing lullabies to babies."

"I'd like to hear that. German for putting babies to sleep."

"Do you know a lullaby in German, teacher?"

Cori blushed slightly and glanced at Ken. He raised his eyebrows.

"Yeah, teacher. Sing us a lullaby," someone said.

"The closest thing I know is 'Silent Night,'" she said.

"Sing it." Several people said this. Ken knew that some of the kids wanted to hear it, while others wanted to see the teacher look ridiculous. He was in the group that wanted to hear it, but only because it was Cori.

She said, "Any German students who know it, sing along." She sang the first verse of the song, and didn't do too badly. She had a good sense of pitch, unlike him. A couple of students clapped.

The girl who had brought up the whole language idea said, "It sounds weird, but not rough like you usually hear it."

Cori said, "I don't know if we can answer the question about the language connection. It's worth looking into. Thank you for bringing it up."

Class went on to a smooth conclusion. Cori walked to the back of the classroom and collapsed at the desk beside Ken. "I never sang for a class before."

"I couldn't tell. You were completely poised."

"Thank you. I have a preparation period, then one more class. You can go home if you want to. I'm sure you're bored."

"Not at all. I will get out of your way so you can go over tomorrow's lesson. Will you work tomorrow?"

"I don't know yet. I don't like that one thing about subbing. I never know."

"Better go over the lesson anyway. I'll take a walk." He stood and stretched his back. She stood and peered to the front of the classroom before she kissed him.

Ken came back in for the last class of the day and took his place. These kids were a little noisier. She stared around the classroom, waiting for quiet. She did not smile and she answered every smart aleck as if they were dead serious. They calmed down quickly. One boy raised his hand and kept it up while another student talked. Cori called on him when the other finished.

"Teacher, did you lose anyone in World War Two?"

Someone giggled. Another guffawed. Cori stared at him before turning back to the one who asked the question. "It was before my time. But my grandfather was writing to cousins who lived in Germany and he lost track of them during the war. Afterward he could find no trace of them, nor of their children. He checked official records and there were no death certificates filed."

"Were they soldiers?"

"No. Civilians. Jewish civilians." The class was very quiet.

"How many people?" a quiet voice asked.

"Six first cousins, four spouses, eleven children. Twenty-one people."

"So it really did happen. I read in a paper I found that the holocaust was fake."

Cori's blush this time wasn't related to embarrassment, but she spoke in a normal tone. "Maybe that paper is written by people who wouldn't mind if it happened again." She paused. "And who might be next?"

None of the students wanted to say much after that, so Cori taught from what the text had to say until there were more comments.

Near the end of class a boy said, "Teacher, this is off the subject, and maybe personal."

She nodded.

"Are you Jewish?"

"About an eighth."

"And you tell people. I'm Jewish and I don't tell anyone because some people are prejudiced."

A girl shouted, "I'm black, and I don't care who knows it." People laughed. Ken grinned.

Cori said, "You just told us that you're Jewish and I'm glad you had the courage. Your heritage is only the beginning of who you are. You make up the rest, you write a part of your life every day."

"I just hope everyone can read my writing," he said. Some laughed, others agreed. Several slapped his back as they filed out.

Cori shook hands with several students as they were leaving. Ken came up to the front of the classroom last. "Wow. Cori, you have a gift. If you could be with these kids every day you'd have a huge impact on them."

"I don't know, Ken. I like the flexibility of substituting. I don't think I could go back. I guess I'm just selfish."

"Not at all. I never heard that stuff about your grandfather."

"I heard it from mom. It was so sad I tried not to think about it. But today, for some reason, I had to tell it."

Ken waited while Cori finished up what she needed to do in the classroom, gathering assignments, recording who turned them in. The principal came in and nodded to him, then turned to Cori. "Mrs. Schiller, thank you for coming in today. We won't need you tomorrow."

"All right. I'll just organize these for the teacher, then."

"I heard you did an excellent job today."

"Did you?"

"From one of the students. Ryan Moore."

She shook her head. She didn't remember which one he was.

"He's over six feet tall, has a knack for imitating people."

She laughed. "Oh, yes. He's a lot of fun."

"Not what most of the teachers say about him. Well, I hope the rest of your day is pleasant."

"Thank you."

He walked up to Ken. "What do you think?"

He nodded. "It was a great experience, but it's really not for me."

"I'm sorry to hear that. It was good to have you here today."

On the way to the parking lot she asked him, "What's really not for you?"

"Teaching. When I checked in at the office this morning there was a line asking the reason for my visit, and I just said I was thinking about becoming a teacher." He shrugged.

Cori laughed, then quieted. "You know," she said after a while. "You'd actually be damned good at it."

He snorted.

CHAPTER TWELVE

*K*en sat in an overheated gray and beige office with sedate tropical plants in the corners, gazing around at the pictures and certificates on the walls while his psychiatrist talked. He sat with his hands clasped, his ankles crossed. He nodded slightly while he listened to this thing the doctor mentioned every appointment. "This is the thing that most concerns me. It indicates that you haven't sufficiently dealt with the shooting. And failing to tell your girlfriend about it concerns me nearly as much. You love her, don't you?"

Ken met his eye. "Yes, I do. And that's why I haven't told her."

"How so?"

"Because I don't want her to worry about me."

"That sounds good, but are you sure it's not because you're too proud to let her know how much you're still hurting? That you wake up crying?"

He studied the mixed blue, red, purple and yellow specks in the carpet that made it gray. The doctor waited. Ken blew out his pent up breath. "That could be part of it."

The doctor shifted forward in his chair. "Now we're getting somewhere. You handled last week's assignment very well. This week I want you to talk to," he flipped up a page on his legal pad, "Cori and tell her you're having bad dreams. And another assignment."

Ken sat up straight, stretched his shoulders. Two assignments. Wonderful. "Your other assignment is optional, since it doesn't have to do with the shooting." He smiled and Ken was wary. "Go on a long car ride and let somebody else drive."

Ken buried his face in his hands and shook his head, cringing and chuckling at the same time. "You have no idea what you're asking."

"I leave it up to you. Maybe you'll want to take two of these before you set out." He opened a drawer and extracted a foil and cellophane package and tossed it to him. Ken caught it. The name on the pill package was not familiar. He looked back at the doctor. "It's a tranquilizer."

Ken tossed them back to him. "I already told you. I will not take any chemicals to help my recovery. I get over this naturally or not at all."

"Suit yourself. You're making good progress without them. But this driving thing of yours is different."

Ken tapped a finger on the arm of the chair while he considered. "Oh, give them back. I might maybe give it a try. Cori'll laugh at me, though."

"You mean, you'll tell her? I applaud you, Mac." Ken made his next appointment on the way out. He liked it that the doctor always called him Mac, his department nickname. Almost made him feel like a cop again, which was probably his intention.

On the way back to Cori's, a place he was thinking of as home more and more of the time, he stopped at Fred Meyer, that great one-stop store where you could buy anything from hammers to champagne. He wandered the aisles picking out things that looked good. He got a Snickers bar for himself and planned to eat it before he picked Cori up after work so as not to torture her with the sight or smell of chocolate. He got her some flowers, a big bunch of white mums and baby's breath with a few red tulips.

It was a big store with an apparel section. He stood with his groceries for a minute, then put them back in a cart and headed over to the men's department. He was tired of the five shirts he'd brought along. Needed something new. He found three shirts he liked.

Since he hadn't bought anything in danger of melting, just for the fun of it, he walked over to lingerie. He had always liked that stuff. He knew better than to get Cori anything from this department, but someday she wouldn't mind if he did. It didn't hurt anything to look.

A helpful, or maybe she was a nosy, clerk asked if she could help. She appraised him from head to toe, glanced at the flowers in the shopping cart he'd parked in the aisle. "Something for your wife? You're newlyweds, I gather?"

Ken didn't know why, but sometimes his ornery streak got the better of him. "Heck, no. We just had our first grandchild. I'm just looking."

"If you tell me what you're looking for, I can aim you in the right direction."

Sounded reasonable. "A pretty nightgown. Nothing frilly or lacy. She's very elegant and doesn't need any decoration."

She smiled and led the way to an area full of silky things. "Enjoy."

She started to walk away. "Oh, ma'am? How do I know what size to get?"

"What's her dress size?"

"I don't know." He pondered. "I know her jeans size."

"Is she consistent from top to bottom?"

"Pardon me?"

"Some ladies are a lot larger on top, others are larger on the bottom..."

"Oh, everything hangs together just right on her." He knew he wore a dopey grin, but couldn't help it. The clerk smiled as she showed him the right size.

Ken skimmed through all of one rack and started on another when he saw a bit of purplish blue material on the next rack. He went there and pulled out a nightie he was sure they made just for Cori. The color would make her eyes glow. It was soft and smooth, and embossed all over with some kind of flower. He held it up to himself. It would hit her just below the knee. It would be a summer thing, he guessed, since it had no sleeves and came down in a deep V in the front. If he bought it, would he get to see her in it someday?

No way. She'd be mad at him for getting it. They weren't at that stage yet, and giving her this would foul things up for sure.

He hung it back up. This was a stupid department to visit anyway. He looked back at his grocery cart, saw the flowers and looked back at the nightie. It was a lot like buying flowers, really. Just something pretty to give to his friend. And he'd probably never again see anything quite like this, something so obviously made for her.

He took it off the rack again. Looked at the tag to check the size. Just right. He strode up to that smug clerk at the cash register. "Did you find everything?"

"Thank you, yes."

"We have a card for regular customers. When you buy ten, you get one free."

"Oh... give me one." Ken felt pretty silly while he loaded his purchases in the car. He had no idea at all of how or when to give Cori that nightgown. He knew he had to buy it, but now what? He drove back to the house, put the groceries away. He arranged the flowers and put them on the table.

He took his new shirts and the nightie to his room and took the tags off everything, and put the shirts away in a drawer. He sat on the end of the bed and looked at the nightgown and pictured Cori in it. She'd like it. She'd know he wasn't meaning to be pushy, just to give her something nice.

Maybe. But maybe she'd think he was awful. Or maybe she'd be embarrassed. That would be worse.

After a while he nodded to himself. He folded the gown neatly and put it in his underwear drawer. He'd wrap it up later and give it to her on the day he left for home and ask her not to open it until after he was gone. He'd put in a note that said that he saw it and bought it because the color was perfect for her. And that he was giving it to her this way so she wouldn't punch him. She'd like that.

He swept and mopped the kitchen and bathroom floors and ran some laundry. While the washer and dryer were doing their work, he sat at the desk with the yellow pages. A long car ride? Would the two hours it took to get to the coast be long enough? He looked for motels with an ocean view.

Time got away from him and he'd have to rush to get Cori on time. He'd forgotten to eat lunch but his Snickers bar was on the counter. He grabbed it and headed out the door.

Cori stood in front of the school, grinning at him as he pulled up. He leaned over and opened the door for her. "What timing, mister. I just barely got out here."

"Was it a good day?"

"It was a decent day. I have to do it again tomorrow." She patted her briefcase indicating work to be done at home. She leaned over to kiss him hello. Ken was happy to comply. "Mmm. Chocolate."

"Ooh. Sorry about that." He pulled away from the curb while she buckled up.

"I can have a bite or two without getting a migraine. Is there any left?"

He slid his hand under the edge of his coat where the remains of the candy bar was. "If you don't mind my germs, go for it."

"Mind your germs, indeed. We're kissing all the time."

"Yeah. I love it."

* * *

Cori was delighted with the flowers though they reminded her of her stupid tulip-eating squirrels. She was pleased with the clean floors, too. They didn't look any different but she could smell the light fragrance of the cleaner.

The yellow pages were open on the table, open to motels. "You going somewhere, Ken?"

"Only if you'll go with me. Best thing I could find, closest to the weekend, was Sunday and Monday night. I don't know whether there'll be any storm to watch, but I'd like you to go with me to the coast and watch the waves."

"I'd like that."

"I don't want to interfere with your work."

"I can get off the list any time I want to. Remember I offered to stay off for your whole visit."

"You're good to me. Then we can do it?"

"Sure."

"Good. Because I already have reservations."

"You're sure self-confident."

"No. I'm Cori-confident." He enveloped her in a bear hug and felt her laughter against his chest.

* * *

After dinner Cori sat on the couch and corrected papers to Beatles music while Ken took his turn at the computer answering his e-mail. She heard him walking around the kitchen singing softly when he was done at the computer. She spent a lot less time online now that he was here, and she knew he did, too.

Ken brought two mugs of herb tea in and set them on the coffee table along with his sock feet. She sat the same way, clipboard and papers on her lap. "Thanks for the tea, Honey Bear."

"You're welcome, CoriOlis. I put a little honey in it for you."

"Good. I'm almost done."

"No rush." He sat silently beside her while she worked. She knew he didn't mean to be a distraction but she knew he was there and he was far more interesting than her work. She kept working. He smelled good. She smiled and laughed at herself.

"Kid write something funny?"

"Oh, not really." She counted papers. "Six more."

"No hurry. No fooling. Am I in the way?"

"Not at all." She straightened, and reached to get her tea. It was good. A kind with chamomile in it, so she'd be sleepy soon. So would Ken, which was good, since he was looking tired.

She finished the papers and marked the grades in the book, put it all away in her briefcase. She smiled over at her handsome and patient friend. "Now."

"Now? Now what, pray tell?"

"Whatever you're patiently waiting to do."

"I'm just relaxing, listening to the music, looking at a pretty lady."

"Want to dance?"

"Will if you want to, but I'm happy just sitting." He took her hand and kissed it. What Cori wanted to do was some recreational smooching, but she couldn't just come right out and ask for it. Some of their conversations were outrageous, but she was still shy in spots. She scooted closer and snuggled up to him. She rested her hand on his chest. He seemed to like that.

Cori noticed that Ken looked a little bigger than he used to. She slid her hand down over his belly. Yup. Bigger.

"What are you doing?"

"Oh, I'm just looking around. You're still nice and slim, but didn't you used to be slimmer?"

"Yeah, darn it."

"Well, we're not getting a lot of exercise. And I admit that I fix comfort foods for you."

"And I admit that I sneak candy bars."

She patted his stomach. "I like it fine. It's a nice stomach."

"Glad you think so, since you did this to me." He placed his hand over hers. "Yup. This is your fault."

"What shall we name it?"

He pretended spluttering outrage.

She laughed and tickled him.

"Cut that out. No fair," he cried amidst gasping laughter.

She slowed the tickling and he grabbed her leg and pulled her foot into his lap. "Oh, no," she yelled as he began stroking the bottom of it. She wiggled and laughed and tried to get away and keep on tickling him all at the same time. He got hold of her other foot and gave it the same treatment. She swatted his arm while trying to catch her breath. Ken pulled her socks off.

"No, no, no, Bear. I'm afraid I'll wet my pants."

"I'll be nice now. Relax." He restrained her with one hand while massaging a foot with the other. Cori sighed and lay down. "These are hard-working feet. I saw how you pace in the classroom."

"Keeps the kids from falling asleep. Heck, it keeps me from falling asleep."

"Mm-hmm." She liked the way he sounded. And she loved what he was doing to her feet. He moved to the other foot as soon as the first was feeling happy and loose. She could almost fall asleep with her feet in his lap. Almost. He finished and stroked her legs with a light touch.

"Thank you. I feel good now."

"That's what I was aiming at."

"Bull's eye."

He winced and she realized what she'd said. "I'm sorry."

He shook her foot. "No problem."

"What did the shrink say today?"

"Says I'm to take a long drive with somebody else driving. I elect

The Kansas Connection   Kathleen Gabriel

you."

"I don't want to be abused. Elect somebody else."

"How can you think I'd abuse you when I was so nice just now? And when I have your bare feet at my mercy in case I'm falsely accused?"

"I remember the stuff you said last time you let me drive. Ain't no way, baby."

He ran one finger gently up the sole of her foot. She squirmed. "Maybe if you promise to keep your mouth shut..."

"Maybe is all I expected out of you today. I'll wear you down more later." She swung her feet off his lap and sat up. She lifted her mug and found she had a little cold tea left. She drank it and got up. She took his mug with hers to the kitchen, then went to the bathroom. She heard him climb the stairs and do the same thing. They were getting so much like old married people it was funny. So much like married except for one critical way.

Cori added a couple more CD's to the stack and took her place on the couch again as Ken came in. He eased himself down beside her and put his arm around her shoulders. "Hi."

She glanced at him, expecting to see his dimple, but was surprised by the longing in his eyes. He withdrew behind one of his usual expressions, a look of affection and amusement, but she'd seen the other look and knew that he felt what she did. She'd known, but now she had seen.

She laid her hand on his cheek. He turned his head and kissed it, smiled back at her. She tipped her head up and he shifted so that he could kiss her more easily. Cori felt a rush of joy as their lips met.

"Cori," he whispered before he kissed her again.

She smiled as he gave her little quick kisses, then a longer one. All were with lips together. Cori wanted more. She ran the tip of her tongue along his bottom lip, felt his smile. She got another kiss for her efforts but it was the same kind.

"Kiss me, Ken."

"Well, what have I been?" His voice was husky and mock indignant.

She combed his hair with her fingers. "You know what I mean. Don't be so cheap with your tongue."

"Aw, honey. I can't."

"How come?"

"How come I'm not allowed to kiss your neck?"

"You know why."

"Uh-huh. Same deal."

"Oh, really?" This was intriguing.

"Really. If we're kissing and I get past your sweet lips, know for certain that it's foreplay and if you don't want me, you'd better make it real clear."

She tipped her chin up and looked at him under her brows. "Little chance of that happening."

"Of which part happening? Of us kissing that way or...?"

"Little chance of me not wanting you."

"Really?"

"Uh-huh. And you're fishing."

"Am I now." He grinned, seemed to be waiting.

"You know I'm nuts about you."

He hugged her to him. "Well, sure, but I wonder, with your background and all..."

"My background?"

"You know. Being married all those years to the sex doctor." She snorted. "I'm just a regular guy and I don't know any fancy techniques or anything."

"No problem. You'll do fine."

"Now how do you know that?"

"Because you're a loving and generous man. Besides, I'll teach you all the fancy techniques you could want."

He squeezed her. "Mm-mm. Sounds like fun to me."

"You know, actually, I have a doubt or two about myself."

"Come to Honey Bear with your doubts." He tightened his arm about her.

"Well, I don't know that I want you to see me naked, since you were married to the underwear queen. I'm not ugly, I know, but I have wrinkles and freckles and gravity has done its number on me."

"Oh, hush. No problem there. I love everything about you, and one of the best things is that you're real."

"So, my sweet friend, can I get a few more kisses? I won't kiss your neck if you promise not to pester me with your tongue."

"If we avoid those two things we should be fairly safe," she said.

"That's true. Just those two things." He kissed her and she still wanted more but she enjoyed what she had.

Cori slid her hand around to the back of his neck while they kissed. Ken's hand slid up her side and boldly took hold of her breast. Cori broke off the kiss in an astonished hoot of laughter.

He took his hand off and held it up. "Been aching to touch one of those since the day we went to the swimming hole."

"The day you got here this summer?"

"Yes, ma'am. You can beat me if you want to, but it was worth it." He stared at his feet, then sneaked a glance at her face.

She cracked up. "I won't beat you, but don't do that any more."

"We're getting so many rules."

"Think how much fun it'll be when we drop the rules. Don't make me wait too long, okay?"

"Not likely. I'm going to move out here as fast as I can."

"How fast?" She held up a hand. "No, wait. I don't want to know until you're sure."

He looked at the ceiling for a moment, looking as if he were doing calculations. "Okay. I can do that for you."

The Kansas Connection

CHAPTER THIRTEEN

*C*ori went to the utility room to start some laundry after dinner while Ken finished up the dishes. She put all the whites from the hamper in the washer and still had room. Ken usually did his own laundry, but his things were right there in the little basket he used so she put his t-shirts and shorts in with the rest.

Ken made popcorn and put in a movie they'd both been wanting to see. When she heard the washer stop she went out and dried the clothes. After the movie, which wasn't as great as they'd heard, Cori went back to the utility room while Ken got into his e-mail. She folded the clothes and carried them upstairs to put away. She put hers away first, then opened two of Ken's drawers before she found the place for underwear.

She saw a bit of periwinkle blue, a color she'd never seen him in. She moved a pile of shorts aside and picked up the pretty-colored thing and shook it out. Such a beautiful satin nightgown. What on earth was Ken doing with it? She carried it with her and sat on his bed and looked at it, stroking the fabric and admiring the embossed pansies.

Ken liked pretty things. He bought flowers often, and he knew what colors he looked good in. Most men didn't. She shook her head. It wasn't a thing she would have suspected of him, but maybe even the manliest man wanted to be feminine sometimes. She folded the nightie and returned it to his drawer.

She walked slowly down the stairs and rested her hand on Ken's shoulder. He wrapped his arm around her hips and tugged her closer. "Almost done. Want to dance?"

"Maybe later. I want to talk."

He took his arm back and saved his message. Cori thought that showing him would be better than just asking. When he looked up at her, she extended her hand. He took it and walked with her up the stairs.

She took him to his room and walked to his dresser. "You know I'm not a snoopy person, but I was putting away your underwear just now and I found this." She took out the nightie, held it by the top and let it fall full length.

Ken's grin was shy, his voice quiet and cautious. "Do you like it?"

"I do like it, yes." She was cautious. She had expected a guilty look at the least.

"I didn't know if you'd let me get away with it."

"Ken, I wouldn't let a small thing like this throw us off. You're more than the sum of your little quirks."

He tipped his head to the side and put his hands on his hips. "Now you're saying I have quirks? What might those be?"

"Well, there's this." She held up the nightie.

"That's not a quirk. Jumping the gun, maybe, but not a quirk."

Her mind whirled. "Jumping the gun?"

"Well, we're not going to bed together yet, I mean to do more than cuddle, but I bought you this pretty gown because I saw it and I knew you'd like it. I was keeping it to give to you the day I left for home, sort of a hopeful kind of a present..."

"This is for me? Oh, thank you, Honey Bear." She flung her arms around him, the nightie draped down his back.

He hugged her back and murmured against her hair, "What did you think it was for?"

"Well. I thought maybe it was... yours?"

He backed up and took her by the shoulders and stared at her. "You're kidding."

She shrugged. "It sounds dumb, huh? But you never know what another person might like and I thought maybe you liked dressing up in women's..."

"I haven't done that since I was eleven, the minute I was big enough to make my sisters stop doing it to me."

She laughed at the disgusted face he made. "Okay, I believe you."

"Sweetheart, that would never fit me anyway. I'd take an extra-large."

She hugged him again and talked to his neck where her nose was tucked. "Am I supposed to get mad at you now for giving me such a personal gift?"

He groaned. "That's probably next, yeah."

"I'm not going to do it. I think it's a great present. I'll model it for you."

"Don't you dare. Uh-uh. No way."

"Okay." She let him hold her, snuggling into him. She kissed his neck and he growled and she chuckled.

"You gave up awful easy on the modeling thing," he griped.

* * *

Cori stood near the driver's side of her car this gray Sunday morning. She held the keys behind her back. "I'm supposed to drive and you're supposed to sit and look handsome. That was the deal."

"I know it," he agreed while trying to get around behind her to snag the keys. Cori kept turning so he couldn't. "But your town driving is pretty scary. If you just let me get us out of town, I'd be so grateful."

"When would I get to take over?"

"Um... Hillsboro."

"Beaverton."

"The Cornelius Pass exit?"

"No. You're not sincere. Cornelius Pass is still way out there. I'm holding out for Beaverton."

Ken stuffed his hands in his pocket and studied the clouds. After awhile he nodded. "Okay. Beaverton."

She slapped her keys into his hand and kissed his cheek. "I'm proud of you, Ken."

"Don't be proud yet. We know not what this day holds."

"I'm proud of you anyway." She commented on things that they passed as they drove through Portland, talking about places she'd been and things that had happened. Ken was largely silent and she took up the slack, knowing he'd appreciate it.

When they were in the tunnel he reached over and patted her leg. "I know you're nervous, too, sweetie. You don't have to try so hard."

She sat with her mouth open, then laughed. Ken turned the radio on. He seemed to be looking out all the windows and in every mirror all the time when he drove, something Cori was sure she could never learn to do. She checked her rearview mirror once in a while, and that was enough for her. They drove along until Cori spotted a sign that read, "Welcome to Beaverton." She glanced over at Ken who glanced back at her and looked back at the road. Ken signaled and turned into a McDonald's.

Cori got out and stretched and assumed they'd trade places here. "I'm going in to get a drink. You want one?"

"Sure." She caught up with him and stood in line with him. He didn't meet her eye but kept a killing grip on her hand. Poor guy.

Once in the car, Cori in the driver's seat, he handed her her keys. She looked straight ahead. "I want you to know that I will stop the car and trade you places whenever you want and I won't think any less of you as a man. Everybody's afraid of something. Understand what I'm saying?"

"I think you're saying that you think I'm nuts."

Her mouth dropped open and she turned toward him. "No! Not at all."

He shrugged. "I don't mind. I am kind of nuts about this one thing. Lady, start your engine."

She started the car, buckled up and pulled out into traffic. She did a good job, in spite of having a critical audience, because Ken did a good job of saying nothing. She caught him rubbing his forehead a couple of times, and eating the ice out of the bottom of his Coke, but he did little else to show his nervousness for the next two hours.

"That's it up here," he said as they approached the motel. "Take the next right." They parked in front of the motel and Ken practically leaped out of the car. He came around to her side and opened the door. He pulled her to her feet and scooped her into a big hug and held her tight. "I didn't think I was going to make it. I hope I didn't make you nervous."

"Oh, no more than if you'd been flying a remote control plane in the car."

"Aw, Cori. I'll make it up to you someday. But darling?"

"Mm-hmm?"

"I'm driving home."

"Gladly." It wasn't time to check in yet so she locked the car and they zipped up their coats and put on gloves. Ken put on a stocking cap and Cori put on ear muffs and they walked on the beach. Cori put her hand with Ken's in his pocket. They kept trading sides as they walked to keep their hands warmer. The waves were big and the wind was up to standard and then some.

"It's time to go indoors, Ken. I can't feel my lips."

"It's time."

They drove to a restaurant that looked big and busy. After lunch they walked through town stopping at all the little art galleries and shops. They went to a saltwater taffy store and watched the machine pulling the candy, twisting it. They bought several flavors; licorice, peanut butter, lemon, peppermint. No chocolate. They lingered in a used bookstore. Cori found a U.S. history text published in 1902. She had to have it and Ken irritated her by insisting on buying it for her, along with a couple of other books she'd admired. Back walking on the sidewalk, she pouted. "I did bring money, you know."

"Probably. But so did I, and I like buying you stuff."

"I don't get to buy anything when you're around."

"That's the way it's supposed to be. Man as provider." He beat his chest.

"Woman as cook and child bearer, huh?"

"Ugh. You my woman." He grabbed her around the waist and kissed her face with exaggerated smacking noises.

She giggled and looked around to see if anyone was watching. "Cut it out. It's cold out here and you're getting me all wet."

"Ooh. Does this do that to you?" He raised and lowered his eyebrows twice and kissed her a couple more times.

"Quit." She felt her cheeks warm.

"All right! I made the non-embarrassable woman blush." He laughed and she rolled her eyes.

They watched the ocean from their motel room window that afternoon, watching and talking and sometimes sitting in the quiet. Cori sensed that Ken was thinking, probably healing, as he watched the water and changing shoreline. There was no storm, but the waves were big and the gulls were active. Sometimes they could see a fishing vessel far out on the horizon. A few brave people walked on the beach.

She said, "I'm getting hungry."

Ken said, "Me, too. How about we just go to that tavern a block from here? Get pizza or burgers."

"Sounds good. We won't have to dress up."

"Or drive." He gave a mock shudder and she gave him a shove.

Cori enjoyed the warm feeling of having her hand enveloped in Ken's big hand as they walked to the tavern, when he interrupted the silence. "I plan to do some drinking tonight. I hope you don't mind."

She considered, and wondered. She'd never seen him have more than two drinks. "No. As long as I don't have to carry you up the stairs and you don't get messy."

He squeezed her hand. "Of course not."

"Well, I didn't think so. No one has to drive, so I'll drink some, too."

"What are you like drunk?"

She laughed. "I don't know. I've never been drunk. Never had more than three drinks in a row."

"How come?"

"I just never got into it. What are you like drunk?"

"I don't know. Affectionate, probably. Talkative."

"So what's new?"

He snorted. "I guess we won't waste any money on booze. Ain't no point in it at all."

"Guess not. But go ahead, if you want to. We're on vacation."

"We're always on vacation, you and I. Do you think we'll ever get to work?"

She shrugged. "You mean, on something together?"

"The times we've worked together I really enjoyed it."

"Christmas dinner was good."

"And fixing stuff around the house. Even though we were working on different projects I could... You're going to think I'm dumb."

"Tell me," she said, as he pulled open the thick rough-cut tavern door.

"I felt there was a bond between us. A connection."

"I feel that, too. Even when you're back home."

"It feels less like home all the time. My home's wherever you are. Mushy, huh?"

She hugged his arm with the hand that wasn't holding his. "I love mush. But only if it's real."

"Oh, it's real, all right. About scares my socks off." The tavern was less than half full, the jukebox blasting out a country song when they sat down. They decided on pizza and Cori noticed that Ken drank most of their pitcher of beer. He ordered another one while they were still eating, then another afterward. The server asked, "Excuse me for asking, sir, but are you planning on driving tonight?"

"Not me. We're staying at the Gull over here."

"In that case, your pitcher's on the way."

Ken watched him walk back to the bar. He leaned across the table toward Cori. "Nosy, isn't he?"

"Oregon law. A good one, I think."

"Is that open space there for dancing?" He pointed to a square of bare floor.

"Looks like it. Nobody else is dancing, though."

Ken's smile was crooked, almost shy. "An opportunity for us to work together. Get these other folks moving." She wrinkled her nose and he got up and walked to the jukebox, digging in his pocket for change as he went. He was still doing a good job of walking. She sighed.

Ken sat down again and drank a few sips of beer while he waited for their song. Cori asked, but he wouldn't tell her what it was. He said, "You can drink some of this, too, you know."

"What, to keep you from drinking it all?"

"I won't need a whole lot more."

Alarm coursed through her. "Need? Did you say, 'need?'"

"To help me sleep. Doc said for me to tell you that I have trouble sleeping sometimes." He twisted his mug around in circles.

"I thought you did. You look pretty tired some mornings."

"You never asked about it."

"You never told me anything, so I thought you didn't want to talk about it."

"You're right. But we have to stop assuming things about one another. You're no mind reader, you know."

"That's true."

"I didn't like what you assumed about me and the nightgown the other day at all."

She laughed and reached for his hand across the table. "That was funny."

"It was scary." He tipped his head. "Here's our song." He got up and pulled her to her feet. Cori glanced at the other people in the tavern as she followed him to the middle of the dance floor.

Once there, Ken got all her attention by pulling her close and singing by her ear as they danced. This one he knew the words to, and she wasn't laughing, just smiling as she listened. "When a man loves a woman..." Two other couples got up and danced, and Ken didn't seem to notice them at all.

When it was over, he kept hold of her. He hunched down so they stood with their foreheads together. "There's something I've been wanting to tell you."

"Yes?"

"You're pretty observant, so maybe you already know."

She took a deep breath, slowly let it out. "Maybe."

"What do you think you might know? Hmm? Tell me."

"I don't know. You tell me."

"I wasn't going to tell you 'til later."

"So tell me later. Or tell me now."

"You don't care?"

"I didn't say that."

"Mm-kay. I think you'll care to know that I love you."

She smiled and moved her head back so she could see him better. The next song began, a foot stomping country song. They stood still. "I knew that," she said. "You're kind of obvious."

He chuckled. "So are you."

"It's still nice to hear. I've had to bite my tongue to keep from telling you I love you."

The Kansas Connection   Kathleen Gabriel

"Don't bite it any more. Save it for better things."

"Okay. Are we going to dance, or are we going to sit?"

"Lady's choice." She gave him a quick hug, backed up and started dancing. He did the same. They hugged at the end of the song and Ken led the way back to the table. "Don't want the beer to get warm."

Ken poured her another glass and she sipped. Ken poured one for himself and guzzled.

"Beer's for sleeping, sweetie?" she asked. "I could help you sleep."

He shook his head. "It's still not time, no matter what we know about what we feel for each other. I still live in Kansas."

"That's not what I meant. I could lie down with you until you fall asleep, or read or sing or give you a massage."

"You're good to me. But what if I get used to that and then I go home..."

"And there's no one but Sylvester to cuddle with. I see."

"Damn straight."

"But I'd do just about anything for you, you know."

"I know you would. Tonight I just need to drink a couple more beers and I'll be fine."

"Why tonight?"

"Well, I make noise when I can't sleep, and I don't want to bother you."

"I've never heard you at night."

"Good." He poured and downed another beer. "Want to dance?"

"Think you can?"

"We'll see." They danced a few more times and he definitely did better on the slow ones. When Cori noticed a little of his weight on her shoulder she said, "Let's go back, now, Ken."

"Why?"

"If I hurt my back carrying you up the stairs I'm going to be ticked."

He frowned for a moment, then looked surprised. "Oh, boy. It is time to go, then. I forgot about the stairs."

They helped each other into their coats and Cori stealthily removed a fifty dollar bill from the table that Ken had left as a tip and substituted something more reasonable. They walked back arm in arm, Cori helping Ken with his balance. She did the same on the stairs. "I 'preciate you, sweetheart. I overdid it, I think. I've never felt quite this good before. I mean bad. You know what I mean."

"Yeah, I do. I hope you're not going to be sick." They made it to the top and to their room and while Cori unlocked the door Ken said, "First dibs on the bathroom."

While he was in there, Cori got out what she needed to get ready for bed, looked at her pretty new nightie and left it in her bag. She also got out one of her new books, a medieval romance. She liked knights and castles and intrigue. She was hoping there would be a sword fight or two.

Ken came out and sat on the bed nearest the bathroom. "Any problem with me taking this one?"

"That's fine with me." She went into the bathroom and took care of some basics, then came back out to find him still sitting on the edge of the bed.

"Want some help?"

He sighed. "I'm sorry. I can't seem to get going."

"That's okay. Don't make a habit of this drinking, though, okay?"

"I won't, little darlin'."

She sat beside him and tugged on his sleeve. "I like it when you call me that."

"Little darlin'. My little darlin'."

"My big darlin'."

He chuckled while she helped him out of his turtleneck. She got his shoes off, then got him to stand up and she started to unbuckle his belt. He took hold of her hands and said, "I can do this. I only wanted help getting started. You go on."

"Okay. I'm going to read in the bathtub awhile. Holler if you need me."

"I'm just fine. Good night, my Cori."

"Good night, Ken." He lifted a hand to her cheek and gathered her close with his other hand. He was a little clumsy, but still as loving as ever. Cori clung to him. "I hope you sleep well tonight."

"It'll take time. Having you near is the best thing for me."

"I'm glad."

"I'm glad I had the nerve to tell you I love you. Um... did I tell you that tonight?"

"Yes, you did. And I love you, too." She tipped her face up to him, kissed him without reservation when he kissed her. She felt he offered his heart in his kiss, his heart and all of his life's devotion. There was no better gift, and she gave her own self in return.

"Someday we'll be together," he sang, his voice almost a whisper. She smiled and swallowed as she stroked his rough cheek.

"Go to bed. I'll see you in the morning."

"Good night." She waved from the bathroom door, went in and closed it. She ran a full tub of hot water, added a few bath oil beads in her favorite fragrance, the oriental and floral one that was her signature scent. She stripped down and climbed into the tub and slowly sank in, then took up her book and drew the curtain closed. Wonderful. The very first chapter started with a sword fight.

She was into the third chapter when Ken scratched on the door. "I need to pee. Can I come in?"

She checked that the curtain was closed all the way. "Come on in." He'd have to go several times after drinking all that beer. Ken came in and apologized again before doing the necessary thing. Cori smiled at their familiarity, but there really was only one bathroom.

"Thanks," he said. "Um..."

"Yes?"

"Are you naked in there?"

She laughed. "Of course I am."

"I wish I could peek."

She looked down at herself and tried to see as a man would, looking for the first time. Her breasts were too small, her belly too big. But, oh, what the hell. "Pull the curtain back and look if you want to, honey."

"You're kidding."

"Come on."

He pulled the curtain back a little ways and put his head in. He looked without a word for several long breaths while she watched his face. A smile grew there and he met her eyes. "Thanks, darlin'."

"Sure."

"I know we said we wouldn't yet, but if I hadn't had so much to drink and all, and if you were willing... I'm inspired to see you this way." He shook his head sadly. "Underdog can't handle alcohol, though."

CHAPTER FOURTEEN

Cori could see the ocean from her bed if she propped up on all the pillows. She lay and watched it and the low clouds and the swooping sea gulls. Someone was flying a kite and it flew in and out of her field of vision, finally settling at her far upper right.

A groan came from the other bed. She'd wondered how Ken would greet the day. "Oh, man, oh, man." She heard him toss the covers back and turned her head to see him ease himself out of bed, wearing nothing but his shorts.

He turned his head in her direction and she waved. "Good morning, handsome."

"Ugh. I'm ugly. Excuse me." He got up and went into the bathroom. Cori looked back out at the ocean for a moment, then got up and got her purse. She heard the toilet flush and Ken reappeared shortly. He got back into his bed and laid his head down slowly. Cori went to the bathroom and got a glass of water and came back and sat on his bed next to him.

"How are you?"

"My head hurts, and I'm stupid. Otherwise I'm doing fine."

"Did you take any aspirin or anything?"

"No. Do we have some?"

"I have some of my migraine medicine. It might work on you."

"That's illegal, taking other people's prescriptions.

She stared him down. "Yeah, so?"

"Okay, if it won't run you short."

"No problem." He propped himself up and she handed him a couple of her pills and the water. He took them, handed the empty glass to her and sank down.

"Thank you, pretty one. I acted foolish last night, and I ask you to forgive me."

"You don't need to apologize. You needed to drink, and you did it. It's okay."

"As long as I don't make a habit of it?"

"That's right."

"I remember everything."

"That's good."

"I told you I that I love you. I wasn't going to let that slip."

She rubbed his chest. "And what did I say?"

He grinned, his first of the day. "You said that you knew it, and that you loved me, too. Tell me you weren't just humoring a drunk."

"I wasn't."

"Huh. Michael and Jennifer know. Jennifer said I was obvious." She drew circles on his bare chest with her finger, then figure eights. He stopped her hand with his. "How come you let me see you in the bathtub?"

"Because you asked me very politely and I wanted to make you happy."

"You make me happy all the time."

"Besides, I had a few beers myself."

"Oh, I see. Would you let me see you now?"

"Depends on whether it's safe. How bad is that headache?"

"How long does it take those pills to work?"

She stood up and stretched, knowing that all Ken would get to see was a little strip of belly as the pajama top rode up. "I'm hungry."

"I'm not up to getting breakfast. Do you mind going on your own?" "

"I can bring some back."

"God, no. Please. I don't want to smell it."

"Okay." She dressed in the bathroom and said good bye. Ken was already asleep.

She ate at a café nearby and walked up to a bookstore she'd seen. It was closed. Most of the tourist businesses were closed on Mondays, because they did most of their business on the weekends. She found a florist's shop open and bought carnations, yellow and pink and purple, and had them arranged in a mug with a picture of a teddy bear on it. She stopped at a grocery store and bought orange juice.

She found him sitting at the table reading when she got back, dressed in his pajamas and her oversized robe. He held the book up to her. "You like this stuff?" It was the book she'd been reading in the tub the night before.

"Yeah, I do, and I like to pick apart the history in them, too. Want to be my knight?"

"I could do without the sword fights."

"Okay. I brought you something." She set the flowers on the table.

"Aw. Thank you, honey. For your teddy bear?" He took the flowers and put them on the table, turning them around a few times and carefully sniffing at them.

"My teddy bear. Yes. Want some orange juice?"

"Did you get me some?"

"I did."

"I think you're an angel."

"I think I might have been right about you liking to dress up." She pointed to her robe.

"This is a generic sort of robe. You don't mind, do you?"

"No." They sat together and drank orange juice and looked out the window while the coffee dripped.

"I feel pretty human now. What do you want to do today?"

"Maybe drive down the coast and see what there is to see in the next town?"

"We can do that. Maybe this evening we can go out, have a few beers..."

"Oh, no. I think not."

He bit his lip. "But what if I can't sleep tonight and I keep you awake?"

"Oh, well."

He nodded. "I can see why your students give in to you so easily. When you get that determined look..."

"Uh-huh. I'll use it sparingly so you don't develop immunity." Cori thought several times that day that Ken might have a bit of a hangover still, but he didn't complain, and she didn't comment. They had a good day of goofing off, looking at things, laughing. She kept observing him, thinking how strong he looked, and how vulnerable he really was beneath it. He bought her a pretty scarf and a package of seashells at one of the few places that was open. She bought him a deck of cards with a seagull on the back. They used them to play rummy in the room when it started raining. Ken suggested strip poker, but she declined.

They had Chinese food for dinner, without beer. They rented a movie they'd both seen before and played half of it sitting together on Ken's bed. After yawning three times, the last time in synch, Ken nudged her. "Hey. Time to go to sleep, lovely lady. You want the bathroom first?"

"Mm-kay." She kissed him and licked his bottom lip, laughing when he growled at her. She got ready for bed in the bathroom, putting on her new nightie. He had seen her nude now, so it didn't matter any more.

When she walked back out Ken sat up straight. "You wore it. You sure look pretty." She felt unaccountably shy. When they had said good night Cori listened until Ken's breathing was slow and regular before she fell asleep herself.

She awakened with a start in the night, thinking she'd heard a noise. She listened and glanced at the clock. It was scarcely an hour since she'd fallen asleep. She heard a sob coming from Ken's direction. She tossed the covers back and went to him. Kneeling on the bed, she shook his shoulder. "Ken? What is it?"

He rolled toward her, reached for her and pulled on her arm. Cori collapsed onto him and the bed. "What is it?" she asked again.

"I saw him again. I saw him and he was a little boy and he was bleeding and I knew I did it to him... God, Cori."

"Oh, honey. I'm so sorry. Let me in." He let go of her enough for her to get under the covers with him, then he clung to her harder. She took a bit of the sheet and wiped the tears from his face. "Do you dream often?"

"Almost every night."

"Is it always the same?"

"No. Sometimes I shoot Michael. Once it was Jennifer."

"Oh, Jesus. How horrible. I wish I could help you."

"You are." He kissed her cheek and she kissed him back. He lay still, holding her tight, his head on her shoulder. She felt a fresh tear through the fabric of her nightgown. Her eyes filled with tears but she blinked them back, not wanting to make him feel worse, if that were possible. She stroked his back with her hand. Gradually his grip on her loosened. Cori matched her breathing to his and fell asleep.

* * *

Ken held Cori as he fell asleep, all of the wickedness of the world held far away from him by the strength of her arms. He dreamed that they sailed together on a huge boat all their own. The sea was calm, a light breeze blowing, clouds high in the stratosphere, like pulled-out taffy. They stood together at the wheel, the wheel for steering the boat, both of them with their hands on it. It was a strange wheel, it had none of the handles sticking out that ships usually have, but it was smooth, polished wood. No, it gave more than wood does, and it was warm.

And here was Cori at his side, his friend, his love, and he put one arm

The Kansas Connection   Kathleen Gabriel

around her and her waist was smooth, more pleasant to run his hand over than that smooth, smooth wheel. Both were good. Everything was good.

* * *

Cori woke in stages. She was aware of Ken's hand moving on her back, rhythmically stroking her back and waist and hip. She felt her own hand stroking his back, his lower back and hip. Awake now, she kept on, enjoying the contact with him. She lay on her side facing him but couldn't see his face, yet she was fairly certain that he was asleep. Dreaming again? But surely this was a better dream, a healing dream, a dream he needed. She ran her hand over his back as far as she could reach without disturbing his hold on her and his constant stroking.

Ken's hand moved down her thigh where he fingered the hem of her nightie, then slid it up over her hip. Cori scarcely breathed until he went on as he had been doing before, now on bare skin. His fingers brushed her bottom, then lingered on the place where the back of her thigh becomes bottom.

He stroked her side as far as the pushed-up gown allowed, then touched her arm, rubbing it lightly, then gently moved it back, out of his way. Cori permitted it, anticipating what he would do next. He ran his hand over the front of her shoulder and onto her neck, then down over her breast and sketched a circle on it, then rested on her chest for a moment. He drew his hand up the middle of her chest and slipped it into her gown and fondled her breast.

Cori had no doubt of where this was going, but she wondered what to do about it. Ken still seemed to be asleep, probably dreaming. After the bad dream he had earlier, she would do anything to comfort him. She was completely in favor of helping him have a good dream. But they had agreed not to make love yet, saying that it was too soon. But it was too soon only because they didn't live in the same state, not because they weren't close enough. They loved each other. Surely this shared tenderness would do no harm and would bring him the comfort he needed.

Cori enjoyed his affectionate touching, this gentle handling of her breast. But what if his dream was of another woman, or of some fantasy not related to their love? She wanted him to have a good dream, but she was selfish enough to deny it to him if it wasn't about her. She wouldn't stand in for anyone else.

But he couldn't mistake her for the underwear queen, even in his sleep. Would it matter to her if it was anyone else he dreamed of?

Yes. It would. Even at the risk of waking him and ending it, she had to know. She took three slow breaths while Ken rubbed her nipple between his

The Kansas Connection   Kathleen Gabriel

fingers. She spoke softly. "Ken?" He moaned, a soft, happy sound. "Ken?"

"Cori, love," he sighed. She smiled and raised her hand to his head. "My Cori."

"Yes," she whispered. He put his hand on her thigh and ran it up to her waist again, then tugged upward on the nightie. Cori hesitated only a second, then rolled to her back, sat up just enough and carefully, so she wouldn't bump him with her elbow, pulled the nightie off over her head. Ken rolled to his back at the same time and she saw him half-sitting, then lying down and lifting his hips.

They rolled together for a warm hug, their first nude one. Ken hummed and rubbed her back and bottom before pushing on her shoulder to get her to lie on her back. He kissed her forbidden neck, while Cori rubbed his arms and shoulders and hoped with all her might that he wouldn't stop. He kissed her chest and both breasts, then suckled as she struggled to control her breathing and ran her fingers through his hair and over his neck.

He pulled her onto her side again and kissed her face. Cori sought his lips and kissed them, kisses Ken returned with lips only, the way he always had. "Kiss me, Ken."

He didn't move for a moment, then kissed her as she longed to be kissed, all passion, no holding back. Tears came to her eyes. Soon they would be together.

All of his being seemed concentrated on their kissing for some time, then his hand sought her nipple once more. She enjoyed that until she wanted more and guided his hand lower. Ken gently pushed at her hip to get her on her back once more and moved closer so he could keep kissing her while he fondled her intimately and well.

Cori no longer cared whether he was awake or asleep, or whether their lovemaking would cause them distress later. She wanted Ken, she wanted only Ken for always, and she wanted him now.

She moved back enough to get her hand between them and took hold of Underdog.

* * *

Ken woke with a start. He had been having such a beautiful dream, and now Cori seemed to have a grip on Underdog in person. He thought about it for about five seconds, then started to chuckle low in his throat. He noticed that his fingers were in a certain warm, moist place - that part of the beautiful dream was true, too.

Cori needed him or she never would have acted this way. And if Cori needed him, he would find a way to deal with his broken heart later. Ten

The Kansas Connection   Kathleen Gabriel

thousand pieces to gather up and carry back in a bucket. Well worth it to give her what she needed, no matter what.

* * *

He kissed her deeply and murmured, "Do you need me, Cori?"

"I do, yes."

"I'm going to be awful quick. I need to satisfy you first."

"Yes." He was talking now, so he had to be awake. And he wasn't stopping, so he had intended that they make love. She was so ready, ready on every level, ready to take him into her body as he'd come into her heart and her life. But now he seemed to be leaving. Befuddled by passion, it took her a moment to realize where he was going and to moan in approval.

He knelt between her legs and nestled his mouth into her most private place. She felt him there and the joy building within her rapidly grew to a peak, the pleasure crashed over her in a sudden wave and she arched her back and cried out.

As the throbbing subsided, Ken came up over her. "Talk about quick."

"I was so ready. Come on now."

"On top okay?"

"Yes. Now."

Ken guided himself in in one slow, smooth thrust. He held still and Cori did, too, knowing he had a good reason. "Aw, damn," he groaned. Cori smiled in the dark as she helped him do what was inevitable. She felt her own pleasure building again, but in no time, Ken released his seed into her with a shout. He held onto her as he collapsed, then pulled her with him when he rolled onto his side.

He kissed her and chuckled as the connection was lost, then kept kissing her. "You couldn't wait, huh?" He kissed her. "It was about killing me." She nodded while they kissed again. "I'm so glad."

"Me, too, Ken. Oh, man."

"I love you so much. I'm not alone any more." He held her head and kissed her thoroughly. "And you're not alone either."

"No more."

"I'm going to take care of you in every way I can think of. Promise me."

She kissed his nose. "Promise you what?"

"Promise that if you think of any way I can take care of you that you'll let me know so I can do it."

"I will if you will."

"Will what?"

"Let me know how I can take care of you."

"All right." He kissed her left eyelid. "But it's mainly my job to take care of you."

"What is my job, oh wise one?"

"To love it."

"I can do that."

"I'm not just talking about sex here."

"I know." She trailed delicate fingers across his bottom. "You have a nice butt."

"My best part?"

"Uh-uh."

"What is?"

"You are made up of one hundred per cent best parts."

He squeezed her. "Is Underdog adequate?"

"Quite."

"Sorry he was in a hurry, the little dummy."

"It's okay. We have years to get it all figured out. And you sure made me happy."

"Oh, is that what you call it?" he teased.

"Yup."

"You made me happy, too. Mm-mm."

"I noticed."

"Oh, Cori, I'm so glad we did this tonight. Man, it's beautiful to be together."

"It is."

He slid his hand in and massaged her breast, then played with her nipple. "Is it sore, the pretty thing?"

"Trade me sides." He climbed over her and got a grip on her other breast, then kissed her some more. Cori hung onto him and played with his hair when he lowered his mouth to her breast. Soon she was wanting him again and he was ready.

She mounted him and began to learn to read his body's cues in the closest dance. She lost the rhythm as she came to a shuddering climax, which triggered his. She lay down on him to rest and to share slow, loving kisses with him.

Ken brushed her hair off her face. "I don't know how you got this started, but man, it sure is sweet."

She chuckled. "I thought you weren't entirely awake when you started it."

Ken's hands were still and he stopped breathing. "Honey, you started

The Kansas Connection   Kathleen Gabriel

it, I didn't."

"No. I was sleeping with you because you had a bad dream..."

"I remember that."

"And when I woke up you were petting me..."

"You're kidding."

"No. I thought maybe you were asleep, but I talked and you answered, so I decided..."

"You decided that I was awake?"

"Well, truthfully, my main concern was that you knew it was me. And you did."

"Now who the hell else would I have thought it was?" He didn't sound angry. But he didn't sound playful, either. She felt a little afraid. Of what, she didn't know.

"I don't know. A dream of some kind."

Ken lay still, then patted Cori's bottom. "You're getting heavy, sweet."

She rolled off and lay beside him, her hand on his chest. He had his arm around her, his other hand lay on his mouth. She waited.

"I did have a dream. We were sailing a big beautiful boat with shiny hardwood planking. We stood and steered together, then I had one arm around you, then I was sort of rubbing your side and all."

"My hip? Back? Butt? Boob?"

"Yeah. And I remember you asked me to kiss you. That was clearer than a dream."

"I did that."

"But I had already been petting you and playing with you..."

"And you already had my nightgown off."

"You're kidding."

"No."

"I'm going to have to think about this. If I started it, it puts an entirely different light on things."

"You're kidding."

"No, I'm not. I thought you needed me, but if... why did you let me get away with it anyway?"

"Because I thought you needed some comforting..."

"Comfort? You would give yourself just to comfort someone?"

"No, only to you, because I love you."

"I know you do, and I love you so much. But I've really been thrown for a loop." They lay still for a few minutes, Cori afraid to move. He pulled his arm from under her neck. "You'd better go back to bed."

Cori was dismayed. She spoke quietly. "I am in bed. I'm right where I belong."

"Whatever," he said and rolled onto his side. Facing away from her.

CHAPTER FIFTEEN

*C*ori fought to wake up, knowing something was wrong. When she remembered, she was surprised she'd been able to sleep at all. She shouldn't have said that about comforting him. She knew it, but couldn't take the words back. It was only one of the reasons she'd gone along with making love with him, and not the most important one. Why that had to be the reason that popped out of her stupid mouth, she didn't know. She did know that he'd been through something horrible awhile back and it seemed to be warping his thinking. That was the most likely explanation. She remembered several of her other ideas about what went wrong, but had reached no conclusion since Ken could not be consulted. His cold treatment of her had made that clear.

She didn't sense him near. She turned and looked around the room, and found him lying in her bed by the window, on his side facing her, his eyes closed. She quietly got up, took clothes out of her bag and went to the bathroom.

In the shower memory washed over her as the warm water and soap lather did. Ken had touched her here, and here. As she dried herself, she spotted her nightgown hanging on the hook on the back of the bathroom door where he must have put it. She held the towel against her with one hand as she caressed the pretty fabric. She wanted to put it on and go back to Ken in it, but she couldn't. If he turned her away, she would be torn beyond repair. She dressed in jeans and a long sleeved tee shirt. She didn't put on a bra; that was as daring as she could make herself be.

After combing her hair, she went back to the room. Ken was awake now and watching her. "Hello, sweetie."

Her heart caught at the familiar greeting. She almost asked if he slept well, but she knew that he hadn't. She dropped her things into her bag and walked over close to him. "Hi. Been to the shower yet?"

"Yeah." He scooted back on the bed, making a place for her to sit. She sat, keeping a close eye on him.

Ken took her hand. "Please forgive me. I was stupid last night."

"The only thing you did that was stupid..." She glared at him. "was trying to get rid of me after we made love."

"Um... I was confused?" he said.

"Uh-huh. I'll say."

"So, will you forgive me?"

She shrugged and nodded. "As long as you never do it again."

"Oh, I won't. That was shitty of me." He sighed. "Cori, I love you, but I wish we hadn't done what we did last night."

"Why?"

"It was too soon. I've been thinking about it most of the night. I think we can go back, and let our love develop naturally."

She scoffed. "Ha. We were as natural as can be last night. And I darned near tried to get some more this morning."

His face lit up. "Really? Even after I practically pushed you away?"

"Remembering that's what stopped me. I figured you wouldn't want me, though I have no idea why not. I'm not going to force myself on you."

"Well, of course not. A woman wants to know she'll be welcomed. And Cori, I shouldn't tell you this."

"Oh, should, shouldn't... Our parents are nowhere in sight. Knock it off."

He smiled up at her. "I welcome you. Permanently, okay? If you really need me, for anything at all, you'll be welcomed."

She leaned over and kissed him. "Oh, excellent. I feel welcomed already. None of that going back crap."

"Actually, darling, we do need to go back. We really do. I know only one way to do that short of a time machine."

"Now what are you talking about?"

"I am definitely moving to Oregon. When I get moved, we can be together, but not before. I can't be sure of exactly when it will be, and you said you didn't want to know a date until I was sure. Is that still true?"

"Yeah. It'd drive me crazy to have the date keep changing and to hear how it keeps changing."

"Okay. So, you're going to be pretending that I'm not coming out, sort of."

"Um, well, I guess I sort of am. Yes. To keep myself sane."

"So pretending games aren't beyond what you're willing to do for the sake of," he wobbled his free hand beside his head, "mental clarity."

She rolled her eyes. She sensed a set-up. But she had to agree with the principle. She had, in fact, thought of it to protect herself. "Well, in principle. Why?"

"Oh, oh. By the way," he said, "when I'm close to moving and have a definite date I'll ask you to get me an apartment..."

"What?" she demanded.

"I said..."

"I heard what you said. Where are your marbles this morning? What do you need an apartment for?"

"Um, for a place to live." He was grinning.

"No way. If you were moving out to be in scenic Oregon, I could see it, but if you're moving out to be with me... you are moving out to be with me, aren't you?"

"Well, duh."

"Well, then, don't let me hear this apartment crap. Why not move in with me?"

He spoke softly, his eyes never leaving her face. "Because you haven't asked me to. Or are you asking me now?"

She rolled her eyes. "Ken, will you move in with me? I just assumed you'd know that I wanted you to."

"Too damned much assuming going on between us, you know it? And yes, I'll move in with you. Nothing I'd like better."

"Will you help me with the back yard?" She narrowed her eyes at him and took on a sarcastic tone. "I'm assuming that you will."

"Sure, I will. And I'll fix stuff, and paint, and whatever you like. Within reason."

"Would it be within reason to get your handsome butt dressed and take me out to breakfast?"

"I can do that."

"Good." She stood up and pulled the covers off him, was a little disappointed to find him in pajama bottoms. He scooted and got up and stood beside her. She slipped her arms around his waist and rested her head on his neck. He cradled her for a few moments, then squeezed her and released her and padded off for the bathroom. Cori sat on the bed and remembered what she could of their recent disjointed conversation. Most of theirs were like that, but this one was particularly weird.

Ken emerged dressed and combed. He looked good, older and more tired than usual, but good. She understood now why he looked so tired in the mornings; she wished she had known before about his bad dreams.

"Ready?" he asked, reaching for her coat.

"Ken, I want to apologize." He looked astonished as he crossed to where she sat on the bed. She watched him and patted the place beside her and he sat. "You had a bad dream last night. Have you been having them all the time you've been with me this trip?"

"Yeah, except for that first night when I was so tired. And night before last when I was too drunk."

She took his hand. "I feel bad that you were suffering and I wasn't more help. I knew you looked tired a lot of mornings, but I never asked, just waited for you to tell me, assuming you would, if it was important."

"What good would it have done to tell?"

"Maybe I could have slept near you and talked with you when you had one."

"And we would have ended up in bed, doing what we have no business doing."

She thumped their joined hands together on his lap. "We're not agreed on that point."

"We were agreed on it, before last night."

"Yeah, well, things have changed now."

"I wish we could just relax and go on from here, but it's not going to work." She saw his determination.

"How do you figure?"

"We have to go back, decide that we are not going to make love until I get moved out here. Already I feel so close to you that it's going to be the hardest thing of my life to fly out of here. The hardest. If we keep on..." He jerked his head toward his bed, "...I won't make it."

"Well, we did what we did. And we can try not to do it again, but..."

"We can't just try. We have to succeed. I have an idea that I plan for us to put into practice."

"Oh, really. Just like that. You have a plan, and we are going to do it."

"Trust me on this, honey. I think it's the only way to go."

"I'm listening."

"I want for us to pretend it never happened."

She blinked. "Excuse me?"

"Well, you're okay with pretending things, I know that. I want us to pretend last night didn't happen. That way we can go on and stay in the same house without..."

"What?"

"If we go on making love, we'll grow closer, right?"

"Well, probably. I mean, that's part of what it's about, you know. Beside being a lot of fun." She thought about it for a minute. Yes, they would grow closer. And they'd get used to having each other around, and then... Oh, shit. He was going to have to go back to Kansas eventually. She could hardly stand that idea.

He kissed her cheek. "So... when I go home it's going to be hard enough as it is, but if we're making love all the time, then it'll be worse." She was nodding now, and he took a deep breath. "It's going to drive me bonkers not having you in my bed every night from now on. If we had never made love, at all, even once, then we'd both be better off, don't you think?"

She could see that it was logical, in a fascinating, sick kind of way. "So. You're saying that we just pretend? You'll pretend it to yourself and I'll pretend it to myself and we won't mention it to each other?"

"Yeah! I think it's the only way to go."

"That is so incredibly warped. But it might work. I mean, I've got pretty good mental discipline when I put my mind to it, and I know you do, too. It might work."

"You bet. It's our only hope."

"I have one problem with it."

"What's that?"

"I don't know if I'm going to be able to instruct my hands in the new regime. I might not be able to keep them off you."

He grinned. "I kind of like the sound of that. But it won't be for long. I'm moving to Oregon, absolutely as soon as I can. I promise."

"Swear."

"I swear on..." He got a far away look in his eye, then met her gaze. "I swear on Mt. Hood."

She laughed. "Can't get a higher authority than that in Oregon." They snuggled and she turned her face up for his kiss. He searched her eyes and bent and kissed her. He kissed her with lips only, darn it.

"I guess we can do the let's pretend deal. But can we have one more time..."

He was shaking his head. "I wish. But I don't dare. I'm sorry."

"And I suppose real kisses are out."

"Didn't I give you some last night?"

"Oh, yes."

"And did I pay enough attention to these?" He lightly rubbed his hand against the side of her breast.

"You did."

"I wonder... it's okay to talk about it right now, then we'll start pretending after breakfast. Or after we get home, whichever you think."

"I'm going to get to decide something? O, be still, my heart!"

He shook his head. "Cori. Did you want to say anything, or ask me anything about..."

"I love your kisses. You are so good. Everything was wonderful."

"But I was too quick the first time..."

"That's sort of a compliment, really."

"Huh. And you're so sweet, so easy to love." Cori felt the wanting building again as he held her close and told her how he enjoyed making love with her. His voice grew husky and she knew he was in the same state.

"Right now, Honey Bear."

"What?"

"We need to start the let's pretend game right now, or else."

"Dare I ask what the 'or else' is?"

"On your back, mister."

He laughed. "Oh, boy. Can I expect treatment like that once we're together?"

"You'll never know if you don't get your butt moved out here."

"I will. Shall we start now?"

"Start what?" She raised her eyebrows and blinked, pretending ignorance.

He grew solemn. "All right. Let's go find us some food. And Cori?" She raised her eyebrows. "Thank you. I will never forget."

She shook her head as if she didn't know what he was talking about. He kissed her tenderly. She patted his butt.

She was sure they were about as down to earth as Pluto with this scheme, but she was going to give it her best shot.

* * *

At breakfast and on the drive back to town they talked and laughed as they always had. That night they got ready for bed, her in pajamas and robe, and she met him in the hall, as she often did. He was wearing sedate pajamas, both halves. She remembered him without them and preferred him that way but this was easier on both of them, darn it anyway.

She walked into his arms for their good night hug and he nestled his face into her hair. "Good night, pretty one. Sleep well."

She remembered his dreams. "Ken, you call me if you have one of those dreams."

His grip tightened. "I'll be alone with them once I get home. I might as

The Kansas Connection   Kathleen Gabriel

well get used to it."

"I'm here, Ken. If you need me, need me for anything."

"I know. I appreciate it." He drew her closer. "And if I'm feeling really awful tonight, I'll call you. Okay?"

"I'll be here. I wish..."

He looked suspicious, "What do you wish?"

She stopped herself. "Gee, I don't remember what I was going to say. Good night, Bear."

"Good night, my love." As he started to slip away, she put one arm around his neck and drew his head down with her hand. She kissed him, intending a sweet good night kiss, but her heart was too near tonight. Her love went into that kiss. She sensed his longing and dared to let her lips part, not expecting him to respond. But he did, kissing her deeply as her heart sang. Hearts pounding, they broke off the kiss and clung to one another. His voice was a fierce whisper, "Don't you ever..." he dragged in a deep breath, "...do that again."

She growled, "Like hell I won't."

"Whoa," he said, shaking his head as he backed away. As he walked to his room, she heard him say, "Down, Dog." She chuckled.

Cori waited a half-hour before getting up and opening Ken's door. She wanted to hear him if he woke. She left her door open as well and went to bed. She heard nothing from Ken all night, but in the morning, his door was closed.

She showered and dressed and smelled coffee as she headed down the stairs. Ken was flipping French toast. He looked her over while she did the same to him. She liked him in turtlenecks. "Is that a new shirt?"

"Yup. How are you?"

"Doing good. You?"

"Good. I felt international this morning. French toast, Canadian bacon, coffee from Brazil."

"And orange juice from... Florida?"

"Probably Florida."

"Good stuff. Though French toast isn't really French." She set the table and poured juice, got out the syrup and warmed some in the microwave. "And did you know that English muffins are unheard of in England?"

"Do tell," he said.

He was busy with another batch of French toast and she took the opportunity to tug his turtleneck's turtle down and kiss his neck.

"Hey, hey, now. None of that."

"Huh. Will if I want to."

"Unsporting of you when my hands aren't free."

"Why don't you put the first batch in the tortilla warmer?" She retrieved the little Styrofoam invention from a lower cabinet and put it beside him on the counter.

"You're full of good ideas."

"I want you to remember that."

"Oh, I will. Will you please pour me some coffee?"

"Sure, babe." She got his cup and filled it up. She took a sip of it herself before giving it to him. She was in more of a tea mood. She started some water in the kettle.

"How come you don't microwave tea water?"

"It tastes better if it boils."

"How come you're making tea when there's perfectly good coffee?"

"You're full of questions. International theme. Tea from Darjeeling."

"Is that in India?"

"Yup."

"We're sure getting fortified. Is this a big day?"

He put the spatula down and caught her by the arm and pulled her to him and kissed her lips, three quick kisses. "I have another hurdle to get over and I sure would appreciate it if you came along."

CHAPTER SIXTEEN

*C*ori adjusted her ear protection, big things that looked like demented earmuffs. She held the gun straight out, her left hand supporting her right wrist. She hadn't hit the target yet, but it was shaped like a person so she didn't feel too bad about missing. Ken was patient with her. She hoped he didn't encourage every new recruit with his arm around their waist.

She concentrated and put together everything he'd told her and this time she hit the thing. She looked over at him, saw him say, "Yes," give her a thumbs up and roll his finger in the do it again signal. She did it again. Then she missed, then she hit it again. When she was finished with her ammo, she turned the gun over to him.

He smiled and kissed her.

He reloaded while Cori watched. She knew this would be hard for him. Teaching her had been to ease himself into it. He hadn't fired a weapon since before Christmas when he had to shoot the robber.

He stepped up to the counter and she watched the target, glancing at him occasionally as he shot. He hadn't forgotten how to do it. Every shot was a lethal hit. He reloaded and emptied the weapon again into another target. He had to take proof that he had been here back to the police department, as every officer did. Cori was reassured that he did intend to go back to work, that he could be a cop again. It was a fear he had voiced to her right after Christmas. He didn't know what else he could do. He'd always been a cop. Always. Now it looked like he still was one.

She watched and waited, and when he had fulfilled the requirements they left, Ken driving, of course.

"Hey, you taught me to shoot," she said.

He rolled his eyes over at her. "You have a ways to go."

"I know it. But I have a start. Those squirrels better not get fresh with me."

"Darn tootin'. I have to take the weapon back to the person I borrowed it from."

"The gun's not yours?"

"I borrowed it from a deputy at the county sheriff's department."

"Pretty generous of him."

He grinned. "She kept my badge and a hundred dollar bill as security."

"Oh." She waited in the car at the sheriff's office and noticed that Ken took one of the targets in with him along with the gun. He'd told her he always shot like that, but maybe he wanted to brag. Or to prove to the deputy what he'd used her gun for.

When he got back in she asked, "Did you get your hundred dollar bill back?"

He shook his head. "She gave it to me in twenties. Seems she borrowed it over the weekend."

"Ah. Well, I can't blame her. We had a good weekend ourselves, huh?"

Ken raised an eyebrow. "Not precisely a weekend, but it was good."

"I wanted to ask you about Sunday night. What was all that drinking for, anyway?"

"I told you it was so I would sleep."

"And you did."

"Boy, did I. I didn't want you to know about the nightmares yet. I wanted to tell you after they were over."

"Did you have one last night?"

He nodded and signaled for a turn. "It wasn't one of the worst ones."

"I'm glad. What does the shrink say about those?"

"That it means I haven't dealt with the shooting adequately. Also said I had to tell you about them."

"Oh, yeah? What does he know about me?"

"He knows where I'm staying. He thinks we're being..." He stopped and licked his lips. Cori waited, but he didn't say anything else.

"What, Ken? He thinks we're being what?"

"Well, he told me that if we're as committed as I say we are that we're being dishonest by sleeping separate."

"Oh." She wondered how much she could say without referring to the thing that they agreed hadn't happened. "I agree with him."

Ken hit the steering wheel with his fist. "Damn it."

She ignored his outburst and went on. "But a little dishonesty now is necessary, considering that we can't live together yet. It would drive me nuts to have you now and then you move back home."

"I see what Sandi goes through every time they ship Jerry overseas. I wouldn't want you to suffer like that."

"I know." She reached over and patted his leg. She couldn't resist getting a little dig in. "I wonder what the shrink would make of what we didn't do this weekend?"

His mouth dropped open, then he closed it. She saw his throat working, then he burst out laughing. She laughed with him.

* * *

Cori stood in the kitchen re-potting some of her more root-bound houseplants when Ken got back from his psychiatrist appointment. "You just can't wait until spring, can you?" he said behind her. He placed his hands on her hips, then slipped his arms around her waist and rested his chin lightly on her shoulder.

"No fair when I don't have my hands free."

"I like you this way." He slid his hands onto her breasts for a moment, then wrapped around her waist again. It was the first time he'd touched them since they didn't do the thing they did. She liked it that he was relaxing more.

"You're sure cuddly."

"Us teddy bears are like that. And you know, I think I've figured out what cute little critter you are."

"Pray tell, what would that be?"

"A bunny. A honey bunny. A sunny bunny."

She wiped her hands off on a towel and turned in his arms, her arms fitting around his neck. "Aren't bunnies afraid of bears?"

"You tell me."

"This bunny ain't afraid of diddly."

He laughed. "I've polluted your perfect schoolteacher language."

She wrinkled her nose. "You're awful lucky I'm not an English teacher. Excuse me. I mean 'Language Arts.'"

"Uh-huh. And you're lucky I'm not with the fashion police." She stepped back and looked down at her gingham apron, flowered shirt, sweat pants and fuzzy slippers.

"I look nice from the neck up."

He shook his head, wet a finger and drew it down her cheek, then showed her his black fingertip.

"I'll finish this up and then we can have tea and you can tell me what the shrink said." She went back to the ivy she'd been working on while Ken started pouring water into the tea kettle. "You're getting pretty good at taking hints."

"Yeah, I am. You know what the doctor said?"

"What?"

"He says I'm making progress."

"That's good."

"Yup. And he..." He seemed to be concentrating on starting the burner.

"What did he say about the dreams?"

"That they may take a while to go completely away."

"Makes sense. It's been less than a month, you know, since it happened."

"I know. And except for the dreams and times I remember the shooting too vividly, this has been one of the best almost-months I've ever had."

She turned toward him, dirt-covered hands resting on the counter behind her. "Had?"

He looked down. "He released me to go back to work. I have to report Monday."

She turned abruptly back to the ivy, stuffed it into its new pot. She had known that he would go home sooner or later. But so soon? Her eyes filled with tears. She took a deep, steadying breath and kept her eyes down. "Well, good. Then you can be a cop again, and everything will go back to normal for you."

He laid his hand on her shoulder. "I'll never feel normal, until I'm with you for good."

She nodded. "So hurry up and move out here, will you?"

* * *

Cori answered a knock on the door to find her mail carrier with a certified letter. She looked at the return address, that of the textbook publisher she exchanged e-mails with a few months ago. Strange.

"What did the mailman bring you, sweetie?" Ken called from his spot at the computer.

She ripped open the stuffed envelope, found as the first page a letter from Lauren Tate-Rivera, the editor she had exchanged so many interesting e-mails with. She stood and read it. "They've seen my work? What work?"

"What is it, honey?"

"They say they've seen my work and like it... I have a flair for working with teens... Oh! Those community observers I kept getting were from the publisher. So..." She kept reading and Ken stood and read over her shoulder

The Kansas Connection   Kathleen Gabriel

until she was done reading the letter and let her hand fall to her side. Ken snatched it from her and handed her the other pages back. She looked them over, shaking her head and laughing. It was a contract, along with some other things.

"That textbook I bitched so much about? They want me to write a revision."

"Says something about a committee, but they want you to be the head honcho. Who else is on this committee?"

"They're subject to my approval. Wow! I never did anything like this. What makes them think I can write?"

"It says here, your master's thesis and your doctoral dissertation... Have I been kissing a doctor?"

"No. I never finished my doctorate. Dad hounded me about it for years." She flipped through the pages until she found a list of names. "This must be my references, because Dad's at the head of the list. But I don't know most of these..." She started laughing.

"What?"

"This is the committee. I'd be my dad's boss. I love it."

"Would he love it, I wonder?"

She sat on the couch and read every bit of the contract and paperwork they sent. It sounded reasonable, but she wanted to have a contract lawyer look it over before she decided anything. Ken sat beside her and read everything after her. When she laid the last page down they sat and smiled at each other.

"I'd do it in a heartbeat, if they were asking me."

"I'm leaning toward yes. Maybe I can use the extra money to finish up my doctorate, make my daddy proud."

"I think we need to celebrate. I'll take you out for lobster."

"But we were going to stay home our last evening this trip. To say goodbye your first trip out we kissed for the first time..."

"And this trip we'll eat lobster." She remembered something else they'd done, but they weren't allowing themselves to talk about it. "Who knows what we'll do next trip?"

He shook his head. "There will be no more trips. This is my last one."

"What? I thought you were moving -"

"Of course I am! A trip means like a vacation. Moving isn't a trip, they're two different things."

"Man, you talk funny," she grumbled.

Ken drew her close with his arm around her shoulders and kissed her temple. "I'm so proud of you. Whether you decide to take this job or not, I'm so proud that they picked you. Out of all the good teachers in the country, you have to be one of the best to be chosen for this."

"I don't know. It would be a lot of work."

"But you can do most of it from home. The committee doesn't actually have to meet physically, do they?"

"We can use e-mail and conference calls... unless I want an excuse to travel..."

"And then they'll pay for it. This is so cool. Hey, Wichita's only an hour or so from my house. Get yourself a committee member in Wichita and find reasons that you have to confer with him."

She met his eye. "So you still like me?"

"Well, duh. I only love you from my hair down to my toenails."

"Hair and toenails are both dead."

"Not mine. Not when I'm around you." He tickled her and she squealed and he moved the coffee table and she obligingly fell on the floor so he could tickle her better. She tickled him whenever she could, but he was fast and trained in hand to hand combat. He foolishly let her get her face too close and she bit his ear.

"Ow!" While he clutched at his ear in mock agony, checking his hand for blood every two seconds, she pulled his shoe off and started tickling his foot. It was a battle she could only lose, both her feet his captives. He held them and rubbed them.

"You know, if you want your feet massaged, you could be conventional and just ask," he lectured.

"You started the tickling crap, Bear, not me."

"Well, you escalated it but good when you took my shoe off, Bun."

"Bun? Now you call me Bun? I don't think I like this."

"Get used to it. It's short for bunny, my cuddle bunny. If I was going to make an anatomical reference, I'd call you Buns. Or Sweet Cheeks."

"You might forget and call me Bun in public and that doesn't sound too good."

"I won't forget, and so what if I do?"

"If you do, I'll call you..." She cast around for something outrageous enough. "I'll call you Underdog."

"Oh, no. But no one would know what that was."

"Of course they would, when they saw you blushing, just like you're doing now."

"Am I?"

"Yup."

She watched his face as his mind withdrew somewhere, maybe trying to find a safe turn to the conversation. "Is that a basketball I hear?"

"It is. The kids across the street are playing."

"Let's us go out and see if they'll let us play. The shrink told me I'm supposed to interact with teens, especially boys, whenever I can until I'm comfortable with it again."

It sounded like an escape to her, but she played along until they got to the door and looked out. There were five teens playing and she knew she'd only hinder them. "You go ahead, Ken. I'd make the teams uneven."

He kissed her. "You sure?"

"I'm sure." He went out and she opened the blinds a little way so she could watch while she sat in her chair. They boys stopped playing as Ken walked up to them. She saw him wave and the boys all look at each other. One looked down and started to dribble the ball. She hoped Ken was ready. He was. When the pass came he caught it and shot. They divided into teams, it looked like it was blond against brown, and Ken was on the blond team, though he really could have gone either way. Cori watched for a while, then read parts of her contract and letter from the publisher over again.

That night Cori set her alarm for two hours before they had to leave to catch Ken's flight. His resistance would be lowest when he was sleepy. She was sleepy right now from the big dinner and staying up late talking about the textbook revision with Ken, but she was sure she could wake up for something important. She wanted to give Ken something that would make him remember this goodbye so well that he'd be willing to crawl back to Oregon.

She woke to Ken scratching on her door, then tapping. "Cori? Honey, are you up?"

She stretched and looked at the clock. "Oh, no," she groaned. Ken opened the door and came in and sat beside her. He was fully dressed in jeans and an olive green turtleneck. His eyes looked green in it. She peered at the clock. She'd been so sleepy she'd set it for p.m. instead of a.m. "Oh, no," she repeated and sank back onto the pillow.

"We still have time to get ready if we don't take a long time at breakfast."

She sighed. "Crap. I wanted to..."

"What? What did you want to?"

"I was going to sneak into your bed this morning and give you a nice send-off."

"Really?" He grinned.

"Yeah, really."

"You mean, like a cuddle and maybe a couple of nice kisses."

"Uh-uh. More like some nice fireworks."

"But if I was sound asleep..."

"It's an easy thing to wake up a man. Very simple."

"Gosh, I bet that'd be fun. You show me some other day, then?" His eyes held a challenge.

"I'd show you a thing or two right now, but you'd miss your plane."

He grinned, then bent and kissed her though she felt early-morning scruffy. "You are so sweet. We can't do that, but you suggesting it, and planning to get up early for it makes me feel so happy. Bun, I hope you never want to get rid of me, because you'll have one hell of a time doing it." He kissed her nose. "Hey, are you wearing what you were going to wear when you climbed in with me?"

"Yeah. Want to see?"

"Yeah." He got up and watched her. She felt deliciously wicked as she flipped back the covers and revealed her morning outfit that consisted of skin.

Ken gave out a hoot and turned around, his hand on his head. "I was expecting that famous periwinkle nightie."

She came up behind him and hugged him, rubbing her breasts on his back. She rubbed her hand on his bigger than it used to be belly. "Are the kids going to give it to you about gaining weight?"

"Probably. They find every weakness and pounce at strategic moments. Bunny, are you still naked?"

"Uh-huh."

"I'm getting out of here, then. Get dressed and I'll have your breakfast ready."

"Okay." She stepped back and he stood still.

"Can I look?"

"Sure, why not?" He turned slowly and took her hands and held them away from her sides. Her nipples gathered themselves into knots in the cool air and under his loving scrutiny.

"Would you really have done that this morning?"

"Believe it."

CHAPTER SEVENTEEN

*C*ori leaned back in her chair, or, more accurately, Mr. Wilson's chair, after a long day of teaching. The kids kept her on her toes. She looked over the last class's homework and corrected it as she sat. She didn't want to take anything home tonight. She was having a long talk with her dad about the textbook revision tonight. He was making dinner, a rare thing, and she wanted to have her whole mind available for talking.

She was grateful to have these days of teaching, because keeping busy was the only thing that kept her from mourning Ken's absence. He'd been gone for a few days now and she felt like crying whenever they talked on the phone. He didn't say anything about when they would see each other again, and that made her sad.

She finished correcting papers, two classes worth since she had done the others during her preparation period. Mr. Wilson would be back tomorrow and she would be off to another school. She'd be teaching German there, a thing she might have been silly to volunteer for since she was so rusty. Still, busy was busy and she was qualified and they needed a sub.

At home, she read an e-mail from Ken. She smiled as she read about Jennifer's latest love interest. She was always talking about him, and she was dreamy when she wasn't on the phone with him. She was more affectionate than usual with her mother and uncle, but her brother she treated with disdain. She wrote to Jennifer, just saying hi and asking if there was anything new. She hoped she'd get a firsthand account.

Cori took time to write Ken an e-mail about her day and what she would be doing the next day, and commented on Jennifer's behavior. "She reminds me of me. It's all I can do to keep from saying, 'Ken said...' and 'Ken and I...' I don't know for sure if I'm feeling more affectionate, but I suspect that if I had a cat he'd get a good mauling. Tonight I'm going over to see Dad. We'll see if Sweetheart can stand up to it."

Henry wanted to see the letter and contract right away, but Cori made him wait until after dinner. "I don't want to eat something made the way Grandma used to."

"I see your point." His mother had always burned everything. After the dishes were cleared, she left him to read all the material. He cleared his throat several times, and accepted a cup of tea without a glance or a thank you. Cori played with the cat and cuddled her, looking at her father occasionally to see what he was thinking. His face gave her no clue. After some time he stopped and stared across the room.

She got up and joined him at the table. "The money's good," he said.

"Yeah, it is."

"Do you have a copy of this text with you?"

"I knew you'd ask." She got it from her bag on the chair beside her and handed it to him. "Take a look at chapter seventeen."

He was looking at the index. "I will. I want to look at something else first." Cori went back to the cat. They talked for a long time after Henry read a few passages. She still wasn't one hundred per cent sure, but thought she would say yes. Eventually, he said, "If you're in, I'm in. I'll help you all I can."

She jumped up and hugged him. "Thank you, Daddy."

"These kids deserve a lot better than this." He flicked the book with his finger. "It's laid out well, but that's all I can say for it."

"We'll keep the chapters as they are, and the format of the study suggestions."

"You'll explain assignments better, won't you?"

"Of course."

"That's the spirit. The teens of America will be able to understand American history better because of what you're going to do."

"I haven't said I'd do it yet."

"Oh, but you will. I know you will. You can't let a challenge like this lie when you could make a difference."

They talked for a while longer, Cori accepting his sympathy about Ken being gone. "I have to get up early. Got a job tomorrow."

"Where?"

"Adams High. Teaching German."

"Good grief. Do you know what you're doing?"

"Officially, yes. In fact, no."

The Kansas Connection   Kathleen Gabriel

When she got home, she found an e-mail from Ken and read it before she even took her coat off. "I could stand up to it," it said. "Call for details, no matter how late." She had to go back and read what she'd written to know what he was talking about. Oh, yes. She'd been wondering if Sweetheart could stand up to the affection she'd give her.

She hung up her coat and dropped her bag on the couch and dropped into her chair at the desk. First she checked to see if he was online. He wasn't. It was late in Kansas, but he'd asked her to call. She punched in his number and waited.

"This is Sergeant Honey Bear, in his underwear."

She laughed. "You got caller ID."

"Now how did you know that?"

"How are you doing?"

"Pretty good. Did Henry's cat survive the onslaught?"

"She did. She was tired of me when I left, though."

"What does your dad think of the book deal?"

"He likes it. He said that if I was going to do it, he would, too."

"That's great. So?"

"I might do it. I just might do it. I'll have to think about how it fits in with the rest of my life, or what I can temporarily toss out of my life to make room for it."

Ken made whimpering noises. "Aw, Honey Bear. I won't toss you out, temporarily or otherwise."

"I'm relieved. Hey, sweetie bun. You're going to teach German tomorrow?"

"That's what they say."

"I hope that goes well for you."

"You and me both." It was quiet and Cori listened for Ken's soft breathing on the other end.

"Are you in bed?" she asked.

"Yeah. It's almost midnight. Why aren't you in bed?"

"Why aren't I in bed with you? That's the larger question."

He was quiet, then he chuckled. "Like a dog with a bone, you are."

"Mm-hmm. Something I need to tell you."

"What's that?"

"Next time you come out here? Since it won't be for a visit, I'm not going to spoil you like I've been, like you're some honored guest."

"What won't I get? Massages? Home-cooked meals? What?"

"You might get that stuff."

"Hmm. What then?"

"You aren't going to get to have your own room."

His voice came through low and silky. "You're so mean to me."

"Like hell I am."

"Bunny, crawl through the phone and tell me that in person."

She sighed and smiled. "Are you getting ready to come out here?"

"I am getting ready."

"How long will that be?"

"You said you didn't want to know when."

"Okay. I did. But can you give me a hint?"

"It'll be close to our anniversary."

"We have an anniversary?"

"We do. I'm so hurt that you don't remember."

"Help me remember, handsome."

"We met during your spring break..."

"In March. Two more months?" She might be able to stand it for two more months.

"Not even two more months. But I'm not sure exactly when. Might be sooner, might take a hair longer."

"I'm so glad. I'll be glad to have you back to stay. But my offer to come out and help is still open. Don't fail to take me up on it if you want me there."

"What about work?"

"I don't need to work, I have money ahead. And the book I can do anywhere."

"You're going to do the book. I knew you would."

"Probably I will. Probably."

"I'm so proud of you, Bun."

"You'd better quit calling me that, mister."

Ken laughed.

* * *

Cori found that the German classes were all accustomed to singing together. And she found that the principal wanted her to stay on for a whole week while the teacher recovered from laryngitis. *Wunderbar.* She got copies of the songs they sang in class and took them home with her. Six of them she didn't know at all. Since she didn't read music and couldn't remember the tunes from the once through the students gave her, she was in trouble. She spent some time memorizing the words, but knew that wouldn't be enough.

Who did she know who could read music? She sat at her desk after complaining to Ken about the situation and pondered.

Brian. He played both piano and guitar and sang. He could help. She called him at home and got no answer. She tried the clinic, though it was after six. He answered the phone himself.

"You're sure turning into a drudge," she told him.

"Hi, Cori. What's up?"

"I'm teaching German this week and the kids all like to sing, and I don't know all the songs and..."

"You want your old buddy to help you out. Never fear, my dear. You still have one of my keys?" He waited while she pulled her keys out and looked.

"Yup. I've never used it, but here it is."

"Use it tonight and bring some Chinese over, your treat. I'll be home about the time you get there."

"We could do this at my house."

"No, we'll want to use a piano. Savvy?"

"Okay. Are you really going to be there soon? I don't want to try to make conversation with your girlfriend since I don't know her."

Silence on the line, then a sigh. "I should have told you. She left me last month. She swiped my angelfish when she left, too."

"Oh, I'm sorry. Poor Brian."

"That was her exact analysis of me. I hear your Kansas cowboy rode off."

"Yeah, he did. But he's moving out here to be with me as soon as he gets stuff wound up at home."

"I want to talk with you about that. Chinese, okay? Whatever sounds good to you. I'll buy. I know you're a penniless schoolmarm."

"Yeah, right. See you in a little while."

Cori set the table at Brian's place, a condo she had spent little time in. It was masculine, all leather and chrome, books and pottery. The built in aquarium looked vacant without the beautiful angelfish Brian liked so much.

They ate first, Cori growing sadder by the minute as she listened to Brian talking about his girlfriend and pretending he didn't care. They were no great love match, but what they had was gone and he was despondent.

"It all comes down to being a doctor, and finding a woman who knows what that means and can accept it. Diane couldn't."

"Maybe you'll have to find a fellow doctor to love, or someone else who's as dedicated to what they do as you are to what you do. Maybe you won't have a lot of time together because of your commitments, but you'll understand one another, and that's more important than time."

He swirled the last of his wine around in the glass, then downed it.

"Maybe. And speaking of commitments, are you going to tell me about this alleged book deal of yours?"

"I'm still thinking about it. Maybe we can talk about it next time, when I'm more sure? I need your help on these songs tonight."

He got up and stretched. "I can take a hint. To the piano." She brought the music to him and set it on the piano. He squinted at it, leaned forward, his elbows on his lap. He looked at her standing beside him and scooted over and patted the bench. "Let's give it a shot. You're in charge of lyrics."

They ran through the first song several times until she was sure she could remember the melody. The kid who played guitar had told her that they were getting ready to have a sing-off with the French class and the Spanish class and that they would do better if they sang in four-part harmony. No doubt they would, but she wouldn't be much help in that area.

Brian looked over the second song and picked out the melody while she looked on. "Beautiful, how about you get me some more wine?"

"Sure."

"Get yourself some, too."

"Oh, I can't. Red wine triggers migraines."

"That's right. Sorry."

"It's okay. You can't remember everyone's idiosyncrasies." She brought him his filled glass and sang while he played. They went over all six of the songs.

"Do you think you've got them good enough now? Or will you torture me again tomorrow night?" Brian softened his words with an arm around her waist.

"I've got them good enough. I'll be singing them tomorrow while they're still fresh. Thank you."

"No reason you can't come over tomorrow anyway. Or I could come over there. I want to catch up on your news. You've heard all mine, such as it is."

Cori heard wistfulness in his words, and felt loneliness in his arm around her waist. What would it hurt? They had been friends for a long time and she would like to talk about Ken and about the book. "I was thinking about making spaghetti. It's ludicrous to make it for one."

"Speak it, sister. I'll be over right after I get free at the clinic."

"You don't have any patients in the hospital now?"

"No. And old Mr. Rosenbaum died last month."

"I don't remember hearing about him."

"He was all alone. No children, his wife died six months ago. He was eighty-nine and the nicest old codger you can imagine. I sat with him every

The Kansas Connection   Kathleen Gabriel

night for his last ten days on earth. Metastasized bladder cancer."

"I'm sorry."

"It happens. Diane said I loved him more than I loved her. And I guess I did. For ten days."

Cori laid her head on his shoulder, her hand on his thigh. He patted her hand. "I'm glad she's gone," she said.

"You are?"

"You deserve better."

He turned her head with his hand and looked her in the eye. He nodded. "I do, indeed." He kept looking until Cori drew back. He dropped his gaze. She gathered her music and got up.

"Thanks again. And spaghetti sauce keeps, so don't sweat it if you need to spend more time with a patient. I understand."

"You sure do. Tomorrow I want to hear about the book, and what developments are with you and Ken."

"All will be made clear."

"You love him, don't you."

She looked back at him, her smile crooked. "I told you that in July."

* * *

Ken swatted at Sylvester when he pounced on the paper he was trying to read, a real estate contract. Sylvester was jealous of anything Ken paid attention to when he felt it was his turn. The cat stood his ground and placed a paw in the middle of the contract, then another. "Is this some kind of a hint, cat?" Sylvester purred.

Ken picked him up and slung him over his shoulder. "You're a good cat. A pain in the butt, but a good cat." He petted him and read the contract to list his house. Everything looked to be in order, but he read everything in it.

He lifted his head when he heard his sister, Sandi, yelling. He frowned and got up, the cat still on his shoulder. He checked the living room, then Michael's room, formerly known as the dining room. Both kids were sitting in there playing a computer game, its music and sound effects drowning out any outside sounds.

Ken waved and went through to the kitchen to see what Sandi was upset about. He found her standing in the kitchen, tears streaming down her face. She held the phone to her ear and listened, nodding and sniffing. Ken caught her eye and raised his eyebrows. She shook her head. He wasn't needed here, then. He went back to his room to get online and see if Cori was around.

She wasn't, and he wrote her an e-mail message after disengaging himself from the cat. Sylvester made himself comfortable on the desk, winding around the monitor, a space a creature as big as he was shouldn't have been able to fit into. Part of him did lap over; today it was a front leg and a nose, a more attractive pose than he sometimes affected.

A sniff alerted him to Sandi's presence. "What's going on, San?"

She came in and dropped down onto the bed. "Jerry."

"Well, duh. Of course it's Jerry."

"He says he might stay overseas another six months. He's not sure yet."

Ken hid his dismay as well as he could. "They can't make him do that. It's against the rules. One year overseas per hitch." Six more months. He wouldn't be able to get to his Cori until August. Or September.

Sandi was nodding. "That's right, but this would be some special thing, he's thinking of volunteering for. Says it's valuable training..."

"Training! Good grief. He's been in for twenty-one years. He's had every kind of training there is. Did they promise to up him a pay grade or what?"

"I didn't understand it all. He was talking fast and I was upset..."

"Boy, I guess you'd be upset. How about next time he calls I get on the phone with him. Maybe he only understands what men say now. You told him not to do it, right?"

"I sure as hell did. He's got no business leaving us all this time. They could send him again before he retires on top of this. He might miss one of the kids' graduations. He might miss more than that if he doesn't get his act together."

"What do you mean, sis?"

"I mean, I've just about had it with him and the damned Marines."

"Oh, come on. Stick it out. You love the big jerk, after all."

"Yeah, I do. I don't know why."

Ken pulled Sylvester out of his carefully wrapped position and carried him to Sandi.

She laughed through tears and gathered him into her arms and kissed his hairy head. "You understand, don't you Sylvester?"

"Kindly do not wipe your nose on him." He watched her pet the cat. When she was little she always wanted a cat when people were being mean. Come to think of it, he was the same way.

"If Jerry does stay over there 'til September, will we be welcome here? I mean, I know you're moving soon, but the kids and I could take care of the house. Maybe you could wait to list it until it's close to time for us to move on."

"I don't want to leave you guys."

"I know. I appreciate that. But Cori needs you, too, and she's more critical."

"How so?"

"I'll always be your sister. But if you wait too long with a sweetheart, she might slip away."

"Not Cori. No way."

The Kansas Connection						Kathleen Gabriel

CHAPTER EIGHTEEN

"*N*o means no when I say it, Brian." The house still smelled of spaghetti sauce and garlic bread. She could hear rain pelting against the windows.

"Friends don't act this way. Remember after Dave died, how I was there for you? I'm the one mourning now and I need some loving."

"I understand how you feel and I sympathize. But I can't help you out that way."

"Because of Ken."

"Even if weren't for Ken I probably wouldn't..."

"Do I detect a note of indecisiveness?"

"No." She folded her arms over her chest and put on a stern face that seventy per cent of her students quieted for.

Brian laughed. "All right. I respect your ties to your man, a good man, as far as I can tell. I understand about the kissing and all. I shall be content to snuggle." She gave him a sharp look and he held up one hand. "Only snuggle, hands above the belt, and off of strategic spots."

Cori debated with herself. Probably she shouldn't. Ken would never understand. But he wasn't here, and if she didn't tell him... No. She couldn't live that way. "We can dance. That's all I'd be comfortable with."

"Well, cool. We both stood all day on the job, now we're going to stand some more. But if it's the only way I can get your sweet arms around my neck... let's do it."

Later that night Cori sat chatting with Ken on the computer. "And he wanted to know about all your sisters and why your parents moved to Georgia when they retired."

"Curious, isn't he?"

"Yeah. I think he was asking because he felt bad about talking about Diane all night last night."

"All night?"

"I mean all evening. I was home by ten."

"Did he ask about your family, too?"

"He already knows about them. He did ask how Dad was getting along with his girlfriend."

"How is he?"

"Doing fine. He and Carolyn are comfortable seeing each other a couple times a week."

"Whatever works for them."

"Yeah."

"Did he and your mom get along well?"

"Mostly they did. They got into a few rip-roaring fights, but nothing serious."

"Amelia painted your castle picture."

"The only castle she ever did. She did it to my specifications, had to find tons of photos of castles and compare them and she did the sketch that turned out to be the rough draft for it while we were in Germany. I took a photo for her of a blooming cherry tree against a periwinkle sky that she used for the colors for the background."

"I think that's so neat you got to go on that trip with her."

"Me, too." Cori watched the monitor for the next message. Nothing came. She waited.

"Honey Bunny."

"Yes?"

"Something is bugging me."

"What is it, Bear?"

"You saw Brian two nights in a row."

"I told you about that. We worked on music and didn't get all our talking done. And he's all lonesome..."

Ken interrupted. "That's the part that bothers me. I don't mean to be a jealous jackass, but I saw you two kiss once, and I'm afraid..."

Cori interrupted. "I know. I would be nervous if you had a friend you kissed. But I don't kiss him any more. I haven't since July, and I won't."

"That's good. I'm just afraid that he's lonely and you're lonely, and somebody might get hurt."

"Somebody. Like maybe you?"

"Damn straight. Or like maybe all three of us."

"I can see that. I won't see him any more except our usual every other week dinner date."

"Once I'm there will you keep doing that?"

"I want to get all the clinic news."

"That could be done at lunch."

"We both have schedules too iffy to plan lunches."

"Okay."

"What does 'Okay' mean, in this instance?" She was not going to get into a big deal over this with him.

"It means okay. I understand."

"Okay."

"Are you still thinking about doing the book?"

"Yes. I'm calling a contract lawyer tomorrow."

"Better get one who does literary contracts. They're a specialty."

"You're right. I'll do that."

"Will you talk to that editor about the things you have questions about?"

"I will."

"I love you. And if you don't accept the job, I'll still be proud that it was offered to you. You were their first pick."

"That's why I want to check out the contract. I can't believe that they'd pick me for something I have no experience doing unless it's a trick or a gyp."

"Ha ha. They picked you for the reason it says in the letter. They want a fresh approach. You are able to deliver that. I'm proud of you."

"Thank you, thank you. (I'm taking a bow.)"

* * *

Today Cori was back to teaching history and social studies, much more comfortable subjects for her than German. She had an assignment that would last maybe two days, maybe more, at Jefferson High. "Have fun," Ken had told her the night before. He knew that she enjoyed teaching, that having fun was what is was for her. She didn't know if she would give that up while she was revising the book or not. It would be a long time before she'd have to decide since the publisher had to recruit the rest of the committee. Cori had told them that Henry was her father, a fact they already knew. He was in. She was looking forward to working with him.

She had all the usual symptoms of her period's imminence, and this was the right day, according to her calendar. She was regular as could be, just as her mother had been up to her early menopause. When she lived at home, they always flowed on the same days. Her dad used to threaten to move out once a month.

One boy in her third period class would not behave no matter what. When she told him to stop doing something, he did something else. She talked to him out in the hall, then when they went back in he interrupted her, used profanity and spit on the floor. One girl laughed especially loud at his antics. Cori took her out in the hall.

"Help me out. Does he always act like that? Or is it something special he does for substitutes?"

"Promise not to tell him I told?"

"Unless it's illegal or immoral."

"He has a bet on with Justin and Andre."

Cori shook her head. "Which ones are they?"

"The redhead and the big black guy in the back."

"Okay. What's their bet?"

"They bet him that he couldn't make you cry."

Cori saw red. "Nobody makes me cry. Thank you. Be sure to act all embarrassed when you go back in like I really ripped on you. Okay?"

"I can do that." Cori opened the door so the girl could go back in. Cori used the faculty phone in the hall and went back into the classroom. A few minutes later the vice principal in charge of discipline came in and beckoned to the rowdy boy. Cori couldn't resist waving to him as he left. The two boys in the back laughed until she called on them to recite the preamble to the constitution.

She had a good long visit with Ken online that evening. When she got ready for bed, she noticed that her period still hadn't started. She double-checked her calendar, re-counted the days. Odd.

* * *

Ken took several runs at saying what he wanted to say to his brother-in-law. Jerry had e-mail capability, but he didn't have his own computer and had to limit personal use. The kids and Sandi wrote him every day, little short notes. Ken wrote once a week or so, mainly to confirm that Sandi and the kids were doing well. He wanted this note to hit home, but he didn't want to be offensive.

"Hey, Jerry. I hear you're thinking of taking some extra training over there, six months worth. I can't advise you on your career, but your family I know some things about. I know Jennifer's in love and could use a good example of what love should be. Michael's decided to be a computer expert and needs a computer expert dad he can look up to, not a dumb cop uncle. Sandi cries easily and flies off the handle at the kids. And not to be selfish or

The Kansas Connection   Kathleen Gabriel

anything, but staying here for six more months really fouls things up for me and Cori.

"Now I know I said I couldn't advise you on your career, but you really do have a lot of training already. Most Marines who retire do it at twenty years. Is this training worth the time and pain to your family? I think not. Get your ass home."

He read it over, decided it said what he wanted to say. He sent it.

* * *

A week later, Cori slowly pushed her cart through the produce department. She wanted something here, but she didn't know what. She picked up a couple of kiwis, some oranges, some ripe bananas. She walked past the mangoes and spotted something that made her shout, "Yes!"

An old lady in polyester stretch pants put down the mango she'd been examining and hustled away. Cori picked up two boxes of strawberries; they had to be hothouse strawberries in early February, and the price was ludicrous, but oh, that wonderful fragrance.

It seemed illogical to go out to lunch right after grocery shopping, but Cori was hungry and didn't want to fix anything. Besides, she felt like being around people. Her house felt empty, accenting the oldness she felt now that she knew she was going into menopause. Like her mother, she was starting into it early. She still felt as if she'd have her period any moment, but nothing happened. She was tired of her empty house. She hoped Ken would hurry up and get out here. Now his brother-in-law was talking about staying overseas longer. She could just cry.

The pizza place was medium busy. Cori ordered the all you can eat salad bar and iced tea. She flopped her coat on one side of the booth and sat on the other. Two young women with a fat baby girl came in and sat opposite her. She watched the baby and smiled when she looked her way. The baby smiled back, exhibiting two little teeth.

Cori liked the combination of spinach, peas, garbanzos, ranch dressing and sunflower seeds that made up most of her salad. She had fruit, too, and would get more on her next trip through. She liked fresh pineapple, but never messed with it at home.

The baby across from her chortled and Cori looked over at her and wrinkled her nose when the baby looked at her. She laughed at Cori and banged a spoon on the high chair tray. Cori ducked her head as the mother took the spoon away. She was going to get the little one in trouble.

She picked up a piece of cauliflower, rubbed it in the dressing and ate it with her fingers. That baby was sweet. She had planned on having children herself - she loved children - but Dave's vasectomy ruined her dream. Dave had ruined a number of her dreams, but she loved him enough that it was worth it at the time. Now that she was officially turning old she was beginning to resent what felt like a wasted life. Menopause was proof of her aging, more than the gray hairs, more than the smile lines.

She peered at the baby again, watched her until she looked over and laughed at her. Cori smiled and waved. The young mother smiled at her. Busted.

A baby. If she wasn't already going into menopause maybe she and Ken could have had one. But no. It was too late.

Late. She stopped chewing. Her period was late, and the most common reason for that to happen wasn't menopause at all. She pushed her plate aside and got her organizer out of her purse. She looked to see what days it was she and Ken had gone to the beach. She counted, and counted again. It would be exactly right. She laughed and felt tears spring to her eyes.

She grabbed her coat and abandoned her salad. She asked permission first, then kissed the baby's fat little cheek and rushed out the door.

Her grocery store was big and had a pharmacy attached. She walked up to the counter, didn't wait for someone to come to her, but called out to the pharmacist, "Excuse me, which is the most reliable early home pregnancy test?"

She gave her a name and pointed out the right aisle, then said, "But if your daughter has an urgent need to know, and it's really early, don't let her rely on any home test. They give a lot of false negatives in the early days."

Cori frowned. "False negatives?"

"Yes, the test will often say a person's not pregnant, when they actually are."

Cori frowned. "Oh. What about false positives?"

The pharmacist shook her head. "Impossible. The test is for a hormone that's produced by the placenta, not a thing a non-pregnant woman has."

"So, if this test says, uh, she's pregnant, then she is?"

"That's right."

"Cool. Thanks." She found the test and took it to the register with the shortest line and bought it and ran to the car.

She left the groceries in the trunk and hurried inside to read the directions on the test while she was still wearing her coat. She took it off and dropped it on the couch and ran the test on herself in the downstairs bathroom. While she waited for results, she got the food inside and put part of it away. She kept checking the time and abandoned the food when the time was up.

The little thing had changed color, indicating a positive result. Cori gave out a whoop, then burst into tears. She hugged herself for lack of anyone else.

She ran to the phone and punched in Ken's number. She would have to use finesse since they had agreed to pretend they never made love. Obviously, they would have to drop the farce in the face of evidence to the contrary. A baby! Ken would be so happy.

The answering machine picked up. She glanced at the clock. Of course it was too early for anyone to be home. She cleared her throat and tried to relax so she'd sound natural. "This is Cori. Call me as soon as you get home, Ken. Got some good news."

She wanted to do something, anything. She wanted to tell somebody. She punched in her dad's number, then hung up. He'd be at the university. Besides, Ken had to be the first to know.

She finished putting the food away, realized she was hungry and poured herself a glass of milk. She needed to have good medical care, as any pregnant woman did, but especially since she was older than most. She would call her doctor, the internist Ken and Brian had buffaloed her into seeing, and get a recommendation of an obstetrician. She picked up the phone.

No. She couldn't ask her doctor. She didn't know her well yet and couldn't trust her recommendation. She wanted someone reliable, someone she knew. She did know a couple of gynecologists, but they weren't doing OB any more. The liability insurance was too high, probably, and the hours were awful.

The clinic had a list of gynecologists. If she called there, though, word would be out in a heartbeat. She couldn't call anonymously because the staff all knew her voice.

Brian. She'd just have to trust him. She could pretend she needed the recommendation for someone else.

"May I speak with Dr. Wright, please? This is..."

"Hi, Mrs. Schiller. I just saw him go by. One moment." She waited a half a minute, then he picked up the phone.

"Hi, Cori. I am a fortunate man. You called because you miss me, right?"

"Sorry to burst your balloon. I just want you to tell me who's the best OB-GYN you know."

"Why? Doesn't your doctor do routine gynecology for you?"

"Yeah, but I have a friend who just got a positive pregnancy test and she's older and wants someone good."

"Does she want an abortion or is she going to keep the baby?"

Cori swallowed. "She'll keep it."

"I'm asking because the best OB I know is also pretty backward about abortions. She won't do them and she won't refer patients out for them. An older patient's more likely to have a baby with a birth defect or Down syndrome, and she'll want to abort if she has a bad amnio."

She swallowed. "This lady won't. She's pretty backward herself."

"Teresa Nguyen. But good luck on your friend getting in. She has a waiting list."

"But babies don't wait. Can you refer me?" She cringed when she realized she'd given up the whole show. "Uh, my friend?"

There was silence on the line, then a soft chuckle. She heard a door close and then he spoke softly. "When are you due, Cori?"

"Oh, Brian. I haven't told anyone yet. October, I guess."

"You'll look so cute in maternity clothes."

Maternity clothes. Another thing she hadn't thought of. That sounded like fun. "Thanks."

"What did Ken say?"

"I just tested myself, just now. He's not home yet and I don't want to call him at work and have it radioed all over Hoskins County."

Brian laughed. "I'm honored to find out so soon. He'll be out here to take care of you, right? Next month or so?"

"It might be September before he's free." It was the first she'd thought of that. She certainly didn't want to go through her pregnancy alone. "We'll figure it out."

"Good. Will I be invited to the wedding?"

"Um..."

"Cori, you are getting married, aren't you? I assumed since you're so head over heels that that's what you were doing when he came out."

"Well..."

"I'm sorry. None of my business. You've just found out you're expecting and here I am giving you the third degree. Well, I'm happy for you. I'll call Teresa and let her know she has to see you. Is that okay?"

"Yes, please. Thank you."

"Anything for you, beautiful. I'll check on you later."

"Okay. Bye." She wasn't happy about Brian finding out before Ken, but it was done. She would have a good doctor to care for her, which was what she was after. She checked the clock. Still too early for Ken to be home. He'd be at the sheriff's office now, doing his paperwork. She looked up the number.

"Sergeant McAllister, please." She waited.

"This is Mac. May I help you?"

She smiled and spoke in her low, sexy voice that he liked so well. "Hi there, Sergeant Honey Bear."

"Good afternoon. What can I do for you, ma'am?" From that, she knew someone else was in the room.

"I need to talk with you about something you already did for me. Is the room crowded?"

"You could say that. I'm interested in hearing more on this subject, however. Contact me in two hours?"

"I'll do that, you handsome rascal, you. I left you a message at home, too. I love you."

She heard papers rustle. "Sympathies on this end are much the same."

She laughed and hung up. He was so cute. Two hours. Time enough to visit a maternity shop.

The Kansas Connection   Kathleen Gabriel

CHAPTER NINETEEN

*C*ori came home and hung up her new clothes. She wasn't sure what all she'd like to have, so she got just a couple of tops and a pair of overalls. She always thought pregnant women looked cute in those.

She made a cup of tea and called Ken while the tea bag soaked. She had been thinking about it while she shopped and decided she had to ease into the news about the baby. She wasn't sure how recently Ken had had his heart checked and she didn't want to take any chances by blurting out the news. Losing one man to a heart attack was enough.

He picked up the phone. "Hello."

"Hi, Ken. How are you?"

"I'm doing fine, now that you're home. I called a couple of times and didn't get you." She could picture him leaning his butt on the counter in a kitchen a lot like hers. She'd watched him lean that way here a lot of times.

"Are you in the kitchen?"

"Nope. Bedroom. You sounded like you might have something personal to say, using that sexy voice and all. Mmm... I love it when you talk to me like that."

She laughed, suddenly shy. "I do have something kind of personal I want to talk to you about..."

"But don't be teasing me, huh, Bun? I've been feeling kind of vulnerable."

"How so?"

"I've been having some strange dreams. Not bad ones just, uh, kind of strange." He cleared his throat and lowered his voice. "You're in them."

She frowned. "Really? What do I do in them?"

"Well, you do some pretty nice things, actually, but, um, nothing I want to think about. And definitely nothing I want to talk about."

She laughed. "Oh! I've had a few of those, too. Very strange, the tricks the mind can play, isn't it?" She wondered how vivid his dreams were, and if some of them were memory rather than imagination.

"So, you see, I'm feeling really impatient to be with you and these dreams aren't making it any easier."

"I'm here for you, Bear. You can talk to me about anything."

"Well, thank you, sweetie heart. But these dreams. No way can we talk about those." He heaved a lusty sigh. "So tell me this good news. I bet I know what it is."

"What do you think it is?" She smiled. Maybe he did know, maybe he was smarter than she was and had considered the possibility at least.

"You've decided to do the book."

She laughed. "Actually, I have. But that's not it."

"It's not?"

"No. I just want to talk with you a little bit about something we promised each other we weren't going to talk about."

Ken said nothing.

Cori waited, then said, "Are you there?"

"I'm here, all right. I'm wondering if your mind is still there."

She grinned. "Aw, honey, my mind is working just fine."

"Well, then I need you to you please just hush about things we promised not to talk about, whatever those things might be."

"Oh, really? Even if I very much want to talk to you about something?"

"Even though. I told you I'm going through something right now, and I really can't take any pressure. And if you go talking about... stuff, I might go over the edge. It's driving me nuts not having you near. It honest to Pete is and I just can't stand it."

She sighed. Maybe it would be too much for him. If Ken needed her not to talk about it, she wouldn't.

Like hell. He was having a baby, too, just as much as she was. "Ken, I don't want to add to your stress level any, but I have to talk to you about something..."

"If it's related to..."

"It sure as hell is. I need you to listen to me."

"Not if it's in any way related to anything we decided not to talk about."

"You're pissing me off, mister."

"So be it. What's so important, anyway?"

"I can't tell you, because that would be talking about it."

"Well, fine."

"Then I can talk about it?"

"No!"

"I guess I'll go find someone else to talk to, then, since you're in such a snit."

"Fine. You do that."

"I will. Even though you're the one I wanted..." Her voice broke on a sob and she slammed the phone down.

It rang. She checked to see who it was. Out of area, Ken's number. Phooey on him. She flung herself face first on the couch and had a good cry, ignoring the ringing phone, then fell asleep from exhaustion.

She woke to a knock on the door and, struggling to remember what was going on, and wondering what she was doing in the dark, she got up and went to the door. She was lightheaded and caught the door jamb as she pulled the door open.

"Hey, Cori. Are you all right?" Brian asked. He was wearing a suit and carrying a bouquet of yellow baby roses.

"Oh, I was asleep and I'm a little dizzy from getting up too fast." She flicked the light switch and met Brian's inquiring gaze.

"You need to be careful. When you're further along a fall could be awkward. You'd be like a turtle on its back and have to call for a crane to help you up."

She laughed and stepped back to let him in.

He came in and turned around and handed her the flowers. "These are for you. Yellow roses are for friendship, and they're baby roses because of a baby." He shrugged.

They were beautiful, lightly fragranced. They came from a florist, not from a grocery store like Ken brought her. Very pretty. She put them in a vase and set them on the table where Brian was now sitting. "Thank you, Brian."

"You're welcome. I thought you might..." The phone rang. Cori didn't move to answer it but nodded toward Brian to continue. "You're not going to answer the phone?" He got up and looked at her caller ID box. "It's out of area..."

"It's Ken. We're not speaking."

"Why not? Is he trying to talk you into aborting?"

"No. He wouldn't even let me tell him." She started to cry and Brian took her by the shoulders and made her sit down.

He drew a chair up close and got the whole story out of her, even the part about their "let's pretend" game that wasn't any fun. The phone rang two more times while she told him. She ignored it.

When she was finished he sat and rubbed his forehead while she watched and waited for him to tell her she was being stupid. Then he held out his arms and she got up from her chair and he pulled her down onto his lap. She sat still while he said nothing for a long time.

He cleared his throat. "Probably..." She waited. "Probably you guys can work this out. But your friend Brian has a contingency plan for you."

"You think I need one?"

"You always need a contingency plan. And I don't think you're going to manage to work things out with Ken if you won't talk to him. No offense, Cori, but you have to talk to him."

"I know. But it's not me who won't talk."

"Oh, really? You're the one who isn't answering the phone."

"True. What about this contingency plan?"

"It's a thing that I've thought about a number of times, but never had the guts to suggest. But now that you have a need... well, I'll just go ahead and tell you. You can laugh if you want, but you should know that it'd break my heart."

She smiled at his solemnity. "What is it?"

"It involves another let's pretend game."

"Yuck."

"Hear me out. If Ken won't do right by you, let's pretend..." He took a deep breath, and blew it out again.

"What?"

"Let's pretend..." he peered up at her, "that it's my baby."

She felt wind on her fillings and closed her mouth. "Your baby."

"Yes. And I will be a happy father and we will be a happy married couple..."

"Married? Is that pretend, too? Or is it real?"

"It's real. That's the part I've thought about a lot of times, whenever I was thinking about settling down and getting married, you have always immediately sprung to mind as the ideal candidate."

"Wow. I had no idea."

"I've told you quite a few times how much I admire you. How I think you're wonderful, how I want you."

"I thought you were teasing about that last part. I'm too old for you."

"Like fun you are. I'd be proud to call the baby my own and to have you for my wife. If you can't tie things together with Ken, that is. I'll be here."

"Wow. But now I feel bad, because Ken is my first choice, you know."

"I know."

"And if you love me..."

He tipped his head to one side, then the other. "Well, I'm not exactly in love with you, but that'd happen eventually. I wouldn't expect you to love me right away."

"Oh, then I wouldn't need to worry about... When would we start having sex?"

"On our wedding night, of course. I didn't say I'd patiently wait on that. We can start sooner if you like. Are you busy?"

She gave him a dirty look. "You've been teasing me. I should have known."

"Oh, no. I'm not teasing. I'm yours if you want me. Do you believe in God?"

"Pretty much."

"Well, you know I'm never more than a week between girlfriends. This time it's been longer and I think maybe the Man Upstairs planned it so that I'd be available for you in your time of need."

"Huh."

"So, do you want me? Even a little bit?"

She messed up his hair.

* * *

Cori paced after Brian left, then ran up and down the stairs to get some blood circulating. Hopefully some would go to her brain and help her think. Brian was a dear to offer his contingency plan, and he really did mean it, which she found incredible. And it was tempting. They were comfortable with one another and she knew how to be a doctor's wife. She was good at the waiting, the changing of plans, the being understanding when he came home broken and needed to be fully mended by morning. She would never have to worry about money, and it was unlikely such a young man would die before her, leaving her alone.

Except for Ken. Ken was her love. Surely she could make him understand and all would be well. He wouldn't talk about what they did at the beach, she was sure of that. And maybe he was under a lot of stress and hearing that he was going to be a father over the phone would be too much for him.

So she had to tell him without referring to their lovemaking. On about the tenth trip up the stairs she remembered that Ken had told her once that some things were too important to say over the phone. She sat at her computer and went online and made airline reservations.

Ken had often told her to call him any time, any time of day or night if she needed him. It was almost two a.m. in Kansas. She punched in his number.

The sound on the other end when he picked up the phone was a cross between a growl and a hum, then he answered with authority. "McAllister."

"Ken. It's Cori."

"Oh, Honey Bunny, I'm so glad you called, I was such a shit..."

"Hush now. Pop quiz."

"Okay."

"Where will you be tomorrow evening, actually this evening, if you count two a.m. as morning, but I feel like it's still night..."

"Huh?"

"The next time there is an evening and it is seven-twenty, where will you be?"

"Um... in my kitchen, having seconds on chili?"

"Wrong. You will be at the Wichita airport picking me up."

She heard a whoosh that sounded like covers being tossed back. "Am I awake? Or is this the dream of the century?"

"It sounds like you're awake. I hope you are because I need you to meet me..."

"At the airport at seven-twenty?"

"Yes."

"Of course I'll be there. Oh, thank you for coming. I miss you so much. Are you coming to see me? Or beat me up?"

"That'll be up to you."

He groaned. "No, really, sweetie. Why are you coming?"

Her eyes filled and she drew in a shuddering breath. "Because I need you, Ken. I need you something awful."

"Aw, Cori. I've been waiting to hear that for years. I'll be there. Seven-twenty." She hoped she was doing the right thing.

* * *

She slept for a few hours, then woke hungry and excited. She showered and ate a bowl of raisin bran then dragged three bags out of the closet. One for carry-on, two for clothes. She didn't know how many clothes she'd need, so she'd take a bunch. She rolled each piece so she could fit more in. She called her dad and left a message at his office and hoped he listened to his voice mail once in awhile, then stood and stared. What was she forgetting?

The car. What would she do with it? She might be gone for two months, or more. She could hardly leave it in long term parking all that time. She had a little money, but there was no reason to throw it away. Maybe her dad would have time to take her in to the airport. She didn't know his class schedule and it was possible. Otherwise she'd take a cab. Simple.

Raisin bran alone was a poor breakfast, so she made tea and ate a couple of pieces of fruit. She'd have to ask her dad to eat what was in the refrigerator. She didn't have time to do anything else about it.

Ken. She would get to see her Ken soon. Phone. She checked caller ID and it was from the university. "Hi, Dad."

"Hi yourself. Are you leaving me?"

"Now, don't think of it that way. Think of it as I'm going to see my true love. I'm not sure how long I'll be staying there yet. Will you watch over things? Eat the food I have in the fridge for me?"

"Well, I'm not sure about your fridge. Is it your usual junk or did you bake something?"

"It's just fruit and milk and stuff."

"If you insist."

"Great. And are you free this afternoon to take me to the airport? I need to be there about one."

"Sorry, kid. I'll be in class. I wish I'd known you were going."

"Me, too. I just decided last night. Something came up..."

"What came up?" She wanted to tell him, but Ken deserved to know first. It was bad enough that Brian knew. Brian. She had to tell him she was leaving, too. "Oh, I'll have to tell you later. It's a thing between Ken and me."

"You're eloping. I knew it."

She laughed, not an altogether natural laugh. "I'll let you know." They said good bye and promised to stay in touch. She called Brian's office. He was with a patient and they'd have him call her back. She called both school districts and got off the sub lists. She signed her book contract and put it in the mail. She wrote a letter to her mail carrier letting him know where to forward the mail and apologizing for not having the proper postal service form.

That pretty much took care of everything. She was glad that she didn't have a cat just now, though she would dearly love to have one, but today she was glad that she didn't have to leave a kitty and try to find someone to take care of her.

She ran to answer the phone. "So, beautiful, have you decided to take me up on my offer?"

"You're sweet, Brian, but I'm going to give Ken a chance. I'm flying out this afternoon."

"Who's taking you to the airport?"

"Um, a cab, I guess. I don't want to leave my car in long-term parking."

The Kansas Connection   Kathleen Gabriel

"I don't blame you. What time do you need to be there?"

"About one o'clock."

"Hang on." She waited, and he came back on in less than a minute. "I have a big gap in my schedule. I'll drive you."

"I don't believe you. Don't sabotage your doctor-patient relationships by rescheduling anyone. I'll take a bus... no, I have baggage. It has to be a cab."

"So, you're planning on being gone awhile."

"Hoping, not planning. I hope he hears me out."

"He will. I wish I'd insisted on a good night kiss last night. I'll probably never get one now."

"Poor Brian. I really appreciate everything, and I mean it."

"And I appreciate it that you didn't laugh at me." He sniffed.

"I couldn't laugh at such a generous and noble offer. Will you keep it available, just in case?"

"Oh, get out of here. Go to Kansas, will you?"

"Okay. Take care." She dragged the suitcases downstairs and left them near the door. She called a cab company and arranged a time for a ride. It was early, but it was always better to be early. She sat down on the couch and wished she could talk to her mother about all of this.

CHAPTER TWENTY

*K*en knew he wouldn't be able to sleep, so he got up and cleaned as quietly as he could. He didn't want Cori to see this mess and he'd have to go directly to the airport after work to make her flight. He wrote the kids a note letting them know they were going to have company and would they please not leave the bathroom and kitchen disaster areas.

He cleared the papers and junk off the dining room table, which now stood in one end of the living room since Michael was sleeping in the dining room. Cori knew how things were here with sleeping arrangements; she'd understand.

Sleeping arrangements. Where on earth would he put Cori? If she was coming to stay, of course he'd put her in his room with him. But if it was just a visit, he wouldn't set them up for the pain of separating by sleeping together for even one night. One night had nearly killed him as it was.

And that one night had done something to Cori's thinking. She was so weird on the phone. They had said they wouldn't talk about it, and now she was wanting to, and all of a sudden she wanted to come out here. Just shows what can happen when you don't keep a tight rein on your thoughts. His thoughts were thoroughly disciplined at all times.

Like hell. Cori. Sweet Cori was coming to see him. He laughed out loud and tackled the bathroom. Towels on the floor, water on the floor, feminine junk on every horizontal surface. He had no clue where to put the latter. Jennifer and Sandi each had their own baskets they were supposed to use for their cosmetics, but he couldn't put these things away for them because he didn't know which stuff belonged to which female. He and Michael were way more organized. They each had small baskets for their things; shaving stuff and deodorant took care of it for them. Not that Michael was a frequent shaver. Now here was some shaving cream on the back of the toilet. Who...? Oh. It was his. He put it away, then cleaned around everything else.

He felt someone watching him and turned around to see Sandi standing there in a fuzzy bathrobe. "What on earth are you doing?"

"Oh, sis, it's such a mess and I don't know which crap is whose and she's coming tonight..."

"Tonight? You mean tomorrow? Who?"

"Cori. She's coming."

"That's wonderful! Oh, shit. This place looks like..."

"Yeah. It's a mess. I'm sorry if I woke you up. I couldn't sleep knowing what the bathroom looked like."

"What about the rest of the house?"

"I took the all the junk off the table. The kitchen's okay. Do you think anyone would have time to dust and vacuum tomorrow? I mean today? I'll have to go straight from work to the airport to make sure I'm on time."

"Okay. I'll recruit someone or do it myself. Shoot, I'll do it now."

"Don't wake the kids."

"Oh, yeah. Let me in and I'll put my stuff away in here." She pushed him out of the way and Ken went out seeking other messes.

* * *

When she got off the plane she walked toward the exit, looking for Ken. She spotted him waving and running toward her. She jogged up to him and dropped her bag as he lifted her off her feet. Ken's arms felt good in spite of the layers of coat that separated them. He set her down and kissed her cheek over and over and she kissed him back until eventually their lips connected and the kissing slowed down a good bit.

"I missed you so much. I'm so glad you're here. Oh, Cori, let's not fight, huh?"

"We won't fight as long as you mind the teacher."

"Oh, yes, ma'am." He kissed her again. "Do you have baggage?"

"Yup."

"Okay. It's over this way." He led the way and they talked about the airport and the weather and the kids and what everyone thought of her coming to visit. They didn't talk about the thing Cori was most thinking of, and Ken didn't ask how long she was staying. When they stopped and she pointed out her bags Ken pulled them off for her. He stood grinning, then pulled her into his arms again and talked into her hair. "If you're bringing this much stuff, you must be staying."

The Kansas Connection   Kathleen Gabriel

"We'll see." She tossed her hair and tried to sound haughty.

He grinned.

She waited with her luggage while Ken brought the car around. He hopped out and put her things in the back, then lifted her into the seat. "Such service."

He got in the other side and started out of the airport. "Where to?"

"Home."

"I like that word, home."

They talked about this and that and laughed on the way to Ken's house. Cori loved hearing his voice. She was sure he'd be pleased about the baby, and she had a plan prepared that would make him listen if he started being stubborn again.

"Sandi took the kids to a movie so we could talk alone awhile."

"That's kind of her. I want to meet them all as soon as possible, but I especially need to talk with you."

She could see him nodding in the dark. "Sandi volunteered to double up with Jennifer so you can have your own room."

"Again, very kind."

"Uh-huh."

She felt him looking at her, but she looked out the window so he wouldn't see her smile. She did not intend to oust Sandi from her room.

Ken carried her bags and dropped them in the hallway, then gave her a tour. She was quiet. It was a nice house, comfortable. Ken seemed embarrassed about some of the housekeeping, but she took his hand and said nothing. "I like it here," she announced at the end of the tour. "But I didn't see the famous Sylvester."

"I didn't, either. He can be shy of strangers, but he'll show up." He showed her to the couch and sat beside her. "Now. What did you want to talk about?"

She took his hand. "I know there's something of our not too distant past that you don't want to talk about, but..."

He held up his hand. "Honey, we can't talk about it until we get other things straightened out. Like, are you staying? Or going back home before I can get moved?"

"I can't answer that until I talk to you about this."

"That makes no sense to me whatsoever."

She gave him the evil eye. "You're stubborn sometimes, you know that?"

"Well, you're mysterious and irritating lately, so I suppose that kind of makes us even."

"Okay. I didn't want to have to do this."

"What?"

"Frisk me."

He was incredulous. "What?"

"Surely you know how to do it. Frisk me."

"What am I looking for? Weapons or contraband?"

"Contraband, in the form of a laboratory specimen. It could be a bag, a bottle or a tube."

Ken slid forward on the couch. "Well? On your feet, ma'am."

She stood and he took a firm grip on her arm and led her to the wall. "Hands on the wall. Feet back and spread 'em."

She stood as he said, then he nudged her feet further back with his. "Geez, Ken."

"No talking." He frisked her up to the waist, then stopped. "Women often carry contraband in their bras."

"Don't be a prude, McAllister." He checked her bra and sleeves and let her go. "Satisfied?" she asked.

"Yeah. Not that I know what that was about." She went to her purse, keeping him nearby. She took a white pharmacy bag out of her purse. "This is a sensitive medical test. I'm taking it with me into the bathroom where I will pee into the cup provided and use this apparatus to do the test. We will have results in a few minutes."

"Okay."

She went into the bathroom and while she was collecting the specimen he shouted through the door, "Is that a drug test? Are you going to try to tell me that I drove you to use drugs? I'm not going to buy it."

She laughed. She came out and asked him into the bathroom where she showed him the little set up. "If this deal changes color, the test is positive."

Ken said nothing and she looked at his face. He was pale, his eyes huge. He grabbed her shoulders. "Is that a pregnancy test?"

"Yes."

"Will it come out positive?"

"Yes." He turned and walked out. She followed and found him standing in the living room, staring at the wall. She touched his arm as she crossed in front of him and stood waiting. He squeezed his eyes shut, shook his head and licked his lips. His next words were barely above a whisper. "Are you sure?"

"Yes, I'm sure."

"You'll keep it?"

She shouted, "Of course we'll keep it!"

The Kansas Connection   Kathleen Gabriel

He drew in a deep breath, laughed it out, then yelled at the ceiling, "Yee-ow!" He started laughing and she did, too, and he bear hugged her until she thought she'd have multiple fractures, then he started kissing her. "Cori, sweetie, darling, love. I can't believe it!"

"Yes, Ken. Oh, yes. I wanted to ease into telling you, but you wouldn't listen to anything I..."

"I'm so sorry. So sorry. No! I'm glad! It forced you to come out and tell me in person and I am so happy and I can kiss your face and..." He kissed her and she caught his face in her hands and kissed his mouth. He responded with enthusiasm that she struggled to keep up with. She had to catch her breath when he let go.

"I hoped you'd be happy, but I wasn't sure and I was a little afraid for us because if you didn't want the baby it would break us up because I won't have an abortion and I love you so much it would just kill me."

"What are you saying? Of course I want our baby. I would never want..."

"I thought so, but I had to think about all the possibilities because it's my worrywart nature and I have made some decisions. And I'd better tell them to you now before I lose my nerve."

He relaxed his hold on her and smiled into her serious face. She couldn't resist snagging one more long kiss. "First. This child, if it is a boy, will not be named after you."

Ken's eyebrows rose. "He'll be a Schiller instead of a McAllister?"

"Of course he'll be a McAllister. He will not be a Kenneth McAllister. And if it is a girl, she will not be named Corinne. That stuff is too confusing. I won't name a child after a living relative."

"I agree. No problem."

"Okay. And I have also firmly decided that this child will have two parents, a mom and a dad, for all of his growing up years. I elect you to be the dad."

"Well, duh."

"This child's mom and dad will not live in two separate states. If you can't move to Oregon for some reason, then it's hello Kansas for me. If we can't live in the same house, we will live less than a mile apart. Got it?"

"Yes, ma'am. I wouldn't think of living more than four feet away from you. No way."

"Good."

"That's it?"

"That's it."

"I totally agree with everything you said. I want to add to that."

"What?"

"That this child's parents will be married to one another."

"I don't know about that." She backed away from him, then walked back out to the living room and dropped onto the couch. Ken followed and sat beside her. He leaned close and looked at her face. She turned away.

"Talk to me. Why did you go away like that? We were so happy, then you left."

"Oh, Ken."

"Don't you love me?"

"Yes, I love you."

"Then tell me what you're thinking. I can't know if you don't tell me." She shook her head.

"Um, would marrying me make you a bigamist because you're already married to someone else?"

She giggled.

"Well, what then? I need to know. I want to marry you."

"You never mentioned it before."

"It wasn't time. I thought it would be nice if we lived in the same state before I brought it up."

"That's always good. But can I tell you the truth?"

"Yes! That's what I'm after here."

"I'm afraid you only want to marry me because of the baby. That you maybe don't want to get married because the underwear queen knocked you for a loop. And not being married is okay with me if you have some reason you..."

"No. No, sweetie, my love. I was going to ask you as soon as I got unpacked at your house."

"How do I know that?"

He frowned. "This'll be a night of demonstrations, I see. Stay right here. Don't move."

Cori sat still while he ran to his bedroom. The minute he was gone, a big black and white cat sauntered out from under the curtain that closed off the dining room. "Sylvester. How nice to meet you." He stood and blinked at her. She got up and scooped him into her arms. He was affable, sniffing her and looking her over before he started to purr.

"Cori? Oh there you are. Damned cat upstaging me." He led her back to the couch by the arm and seated her. She still held the cat. Ken knelt in front of her. Cori let go of the cat but he stayed on her lap.

"Cori, will you marry me?"

"Oh, Bear. I'm still not sure."

The Kansas Connection   Kathleen Gabriel

"Have I been anywhere near a jewelry store since you told me that we're having a baby?"

"No, you've been here with me. Why?"

He took something out of his pocket and she gasped when she saw the sparkling diamond ring. "When did you get this?"

"July. So will you?"

She wept and held her left hand out toward him. "I take it this means yes." She nodded her head and tried to swallow the tears. It didn't work. Ken slid the ring onto her finger and she caught his hand and tugged on it. He got up and sat on the couch beside her and she hugged him and threw one leg over his to get closer. The cat left in disgust.

Cori studied her hand with the ring on it and laughed through tears. "When in July?"

"Right after I got home."

"So... you knew then?"

"I knew how I felt, and I was hoping to persuade you."

"It seems that right before you left you were upset about me kissing Brian, and that you weren't sure about us."

"I knew I could win you away from that damned Brian. How long have you known about the baby?"

"I took the pregnancy test yesterday. It didn't dawn on me that that's why my period might be late. I thought I was going into menopause early like my mother did."

He grinned. "This is better than that."

"Yup."

"Will you nurse the baby?"

"Yes, I will."

"Good. Will you take time off work?"

"I haven't got everything figured out yet, but I think I'll call it a sabbatical and work on the book at home while he's small. I'll stay home and work as long as I can find profitable work to do, maybe other textbook things or helping Dad's grad students with theses. Something. I'd like to be mostly home until he starts school."

"I'm glad. You wouldn't need to work at all, since the house is paid for and I'll have a good job."

She tipped her head. "Will you?"

"I'm going to work for Willis County sheriff's department. It's close to home and I'll have a supervisory job like I have now, patrol and overseeing deputies."

"That's great. You never told me you were looking for a job when you were out."

"You said you didn't want to know the date until it was certain, so I didn't tell you about the details. I hope I did all right."

"You did just fine."

"So, our baby's due in early October?"

"I think so. I haven't seen a doctor yet, but I know who I want, and they have charts."

"I guess you didn't have time to go to a doctor yet. If you're staying with me, we'd better get you in to see someone here. Are you staying with me?"

"If you want me."

"Little doubt there."

"You said something earlier tonight, at the airport, that I wondered about. You asked if I was staying and that you heard something you'd been waiting to hear?"

"Remember the night we decided didn't happen?" She rolled her eyes. "I asked you why you gave yourself, and you said you loved me, and that we belonged together. And earlier you had said that you wanted to comfort me, that you thought I needed you."

"Nothing wrong with that, is there?"

"Not at all. But what I waited to hear was that you needed me. Yes, I know you love me, and that you'll take care of me. But I want to be necessary to your life. I want to be needed."

"You are, sweetheart. I was frantic when you wouldn't talk to me yesterday."

"Then I decided that I'd better hear you out and you wouldn't answer the phone."

"I was busy crying. Then Brian came over with roses..."

"That damned Brian."

CHAPTER TWENTY-ONE

"Yes. As soon as I got the results I called you at the house here," she looked around. It still seemed strange to be at his house. "But you weren't home yet and I didn't want to call you when you were on duty. I wanted to tell someone, but I wanted you to be first. Then I remembered that I'd need a doctor, but I didn't know my internist very well yet and wouldn't be sure of her recommendation, and I didn't want to get someone off the list at the clinic because they all know my voice and so I called Brian. I told him that a friend of mine needed an OB..."

"OB?"

"An obstetrician. A baby catcher, you know."

"A baby catcher. Another technical medical term like plumber. I see."

"And I asked him who he recommended, and he told me a name, but that she had a waiting list. That's ridiculous because babies don't wait and I had a slip of the tongue and so he knew that it wasn't a friend, but it was me. So he's happy for us..."

"For us? As in, you and me?"

"Yes. And he said he'd check on me later and he brought some yellow baby roses over only I had been crying and he... he was very understanding and gave me advice."

"What did he tell you to do?"

"He told me to answer the phone. But you didn't call again, and I didn't know what to say anyway without getting upset and so I sat and talked with him for a while and after he left I came up with the idea to do a demonstration for you and I got on the Internet and got myself a plane ticket..."

"A plane ticket? One?"

"Yes. I bought a one-way ticket."

"They're cheaper if you buy both ways."

"I plan on driving back with you."

"Pretty sure of yourself, aren't you." He was grinning and hugging her to him.

"I'm pretty sure of you. And now you're going to be my husband. When will we get married?"

"As soon as you want to. We can do it right away, at the county courthouse if you like, then no one will be sure that the baby was conceived before we married. Or we can do it back home so your dad can be there. Or, well, we can do whatever you want. It's your show."

"What would you like most?"

"Just to have you in my arms forever and ever and ever and ever..." She silenced him with a whole-hearted kiss. While they kissed, Sylvester came back and climbed onto Ken's lap and put a paw on Cori's leg. He applied a bit of claw.

"Ow. Are you a jealous kitty?" Sylvester played innocent. Cori petted him.

"Bun, I heard something about cats being dangerous to pregnant women?"

"Cats themselves are okay, just something they do carries some germ or something. I won't be allowed to clean litter boxes."

"Aw, darn. I know you love to do that, too."

"My favorite part of cat ownership."

"What will we name the baby? I know what we won't name her."

"I don't know. We'll have to get a baby name book. Maybe you can list me some family names from old dead grandparents and aunts and uncles, and I'll do the same. Your family's bigger than mine."

"Yeah, it is. We don't need to spend a lot of effort on picking a boy's name."

"How come?"

"It's the father who determines the sex of the child, and we McAllisters run strongly to girls."

"Oh, well. We'll pick a nice boy name, too, anyway. You are obviously male, so we might get a boy."

"We'll do that, but five to one it's a girl. I have four sisters, and I'm the only boy. My father had seven sisters, and he was the only boy."

"What about your grandfather?"

"He had a brother."

"Aha!"

"But he also had ten sisters. Five to one, basically."

"Well I'm not going to do this over and over just to get you a son, so you might as well put that idea far away. In fact, I'm so old that this will probably be our only child."

"I'm thrilled to have just one. I never thought I'd be a father. I wished and dreamed, then my ex killed the idea..."

"I know. Mine did the same. But we're getting a second chance. Two second chances. A chance at love, and a chance at being parents."

"Bun, I am so happy."

"Me, too. But Bear, you're going to be bruised up if you keep calling me Bun. I'm going to start pinching you to cure you."

"Oh, pinch me and bruise me. Sure. You haven't got enough strength in those little fingers to hurt a big brute like me."

She slid her hand down to his butt and gave him a pinch.

"Yow!" He grabbed her hand and looked at it. "I thought maybe you were using pliers, Bun."

She broke free and pinched him again, then tickled him. He twisted to get away from her while laughing and got a grip on her wrist again. She pinched his leg with her other hand and he tickled her ribs. The cat leaped onto the back of the couch to be out of the way, or maybe so he could see better.

Ken rolled on top of Cori, then rolled off the couch onto the floor. She felt an advantage in being on top and managed to tickle with whichever hand he foolishly let go of. She tried to get her face next to his. "Oh, no, you don't. I remember you about bit my ear off last time we did this."

She pinned his arms and lowered her face to his while he protested and laughed. She licked his cheek from jaw to temple and he laughed louder. That was when she heard someone coming in the door. There was no way to keep from getting caught, so she held Ken there and stared him down. His eyes held a wicked glint.

"What's this?" said a woman.

"Hey, Uncle Ken. Whatcha doing?" said a teasing young male voice.

"Oh, please," said a young woman. Cori could tell who was who with no trouble. She laughed, let go of one of Ken's hands and got in one last tickle before she got to her feet. She dusted her hands off on her pants and went to the little gathering at the door. She extended her hand to Sandi. "I'm Cori. And I want you to know he deserved it."

"He always does. Glad to meet you. This is Jennifer, and this is Michael."

"Hi," she said. Michael extended a hand. Jennifer didn't, but Cori reached out and Jennifer hugged her. She met Sandi's eye over Jennifer's

The Kansas Connection   Kathleen Gabriel

shoulder and she winked, then started when she saw Cori's left hand.

Sandi reached for it as Cori and Jennifer parted. "Beautiful." Her eyes were big. "Are you going to be my sister-in-law?"

"Yes, I am. I had to wrestle Ken for this."

"Oh, she did not," he said behind her. "I had to beg her to take it. Then she was more interested in the damned cat."

"I was not. It's just that he was sitting on my lap..."

Jennifer said, "Uncle Ken? Or the cat?"

"Both. It was rather crowded," she said.

"Speaking of crowded," Ken said to Sandi, then stopped. "Uh, never mind. I'll tell you when the kids aren't around."

"Get ready for bed now, kids," Sandi said.

"The movie was great, Uncle Ken," Michael said. "Thanks so much for asking."

"Geez. I get you a new aunt and all you can think of is Miss Manners."

"I think it's wonderful," Jennifer said. "I feel like I know you already, Cori, from all the nice e-mails you've sent me."

Michael said, "And from all the nice Master of the Galaxy games you whipped us at. My opinion of you was confirmed the minute I saw you with my uncle pinned to the floor. Way to go."

Sandi said, "Bed, I said. We'll talk tomorrow. You have school in the morning." They hurried out, pushing each other, each calling dibs on the bathroom.

Sandi asked, "When's the big day?"

Cori answered. "We're not sure yet. We'd like to make it pretty soon. So many things are new right now that I'm happy just knowing I have the bear staked out; he's officially mine."

He wrapped his arms around her from behind. "Cori's officially mine, but we'll take awhile to get it all sorted out." He kissed her cheek and Sandi smiled. "I haven't even asked if she'll use my name yet. Will you? Or will you be Schiller, Schiller-McAllister, or McAllister-Schiller, or Giles-McAllister..."

"You dope. I hate hyphenated names. I'll be Cori McAllister, of course."

"Giles is a neat name," Sandi said.

"You stay out of this," Ken growled.

"Mom! Look what I found in the bathroom. What is this?" Jennifer asked, carrying the home pregnancy test in her hand. Cori grimaced. "Michael says it's some woman thing and to mind my own business but it was right in the bathroom..."

Michael stood in the entrance to the hallway, watching. Ken said, a chuckle bubbling up out of him. "Aunt Cori will tell you what it is."

"Um. Well, I hate to have you kids think less of your uncle, but..."

"Out with it, Cori," he said.

"That's a pregnancy test. Besides an aunt, Ken's getting you a cousin, too." Jennifer gasped, then threw herself at Ken. He had to let go of Cori to receive the onslaught. Sandi held her arms out to Cori and they shared a long hug. Cori saw Michael approaching and held out one hand to him. He joined her and Sandi for a three-way hug, then Ken and Jennifer joined in.

"We might as well wrestle," Ken remarked.

"Reminds me more of football," Cori said.

"When?" Jennifer demanded. "When do I get my new cousin?"

"October."

Michael said, "You'll be a good dad, Uncle Ken. I hope the rock eater makes a good mom."

"She will. Now get ready for bed, you two." They left again, arguing about something or other on the way.

"Well, I'm going to bed. It's been a big day," Ken said.

"Me, too," Cori said. "You have to go to work in the morning?"

"I don't have to be at work until noon," Sandi said. "Maybe we can get acquainted in the morning."

Ken said, "Don't count on it. I called in happy."

Sandi looked at both of them. "I guess I won't need to give up my room?"

Ken said, "That is correct. You're very astute for a woman with a mind warped by teenagers."

"Good night, Sandi. It was good to finally meet you." They said good night and congratulations a few more times and it took a while for Cori to get her turn at the bathroom. After she did she stripped down and crawled into bed. Ken's bed. Finally. Sylvester was already on the foot of the bed and she was sure he gave her a dirty look. Cori admired her ring in the lamplight.

Ken likewise stripped and got into bed and gathered her into his arms and held her tight for several minutes. She would have laughed if she could have gotten enough breath to do it. "You'll never let me go."

"Not never, not no how."

"I love you."

"I love you, too. And I don't know if you can hear me, baby, but I love you, too."

"He can't hear you."

"She might be able to. How do you know?"

"I never heard of anyone calling in happy."

The Kansas Connection   Kathleen Gabriel

"I wasn't sick, so I couldn't call in sick. I took a vacation day. I told everybody why, too, and they all want to meet you."

"That's nice."

"Yeah. They want to meet the creature who can tame their sergeant."

"I haven't managed it yet. But I'll keep trying."

"Don't ever give up, Honey Bunny."

* * *

Cori sat at the kitchen table with the phone hoping Sandi wouldn't catch her with her hair all over and wearing Ken's robe. She wanted to call before her dad left for work.

"Hello?"

"Hi, Dad."

"Hey, haven't you left yet?"

"I'm at Ken's. I have some good news."

"Tell me."

"We're getting married."

"Good for you. I knew you two would be all right. Did you talk about whatever had you so upset?"

"Yeah, we did. Which brings me to the other good news. Are you sitting down?"

"Okay. I'm sitting down. You aren't moving to Kansas, are you?"

"No, we'll be coming home as soon as we can. Know what I had to talk to Ken about? I had to tell him first, but I did, so now I can tell you."

"So tell me."

"I came out here to tell Ken that he's going to be a father." She waited, but her dad didn't respond right away. "Dad?"

"You shouldn't tease me like this, Cori."

"I'm not! You're going to be a grandpa. I just found out day before yesterday. Isn't that incredible?"

"You're pregnant?"

"Yes."

"Cori, that is fantastic. I never thought... I'm happy for you. Hell, I'm happy for me! Was this planned?"

"No. Totally unplanned. A surprise to both of us. Maybe I'll tell you about it someday."

"I'm not sure I want to hear. But however it happened, I'm glad. I hope you don't take too long coming back home. I want to see you blooming, and I want to see that little one. Do you have names picked out?"

"We're just starting. I'd like a list of your suggestions. Send them e-mail."

"Family names?"

"Yes. None from living relatives, though. And lean heavily toward female names."

"With pleasure. Can I talk to Ken?"

"He's in the shower."

"All right. I'll talk to him later. Thank you so much. Thanks to both of you. I feel... honey, I feel like my life is being fulfilled."

"Oh, Daddy."

He cleared his throat. "I have so wanted the best for you. I tried to accept Dave, you know that."

"I know."

"But Ken. Now there's the man I would have chosen for you myself."

"Really? You didn't say much..."

"Of course not. I was afraid of putting the kibosh on the whole deal."

"Oh, Dad."

"I even mention it and I'm not Daddy any more, but am demoted."

Cori laughed as she hung up and was still laughing when she joined Ken in the shower.

EPILOGUE

On October sixth, Cori breathed through another contraction while Ken held her and whispered encouragement. Something was feeling different with these contractions; they were awfully long and getting longer and she felt a growing urge to push.

"It's not time yet," the nurse kept telling her. Cori was weary, and her hair was stuck to a sweaty neck that Ken didn't seem to wipe often enough.

"Soon you'll get to see the little rascal who's been playing basketball with your bladder," her dad assured her. He sat near her head to be close to her and as far as possible from what he referred to as "the action."

Two nurses stood by the foot of the bed. Cori thought they looked anxious, but she was probably projecting her own nervousness. A tap on the door was followed by Brian's head. "Can I come in?"

The Kansas Connection   Kathleen Gabriel

"Come on in. We're just taking it easy here," Henry called.

Brian grinned as he strode in.

Cori muttered some rude words, then groaned as another contraction began. Ken rubbed her shoulders and propped her head forward. Brian went to the nurses and talked with them. Cori concentrated on not yelling, as the pressure grew greater. It let off and she let her head fall back into Ken's hand. She heard a nurse say, "...paged her, but she's tied up."

She lifted her head and looked at the nurses. One pushed a cart closer while the other was lifting the covers. "I need to examine you again, Mrs. McAllister. This will just take a moment."

They all waited silently, then the nurse said, "Oh, my! Doctor, if you'll please gown and glove?"

"Me?" Brian looked astounded.

Another contraction was already beginning, along with that pressure. "I'm pushing, damn it." Ken braced her and she pushed with an immense power that was a relief, and a beginning.

She was aware of activity at the foot of the bed. Brian said, "Well, I'm used to seeing clogged plumbing, but this is ridiculous."

"Be quiet," Cori growled. Her contractions came regularly with little respite between. At one point, Henry retrieved his hand from hers and rubbed it, then gave it back with a martyred look. She said, "Sorry, Dad."

After one mighty push, she cried out as she felt a breaking sensation and a splash. All was quiet inhabited with a throbbing relief, then she heard a gasp, then an indignant cry. She held out her arms as Brian presented her with a squalling, red-faced bundle, saying, "Here you go, beautiful."

"Here's my baby. Here you are," she crooned. The little one quieted and blinked at her. Cori gazed at her little one while she looked back at her. Ken gave her his finger to hold and Henry stroked her damp forehead.

Ken kissed Cori and nuzzled into her hair and murmured, "She's great."

"What's her name?" Henry asked. "You never would tell me."

"Amelia," Cori answered, not taking her eyes from the baby.

Henry smiled. "After your mother. Well."

Ken said, "I'm so glad you followed me off that exit, Cori love."

"Oh, me, too."

Henry chuckled. "So am I, now that you mention it."